The
Chalice of Knowledge

S. A. Richardson©

Copyright

Copyright © S. A. Richardson 2015

About the author

S.A. Richardson lives in the historic town of Tutbury in the U.K. with his wife and two children. He graduated from school in 2002 and took a fulltime job at one of the largest poultry suppliers in Britain, where he worked until 2010 when a minor medical problem with his spine forced him to give up the job. Failing to find another job, he took up writing as a pastime and has continued it ever since.

Dedication

In memory of my Granddad

Richard Joseph Fitzsimmons

Table of Contents

Map of Valhanor

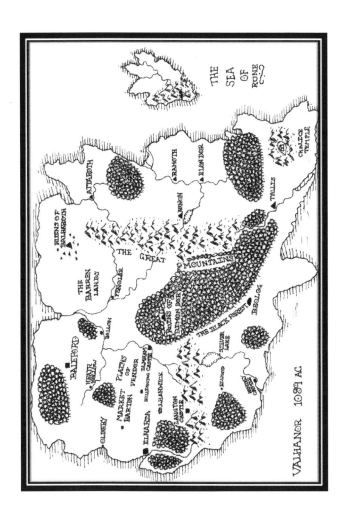

Prologue

It began with the movement of the stars. For so sad was our heavenly fathers at the darkness that grew and tainted men's soul, that they gifted wise men with light to shepherd men from the darkness that plagued them.

The ancient kingdoms of Balharoth and Dimon Dor though mighty, were failing like great mountains crumbling in the wake of time. All kingdoms were infected by the darkness, with no race spared.

Where once there was perfection, now became dark and lesser. Men grew without self-control falling to all kinds of wickedness, with righteousness becoming a memory of old.

Then in the reign of king Shaphir of Balharoth a wise man, Adullam came forth. He petitioned king Shaphir to call a council of all kings, of all the kingdoms. Shaphir the pious went forth and summoned a mighty council made up of all races, with not one race being forgotten.

The great council met in the halls of king Shaphir, at Balharoth where Adullam made his address to them.

"Great kings of old, for too long has the darkness plagued our lands and our souls. Long have wise men wondered the kingdoms in search of answers to fight back the darkness that now lays siege to our very souls, all to no avail. We mere mortals have not a true knowledge to rid ourselves of this darkness that plagues us. Only our fathers in the heavens possess such knowledge. Many leagues have I travelled in search of an answer of how to gain such knowledge, and an answer I found."

At that Adullam pulled forth from his robe an ancient bone flute, a relic once belonging to the Gigantes. "Here within this ancient flute lies the power to summon forth a star from the heavens." Adullam handed the ancient flute to Norlag the Craft Master of the Gigantes and the rightful heir to the ancient flute.

Then once more from within his robe Adullam pulled forth a scroll bound with golden cord. He held the scroll aloft his head for all the council to see.

Then once more in a mighty voice he spoke. "Here within this scroll lies the words of an enchantment of pure knowledge." He then gave the scroll to Georus the Grand Imp and rightful heir of the scroll.

Our heavenly fathers had guided Adullam to this purpose of calling forth a star from the heavens, then to forge a chalice from the fallen star and then place the enchantment upon the chalice. Then all kings were to consume blessed water from the chalice, giving all kings a true knowledge.

To all this the great council agreed and made forthwith atop Mount Gannim, where the Craft Master of the Gigantes played a tune so soft and true that all kings wept and begged our fathers in the heavens for the will to turn aside the darkness. Our fathers in the heavens wept also for men, and being true and just, set alight to a star, sending forth a saviour for all.

A star gave fire and fell down splitting in two as it fell. Half fell upon the land, half into the great waters. The kings rejoiced at the dawn of a new day for the sea had yielded a young boy.

Adullam proclaimed the boy of heavenly descent and would lead men away from the darkness and back into the light.

A wise man named Baal then came forth with an armful of star rock. He persuaded some of the great council that he now possessed the only true body of our heavenly fathers and from it a chalice will be forged, so that kings may gain a true knowledge and end the darkness.

So Norlag the Craft Master of the Gigantes took the pieces of star rock high into the Great Mountains. For eight days the great furnace of the Gigantes burned until the chalice came to be.

Then Georus the grand Imp took the chalice deep into the Great Forest. For three days the Imps chanted and poured their enchantment of knowledge into the chalice, making it glow blue whenever filled.

Thus the Chalice of Knowledge came to be, and men's thirst for knowledge became unquenchable.

A passage from the Chronicle of Elnar.

Chapter 1

The summer had passed and the town of Heath Hollow was celebrating the festival of summer's end. An unusually early snow fell gently on and off throughout the day, dusting the town below in a soft white blanket. A cold wind blew from the north, making the night feel colder than it actually was. However, despite the cold, the people of Heath Hollow rejoiced and made merry, for the occasion was a happy one, which was loved by all.

Lanterns with different coloured glass hung on ropes suspended from roof to roof, lighting the narrow streets below with reds, yellows, blues and greens. Red and yellow quartered banners with the Lord's emblem of two stags locking horns hung from every window, snatching with the light breeze. The smells of freshly baked bread, pies and cakes filled the air, giving the night a festive feel.

The town's folk dressed in their finest clothes and took to the cobbled streets, filling the town with life and noise. It was a good night for the traders in the market, as it was an old tradition to buy loved ones a gift on this night; but it was also a good night for thieves too.

The marketplace was busy with people bustling around and bartering for the lowest price, with Thieves weaving in and out of the crowds, snatching at purses hanging from belts. On this night they could steal a fortune and live well for a few weeks. If caught they faced the hangman's noose or being branded with a T on the forehead as a mark of their crime.

The best thieves were hard to spot; they dressed as finely as other people and portrayed themselves as trusted, wealthy gentlemen. They often worked in pairs, while one would distract you with smiles and flattery, the other behind you would pick your pockets and slip away without you even knowing it. Others were easy to spot, just poor peasants looking to make their next meal.

Henri Richards was such a thief. He came from a poor family whose only money came from what they stole. Most fathers did skilled work in an evening to make enough money to buy their independence from the lord, but not Henri's. His father was a drunk and spent what little money they had in the tavern. So they were never able to buy their freedom from the Lord and were forced to work the lord's fields every day.

Henri had wanted more from life; he felt that he was destined for greater things, better things then stealing or working in the fields. His father had always told him to stop daydreaming and walk in the real world, and to be more like his brothers. His three other brothers were suited to stealing; they were good at it and were even proud of it. The Richards family had a bad name in the town and his brothers tried to live up to that name. A family without honour the town's folk said. And for the most part, they were right.

He sat on an empty beer barrel in a far dark corner of the marketplace, watching, and thinking. He was supposed to be picking pockets, but couldn't think of a good reason of why he should steal someone's hard earned money. His father, nor his brothers, never cared who they stole from, so why did he? He sat looking at the town's folk, their just the same as me he told himself. Though the town's folk would not see it that way.

"Your father has been asking round for you." A familiar voice broke Henri's thoughts.

Henri looked up into the face of his best friend Tom. "Bet the stupid bugger hasn't got any further then the tavern." Henri replied.

Tom was every inch as tall as Henri's six feet and came from a family just as poor. He now lived with his grandmother since his mother and father had died of the plague ten years ago, leaving him alone.

"No, and he's already drunk." Tom said. "He's telling a tale of how a spear took out his eye."

"He'll have run out of money then, and wanting more." Henri spat with disgust.

"Have you any to give him?" asked Tom.

"No."

Tom stooped down and pulled off his boot and tipped it upside down, shaking a few copper coins on to the ground. "Here take half of this."

"Where did you get that Tom?" Henri asked.

"While you have been sitting daydreaming, others have been on the fiddle." Tom said scooping up the coins and offering Henri to take a share. "If you go back empty handed your father will tan your hide."

"Thanks Tom but no, give it your grandmother, she'll need it to keep you fed. Anyway if all goes good tonight I won't be going back empty of coin. "

"You're not going through with that stupid plan of yours; they'll hang you for sure if you're caught."

Henri jumped off the barrel and slapped Tom on his back. "I'll just make sure I'm not caught then. Now let's go see what's about this year then."

"Hadn't you better see your father?"

"No he can wait, besides, 'I've no coin to give him, and I'm in no hurry for a beating."

Henri and Tom walked off into the crowded marketplace. They had to push and shove to make it through the crowd. The aroma of freshly baked goods made Henri's stomach grumble. He hadn't eaten all day and his stomach was as empty as the town idiot's head. They headed over to a stall selling meat pies, but it was not the pies that drew them there, but a girl who worked the stall with her sister.

"So that's why you keep your father waiting is it." Tom said with a mocking smile across his face.

"Tonight I'm going to ask her."

"Ask her what?" Tom knew the answer already, he turned away to hide the disappointment on his face.

"You know Tom; you've tried to talk me out of it enough times."

"She's the daughter of a merchant, a well-respected merchant at that! Look at yourself Henri. A peasant still working the lord's fields! Her father isn't going to allow such a person to marry his eldest daughter, is he?"

Henri looked down at himself. His trousers and tunic were stained and dirty, his boots were well worn with a hole in his left toe. Tom was right he was a peasant, but he couldn't help the way he felt, and he was sure she felt the same way too.

"It's no shame being born in a drainage ditch Tom, though it's a great shame to stay there." Henri said brushing at his tunic with his hands.

Tom shook his head and turned back to face Henri. "Well it's cold and starting to snow again, so I'm going back to the wheel for a warm mug of ale. I've no wish to see a friend making a fool of himself chasing dreams." With that Tom turned and disappeared into the crowd.

Henri pushed past the people and worked his way to the front of the stall. There she was. The most beautiful girl he'd ever set eyes upon. She had long brown hair that was tied back with a blue ribbon that matched with her long blue dress. Her deep green eyes lit up when she smiled and she had a full, but not fat figure that many men admired.

"Elizabeth!" Henri shouted to be heard over the crowd.

Elizabeth turned. "Henri!" A smile lit up her face. "Here try one of these." She said thrusting a small pie at him.

"Sorry I've no money." Henri said, feeling ashamed to admit it.

"It's a gift, and I'll warrant you've not eaten today."

Henri felt a flush of heat rise to his face; he took the offered pie and bit into it. "It's very good." He said with a mouthful.

"It's father's new recipe, pork with a few herbs. They seem very popular, their selling like hot pies." She said with a small, beautiful laugh.

"Father won't be pleased with you giving away his pies." Catharine said reproving her sister. "Especially to him," she shot Henri a look as though he disgusted her. "You know what father said, to stay away from any of the fieldworkers. Besides that its busy and paying custom is waiting to be served." She briskly turned and went back to serving the waiting custom.

Henri finished the pie and wiped his mouth on his back of his hand. He was suddenly aware of Elisabeth's gaze. "Sorry." He said.

"Don't be, she forgets that our great grandfather worked the fields too. So what brings you to the market then?" Elizabeth asked wandering why someone would go to a marketplace with no money.

"I wanted to see you." He said so softly that Elizabeth didn't hear him.

Voices from the crowed began shouting out. "I'll take half a dozen of these." Henri was shoved aside by a man who looked more like a pig. "Get out of the way peasant." He said, waving his hand at Henri.

Elizabeth could see the anger in Henri's face, she felt it too. Though Henri was a peasant, he was still a better man then most, like finding a golden coin in a drainage ditch.

"Elizabeth!" Catharine shouted for help.

"Meet me at the lonely tree after the market closes." Henri asked Elizabeth. She smiled and nodded; then quickly turned and went about her work.

Henri stood for a moment, watching her. He had never felt like this with anybody before, he had never been given the chance. His family were the lowest of all in society, with a bad reputation that had clung to the name Richards for generations. Most of the people of the town wouldn't even look at them; some would even cross the street so they wouldn't have to be near any of them. But not Elizabeth, She had defied society and had become friends with Henri, a Richards, a fieldworker and a peasant. Henri turned and walked across the busy market place to the tavern were he would find his father.

The tavern was old and rundown. The bricks were crumbling and the wooden beams rotting. Once, the tavern had been a respectable place, where the merchants would meet after a day's trading in the market. But those days had long passed. Now the tavern stood as a place for the peasants to drink cheap ale and find an even cheaper woman. The Wagon's Wheel it was called, but the peasants just called it the Wheel.

Henri pushed open the door and was met by a blast of hot air mixed with the stench of stale ale. He closed the door behind him and waited for his eyes to adjust to the gloom. The room was warm, dimly lit and crowded with not a seat spare. Women wearing see through dresses walked the room in a seductive manner, searching for business. A drunk lay on the floor unconscious while a dog licked at the sick on his face.

Henri could see a small crowd in the far corner nearest to the fire. He could hear his father's voice followed by bursts of laughter and walked across to the crowd, pushing his way through to the front. There his father was sat, behind a table littered with empty ale pots red faced from too much ale, with one arm around a woman stroking at her breast, the other around a pot of ale. There Bill Richards sat regaling a story of how he lost his eye.

"I tell you, so many were they that they were beyond what numbers I could count."

"They can't have been that many of them then." Someone shouted out, making the crowd burst into laughter. The crowd settled back down and Bill continued his tale.

"We, the king's loyal followers, were so few that many wanted to lay down their spears and beg for mercy, but not me. I tightened my grip around my spear and with no orders, charged straight for our foe. I was later told that the king himself shed a tear upon the sight of my bravery." He paused to swig at his ale.

"It was now because of me that the king's army found heart, and giving a mighty roar that split the heavens, they charged into the fray. For what seemed a lifetime I fought alone against the rebel horde, thrusting back and forth with my spear until the ground I stood upon was wet with rebel blood. My arms burned as if on fire and my mouth was as dry as a desert. " He paused and took a long dreg of ale and continued on. "I killed at least a hundred maybe more? I killed until none would face me. There I stood in the mist of battle leaning upon my blood soaked spear, drawing breath, when out from the rebel horde stepped a creature, half man half beast."

The crowd fell silent anticipating the climax of the tales ending, children edged behind their fathers not daring to listen, but not wanting to miss the ending of the tale.

Henri looked from face to face in disbelief. Most of the crowd had been in the lord's spear militia. They must have known it was all a lie.

"It was as tall as two men and as wide as three." Bill continued on, showing with his hands how big the creature had been. "It wielded an ancient war hammer of the Gigantes, striking down any who would dare challenge him. Many fled from its wrath until only I stood before it. Its red eyes looked down upon me, full of rage and lusting for my blood, then swung a mighty blow towards me. I flung my body out of the way and thrust my spear deep into its chest.

The beast's blood was as black as an empty night sky and killed the grass beneath where it spilt. The beast pulled my spear from its chest and threw it straight at me. I moved, but not quickly enough." Bill removed the dirty bandage from around his right eye. He reviled a red scar that went as straight as an arrow from his eye to his ear, flanking an empty socket where his eye should have been.

"The blow knocked me off my feet. I lay in a daze with the beast standing over me, his face snarling and foaming from the mouth, preparing to deal the final blow to end me. I drew my dagger and plunged it deep into the beast's manhood. It fell to its knees screaming a terrifying scream. I wasted no time. I picked up the beast's mighty hammer, raised it above my head and struck down upon the beast's head with all my strength. Tired from battle I fell to my knees waiting for death to find me, but it did not come.

With the beast's death the rebels lost heart and fled the field of battle. It was then that King Henri himself came to me and thanked me by giving me a golden crown." Bill fished a thick golden coin from his purse hanging from his belt and held it up for all to see.

Children clapped with excitement and ran off chasing each other pretending to be monsters. The men made comments of doubt with one even shouting out. "Strange, I was there that day and I don't remember any of that happening!"

"Well you wouldn't have seen it, being that far from the fighting Sam." Bill replied returning the crowd to laughter.

With the tale finished, the crowd dispersed to make merry. A fiddle was picked up and a jaunty tune filled the tavern with a cheerful atmosphere. Men sang and danced with the women, waving full ale pots in the air. But Henri was in no mood for merrymaking. He had wanted to get this over with as soon as he could. Tonight he would earn the respect of everyone by pulling off the biggest theft anyone could attempt.

"You wanted me father?"

Bill removed his head from a woman's breasts and looked up with his one good eye. "Henri it's about bloody time!" He turned to the woman sat next to him. "Off you go lass; I'll come and find you later." Bill nodded at the vacated seat beside him "Well you've kept me waiting long enough." He said as Henri came and sat beside him.

"I've been busy." Henri said coldly."

"Good, let's see what you have then." Bill said rubbing his hands together.

"I don't have anything, not yet. But if all goes well later then we should be good for coin all winter."

Bill looked stone-faced at Henri. "I've heard a rumour you plan to steal from the lord himself, is this true?" Bill asked in a hushed tone.

"Who told you that?" Henri said a little too loudly that it made people standing near turn and look.

"You did boy, just now."

Henri felt anger rise in him at his plans being discovered. He planned to go tonight while everyone was busy with the festival. The town guards were few, and what few they were would be dozy from drink. No one would expect it, that's why it had to work. The lord could afford to lose a few coins, and he probably won't notice a few coins missing. Then with enough coin he would buy his freedom from the lord and marry Elizabeth. All it was going to take was to steal a few coins.

Henri sat smiling at the thought of paying for his freedom with the lord's own coin when his father smacked him across his head. "Stop dreaming boy! Do you want to end up doing the gallows dance like your uncle Jacob?"

Though Henri had been small at the time he could remember the hanging. His uncle's face had turned purple with his eyes slowly bulging out from their sockets, and then as his body went into a spasm his bowels and bladder gave way, fouling himself. But the worst of all was the cheering crowd that sneered at his uncle while his life slowly fled from the world. A good end for a Richards they had cheered.

"Don't worry, I know what I'm doing." Henri said rubbing at his head.

"I'm not worrying; if your own stupidity gets you strung up it's your own fault. I'll have one less to feed, so it suits me. But what I care about is that you have no coin yet again. You know your older brother has been in with six purses already tonight." There was an awkward silence between them and Henri wouldn't meet his father's angry gaze.

"Get out there and acquire some coin and don't bother coming back until you get some! I've no need for dead bloody wood in my family."

Henri was about to lash out at his father when a red-faced Tom came and stood by the table. "Worth every single coin that one." He said tying up his lace on front of his trousers. "The kind of women I'd like to marry one day."

"You can't marry a whore Tom." Bill said looking around the room.

"And why not?"

"Because if all the whores married, they wouldn't be whores, but wives, and young fools like you wouldn't have anywhere to spend coin, because married women aren't allowed in taverns." Bill said standing. He turned to Henri. "Remember with coin or not at all. This is your fifteenth winter and time you pulled your weight." He drained the last of his ale and went over to a woman, grasped her arm and took her up the stairs at the back of the tavern.

"He seems cheerful tonight." Tom said.

"Bastard wants a kicking." Henri replied, cuffing away his tears.

Tom knew what Bill was like, self-centred and uncaring. He knew Bill would beat Henri if he went home empty handed again, so Tom tried to offer Henri a few coins again. "Here take these."

"No Tom. My father's right, it's time I lifted my own weight." Henri stood and walked towards the door.

"Where are you going?!" Tom shouted at him.

"I'm going to earn my keep Tom, to earn my keep."

The clouds broke revealing a full moon that shone brightly, illuminating the patchily snow covered hills below. Six Knights of the Order of the Star rode the hill road. They had travelled for days as fast as they were able, pursuing a band of thieves that had stolen from their star perceptory at Baleford. They were tired, cold, hungry and wanting the warmth of a fire.

"Halt!" The Commander called. Though he was a Commander he wore no badge of his rank, and only the confidence of his voice betrayed him as a man of rank.

The five other Star Knights garbed as their Commander, all black with a single white eight pointed star upon their chests, came to a halt behind their Commander.

"What is it Commander?" Orin asked. He was the oldest Knight in the company and because of his experience was second in command.

The Commander took out his telescope from a pouch on his belt and scanned the surrounding hills. "The town of Heath Hollow, four or five miles south." He said to no one in particular. "An hour!" he said. "An hour at the most and we should reach our perceptory at Heath Hollow." He held out his telescope for Orin to take a look.

Orin reined in besides his Commander and took the offered glass, casting his experienced eye on the road that lay ahead. All looked well enough. The snow hadn't been heavy and the road was in good condition. He traced the

28

road south towards the town, then a mile out from the town, he noticed the road ran through a small wooded valley. A perfect place for an ambush Orin thought.

"The road will take us through that small valley Commander, a mile out from the town." He said handing back the glass.

The Commander looked a while through his telescope. He could see no movement upon the road to worry about, but he knew a small army could have hidden in that valley. He trained his glass on the outskirts of the valley looking for a safer way around.

"We could go around and approach the town from the east?" He said, momentarily taking his eye from the eyepiece.

"We could Commander, but it could delay us for a few hours and the thieves won't wait for us. But if they wanted to set an ambush, there would be a perfect place."

The Commander snapped shut his telescope and pushed it back into his pouch. He dismounted and stood staring out at the distant town, thinking. He knew he needed speed to catch up with the thieves, but he also knew they was no better way to halt a pursuit then an ambush on a dark night. He turned and looked back at the knights under his command. They were tired, cold and what little provisions they had carried from Baleford were gone. They couldn't spend another night in the open. Tonight they needed shelter and fresh supplies.

"They're likely to have just headed straight for the town, common thieves wouldn't dare take on six well-armed Star Knights, besides it's too cold a night for waiting around to ambush us." Orin said as though he had read the Commanders thoughts.

"We'll stay on the road, but proceed with caution. Brother Edmond and William take the banks one each side, a quarter the way up. Keep your eyes focused for anyone who might be hiding, but go quietly. The rest will ride in loose formation a quarter mile behind."

With the orders given and each Knight knowing what to do the small company of Knights dismounted, knelt down and said in unison the star prayer.

*"O heavenly stars let your divine light
guide and protect us slaves that
submit before you. Banish all darkness
within us and let the light fill our
hearts. Give us the strength to stand
against the darkness, that we may
bring the kingdom to light."*

Their prayer said they then mounted their palfreys and nocked their war bows, knowing that they were useless in an ambush, but having them in hand comforted them.

Their war bows were an old weapon no longer used in the King's army who favoured the more powerful and accurate crossbow. But the Star Knights could loose at least ten arrows a minute with their bows, an advantage over the crossbow which was slow to reload.

With their bows strung they rode in a loose formation of four while the two other Knights rode on ahead to scout the valley.

They reached the valley in good order and the Commander began to think that the cautious approach wasn't necessary. There was no sign of anybody having even travelled the hill road and the scouts hadn't come back to report any dangers.

They were almost at the end of the valley and the Knights could see the bright coloured lights glowing from the town. The wind carried the noise from the town to the Knight's ears, it sounded pleasant and cheerful to the cold, tired Knights.

"It sounds like the whole town is merrymaking." Orin said.

"It's the festival of summer's end; the whole town will be feasting and dancing." The Commander said breaking away from the others. He walked his horse a few paces in front of the other Knights and blew out a long breath that misted up in front of him.

"Commander is everything all right?" Orin asked as he came and rained his horse besides his Commander.

"It's just doesn't seem right does it?" The Commander said more to himself then to Orin.

"Commander, what don't seem right?"

"The tracks, Orin where are the tracks?"

"I can't see any tracks sir." Orin said, at a loss to his Commanders' point.

"Precisely, nearby merchants would have travelled to the town to sell their goods, at least a handful of wagons must of passed this way. Yet there's no sign of anything other than us to have passed this road. Which is strange, as today is the day of summer's end, and merchants will be travelling the roads up and down the kingdom?"

Orin suddenly realized the danger and said. "They have either covered up their tracks and have set an ambush, or we've come the wrong way." He added.

The Commander and Orin looked at each other with the horror of their mistake written across their faces. They had believed the road empty and now they had a sickening feeling it wasn't.

But it was too late.

A crack and a thud broke the moment's silence. Orin was snapped back by a bolt from a crossbow, his blood spraying high into the air as he fell from his horse hitting the ground with a crack, gurgling unable to speak because of the bolt embedded deep into his throat.

The Commander horse reared as another bolt came whistling from the wooded hills above, striking his horse in its flank. The Commander kicked his feet from the stirrups as his horse fell to the ground, kicking out in a blind panic. He went rolling into the road dazed by the fall, momentarily forgetting the fight around him. He looked over to Orin's body lying lifeless, his blood streaming onto the cold snowy ground. The sight angered him; it was not just for a Star Knight to be killed by a coward behind a crossbow.

"Knights of the Star rally to me!" He shouted in a voice that could have awakened the dead. The two other Star Knights, now also on foot, ran to their Commander side. Together they formed a three man shield wall, standing strong and unflinching as crossbow bolts flew and buried themselves in their shields. They had abandoned their own war bows knowing that this was work for their board swords.

"Is it cowardly dogs that hide their faces in the night? Come now and embrace death as men!" The Commander shouted toward where the crossbow bolts were coming from.

The night fell eerily quiet as the crossbow bolts ceased. Clouds came and drew across the bright moon releasing snow that began to cover the world below with a peaceful beauty. Then a cheer came breaking the calm as a dozen men descended furiously from the wooded hill. This was a mistake that would cost them their lives.

The Star Knights lived for moments like these. They had trained since the age of seven, everyday swinging heavy swords at a wooden post until they had mastered their skill. They didn't fear death as a place amongst the stars was waiting for them should they fall in battle. Now on this cold night the band of thieves would learn this harsh lesson.

Outnumbered, the Star Knights began to move forward to meet the oncoming horde. With swords and shield held ready, onwards they went with a terrifying calmness. The horde came crashing down from the woods and broke against the Knights as the sea breaks around a rock.

The Knights stood back to back wielding their broad war swords with deadly effect. Bodies of the fallen lay at their feet. Even though the Knights were famed as the greatest warriors in the entire kingdom, it was still only a question of how long they could hold out for.

The Commander knew this and shouted out, "Smile, for this night we shall join our brothers amongst the stars." The two other knights gave a cheer and fought defiantly on. Then just when all seemed lost, from down the road came one of the skirmishers. At a full gallop he charged straight into what was left of the horde. The horde scattered in panic and began to fleeing back into the woods.

"Now my brothers, now let us end this!" Came the commander's cry. The Star Knights broke their formation and pursued the fleeing enemy, killing all that remained of the horde.

The Commander knelt down and wiped his blade on the tunic of a fallen enemy and sheaved his sword. He looked around at the ground littered with the dead, tears filling his eyes. "Orin," He said rushing over to the body of a brother knight. He knelt down besides the body and shut Orin's eyes. "Rest well, my brother."

"Commander, a small band went ahead making for the town. I followed them until I heard the war cries behind me, but I followed them long enough to see them head into the town."

"Brother William, we owe you a great thanks." The commander said standing and placing his hand on William's shoulder.

"I did my duty to my brothers' commander, nothing more."

"Where's brother Edmond?" The Commander asked.

"He's here Commander." A voice came from up the hill. A brother Star Knight came from the woods, carrying over his shoulder the body of Edmond; he went and laid it besides the remains of Orin.

"How many of the horses survived?" Said the Commander, feeling suddenly very cold and tired.

"Two." William answered.

"Put the bodies on the horses and let us leave this place of death. There are still thieves we must apprehend."

The Knights placed the bodies of their fallen brothers on the horses and left the valley in silence. They knew they had escaped death and won a victory against the odds, but it was a bitter victory. Two brother Knights had fallen this night and it was not over yet. A band of thieves had slipped away into the night, gaining the advantage over the Star Knights.

*   *   *

"No Tom, I have to do it."

"But if you're caught they'll……"

"I won't get caught."

"Well I better come with you then."

"No!" Henri was sharper then he intended to be, but he'd had enough. Since leaving the tavern Tom had followed him to the foot of the castle trying to talk him out of his plan. He knew the risks, but he was still determined to go through with it. "Sorry Tom but I'll go alone, its better you don't get involved."

Tom tried one last time. "Why have you got to do this? Let's just go back to the Wheel and grab a purse or two on the way. You don't need to do this." But his pleading fell on death ears.

"I can't buy my freedom and marry Elizabeth by stealing a couple of purses filled with a few copper coins. Besides, after my father takes his share I'd be left with nothing. I need gold."

"Can you not just become a tanners apprentice or take up gong farming? I hear you could make up to a silver denar per night."

"It would take too long to save enough coin and my father would take most of it. Besides that, who would take on a Richards anyway?"

Tom knew this to be true; no one would willingly take on a Richards. It would damage a business's reputation. "You know you're as stubborn as your father." Tom said accepting that nothing he said was going to change Henri's mind.

Henri smiled. "Wait for me at the Wheel; I'll be back in an hour with enough money to buy my own kingdom." He said slapping Tom on his arm.

"Alright, but make sure you're no longer." Tom said turning and walking off. He strode a few paces and without looking back he called over his shoulder. "And don't get bloody caught."

Henri stood and watched Tom walk away, it was better to wait till Tom had gone he kept saying to himself, though in truth he was scared. His heart was pounding and he felt sick. He stood at the foot of the hill that was crowned with the castle of Heath Hollow. Looking up he could have sworn the castle had got bigger. He felt suddenly naked as if hundreds of eyes were watching him, daring him to try and sneak in.

The castle of Heath Hollow was old. Its once mighty white walls were now weathered and crumbling. The hill which gave the castle its commanding presence was now covered with bushes and trees. It was a castle that had not seen action, nor expecting any in the coming years.

With a deep breath Henri started climbing up the hill. This was the easy part, anybody could approach the castle walls unseen, even if the guards were looking out in the same direction. Henri moved quickly uphill, snagging his tunic on bushes as he went. Breathlessly he reached the foot of the towering castle walls. They appeared somewhat bigger then he remembered them, despite their crumbling state. He felt as though his heart would burst from his chest and at any moment the alarm would be raised. But the night was almost silent.

The stretch of wall in front of him was in a bad repair. A few years ago a small earthquake had shook the region, causing some stonework to move which left some stones slightly jutting from the others. A year ago Henri had climbed the same stretch of wall. He had been dared to steal a banner from the battlements and bring it back to the Wheel. He had done so, and had found that the wall was scalable, and a yearlong plan began forming in his head.

Henri jumped and grabbed at a projecting stone, he quickly found a foot hold and began climbing the wall. The stones were so cold that his fingers were beginning to numb, making it more difficult to get any grip. But it was easier than he had remembered, even though the stones were slippery with snow. He quickly reached the top of the battlements where he stopped and listened for any movements. He couldn't hear anything, not any guards talking, and no footsteps of them patrolling along the wall. All seemed too quiet for his liking. He poked his head over the battlement. It was clear of any guards, so he scaled over the wall on to the battlement. He was in, and his previous nerves had turned into an excitement that he had never felt before.

The castle was a small square shape with a square tower in each corner. A single gatehouse controlled the entrance on the west wall. Buildings for all the castles needs were built against the outer walls, which gave them extra strength.

Henri looked out across the courtyard, looking for a way to get to the treasury tower unnoticed. Two guards stood beside the doorway to the northwest tower, opposite were the barracks for the lord's Men-at-Arms. No one had seen him yet but he had to move quickly, if any of the guards would have looked towards the south wall now, they would have spotted him. He noticed empty wagons parked below him and he crept quickly down the battlement stairs towards the wagons and hid underneath one.

His heart was racing and he felt certain he had been spotted, but no shout of alarm came. The ease of it all was starting to discomfort him. He peaked between the spokes of the wagon's wheel at the treasury tower. He knew it was the treasury tower from the size of it and by the fact that even on this night it was guarded.

From the courtyard there was only one way into the tower and that was guarded. Henri was unsure how he was going to get past them, maybe he couldn't. He was about to give up and sneak back out before anyone noticed him when he had an idea. He needed a distraction, something that would make the guards leave their post. He looked around from under the wagon, looking for how he could make a distraction, the stables. If he could spook the horses, cause them to panic, but how? Fire! Set alight to some hay that would be enough to panic them. He looked at a torch in its brackets fixed on to the wall. Then looked back over at the guards; they had their backs to him. Now was the time he said to himself. He slid out from under the wagon and dashed over to the stairs. Quickly grabbing the torch from its bracket, he rushed over to the stables and opened a small shutter at the side and threw the torch in. He quickly went and slid back under a wagon expecting a shout of alarm. But none came.

It didn't take long for the fire to take its desired effect. Horses began to thrash about, Rearing and kicking at their pens in a blind panic. The guards suddenly snapped into motion. They left their post rushing over to the stable, shouting as they went. "Fire, quickly fetch some water!"

Henri crawled under the wagons, using them as cover for as long as he could. Then slipping out from under the last wagon he sprinted towards the tower. He got to the doorway to find that the oak door was open; he quickly went inside, shutting the door behind him.

The room was dark with no light. The smell of oil and leather hung heavy in the air inside. It took a while for Henri's eyes to adjust to the darkness. He looked around but couldn't see any gold. The room was full of weapons, blankets, boots and many other things an army would need on campaign.

Henri walked around the room in wonder at the weapons, and then he noticed a spiral staircase at the back of the room. He went up the stairs which bought him out at another room on the next level. Like the room down stairs there was no gold, but was filled with empty boxes. At the back was another stairway. Henry climbed these stairs to see where they went. They took him to a thick, wooden door studded with metal. It was locked with a padlock that was as big as his hand. He tried to shoulder the door open but it didn't move.

Henri cursed himself for not thinking that any of the doors could be locked. Why didn't he think of it? It was obvious. He lashed out and kicked the door in anger. What he needed was a picklock he thought. Then he had an idea. He rushed down the stairs into the room filled with boxes. He began searching around the boxes looking for a crowbar so he could break the padlock away from the door. He found one inside an empty box in a dark corner opposite the stairs.

Just as Henri was about to head back up the stairs a loud bang followed by voices caused Henri to instinctively jump inside an empty box. He wondered if someone had seen him or heard him kicking the door. He took a deep breath to calm himself. The voices suddenly became clear and the flickering light from a torch filled the room with a dull yellow light.

"I assure you my Lord Aide we will be ready come the spring." One of the voices said.

"What of the masons, I trust you have negotiated a more reasonable price?" Said a more privileged sounding voice.

"They won't budge my Lord Aide. They know trouble is brewing and claim every castle in the kingdom will want skilled masons."

"What wretched times we do live in when peasants can make demands to a Lord Aide. Were we in the days of old, then I would have them strung up for their insolence!"

"Am I to tell them that we are agreeable to their price?"

"We have little other choice; the castle is in need of repairs, without them children throwing stones could bring the walls down."

The two figures walked up the stairs taking the light with them, leaving Henri in the dark once more. He didn't know how long he was hiding in the box but it seemed like hours. His legs began to hurt and tighten. He was about to give up and climb out to stretch his legs when the voices returned.

"More is needed if you are to secure your son's position and promote your own."

"I have this very day negotiated an arrangement that shall help fill my own coffers." Answered the more privileged voice.

Henri was now fed up with hiding, he just wanted to steal a bag of gold and go home. His heart was racing and his legs hurt, but it was curiosity that got the better of him. He managed to turn on to his knees in the box and peep over for a glimpse of who the two voices were.

The first Henri noticed was the Lord Aide. He was tall, thin and looked ancient. He wore a long ankle length black robe made of velvet that pointed up at the shoulders. Atop of his head he wore a matching tricorne hat with a long red feather projecting from the back; around his shoulders he wore the symbol of his status, a chain of gold coins with a golden key in the middle.

The other figure was harder to make out as his back was to Henri. He was shorter than the Lord Aide by a good couple of feet and he wore what looked like a grey cloak with the hood pulled over his head. Other than that Henri could make nothing out.

Henri tried to adjust himself to try and get a better look. *Crack*. The noise stopped the two figures in their tracks. Henri instinctively ducked back down. Why had he done it? Why did he have to look? He should have just stayed stooped down hidden in the box. His grandfather had always used to tell him that his curiosity would be the end of him, and now he feared he was right.

The Lord Aide snatched the torch from his companion and held it out peering out across the room. "It's just the boxes my Lord Aide, at night they creek and crack as if they were talking to each other."

The Lord Aide seemed satisfied with the explanation and gave the torch back. "Come with me, I have yet more business this night to attend." They walked back down the stairs and out of the tower locking the door behind them.

Henri heard the door bang shut and he let out a sigh of relief. That had been close. He climbed out of the box and flexed his legs until the tingling had passed. Then, snatching up the crowbar, and feeling suddenly very confident as if his near capture had somehow empowered him, he raced up the stairs. I'm going to do this he kept saying over and over in his mind.

He got to the thick oak door and slid his crow bar through the loop of the padlock. He twisted with all the strength he had. Nothing happened. He tried it again straining until it felt as though is body would explode from the pressure. *Snap,* the padlock had broken.

Henri removed the padlock throwing it to the floor and then pulled back the bolt. He pushed the door open to a room filled with chests and a desk piled with papers at the far end. He went in and opened the first chest he came to. It was full with lots of small bags. He took one of the bags out and opened it. Golden coins glittered in the gloom. The purse was full with golden crowns, how many he couldn't tell. But it was enough. He was rich, and visions of what he would do with the money circled around in his head. But he still had to get out without being caught. Suddenly realizing this Henri pushed the purse into his boot and ran down both set of stairs until he was back in the room filled with weapons. He rushed over to the door and tried to open it, but it was locked. He heard the startled guards on the other side sliding the key into the lock. Henri quickly went and ducked behind a pile of shields waiting for a chance to escape. The guards came bursting through the door holding a torch out in front of them.

"Who goes there?!" one of them shouted.

"Maybe it was the ghost." The other guard said a little nervously.

"It sounded real enough to me. I'll search the room upstairs, you search down here."

"I'm not stopping down here on my own."

"Stop being such a scared child."

"Come on you've heard the tale, and besides that, we've only got the one torch."

"Alright but you take the torch and go first." The two guards, luckily for Henri, went up to search the room upstairs.

Henri crept out from behind the pile of shields and rushed outside. The fire in the stable had been put out and guards were spread out over the courtyard. There was no way past without being seen, but he had to do something. He looked around trying to find an escape route, but guards were everywhere. From the corner of his eye he thought he had seen someone, a shadow seemingly watching him, but as soon as it appeared it had vanished again.

He began to feel uneasy and that at any moment he would be caught and hung. He swallowed down his fears and as he was about to find somewhere to hide, when he noticed an unattended cart full of dung and hay. Without needing to think about it he rushed over and climbed into the cart and buried himself in the dung. The smell made him feel sick, but he knew this was his best chance of escape.

He couldn't tell how long he had been there, but soon he heard muffled voices and the cart began to move. As soon as the cart had begun to move it came to a stop again. Henri heard a brief conversation followed by a bang and a squawk and the cart began to move again. He was through the gate.

The cart left the castle on the road to the town. It was a bumpy uneven road that made Henri bang and bump around in the dung. He waited until the cart was a distance from the castle before jumping out. He landed with a thud and quickly ran into the nearest bush.

Henri took a deep breath of relief. He had done it, and he felt as though he could have taken the kingdom on, as if no one could stop him. Now he could buy his independence from the lord with his own money and marry Elizabeth. He waited until the cart was out of sight before he went and headed for home.

Henri quickly walked down the road and soon came back to the town. The town's folk were still busy making merry, for the night was still young. He avoided the main street and took to the back alleys trying to avoid any suspicious eyes. But since escaping the castle he had felt that he was being watched. Twice he had looked behind him, but had seen no one.

He came to his family home, a squat poor building with a thatched roof surrounded by mud and muck. He could see the flicker of a fire from behind the seams of the closed door and knew it must be his mother. He opened the door and the inside was no better than the outside. The walls were black with damp and smoke, the floor was muddy and wet. In this one room six people had to live, sleep and eat. There by the fire rapped in an old blanket sat his mother. She looked thin and frail like an old spear wrapped in a blanket.

She looked up. "Henri, what's happened to you? And that smell." She said holding her finger to her nose.

"I was walking home and someone emptied their chamber pot." Henri lied.

"Looks like you've been rolling in it." She said knowing Henri was lying.

"I slipped mother nothing more." Henri said knowing his mother suspected there was more to this then he said. "Anyway I came back to give you this." Henri stooped down and pulled the purse from his boot. He opened it and took out a thick golden coin and handed it to his mother.

"Where did you get this?" She said turning it over in her thin hands.

"I've become a tanner's apprentice." The lie was so smooth that Henri would have believed it himself.

His mother shot him a look as though she knew the truth already. "Where did you get this?" She asked once more, standing and staring Henri straight in the eye.

Henri couldn't lie anymore, but he didn't want her knowing the truth either. "Does it matter? Just take it; you need it more than I do anyway."

Despite Henri being covered in muck his mother hugged him tightly and said. "You're a Richards in every way, yet at the same time you will never be like them." She turned back to the fire, placing more wood on, which caused red ambers to fly up and around the room. "Are you hungry? I have some bread."

"No you have it; I'm going back to the Wheel, I'll get something to eat there and take a bath." Henri added suddenly very conscious of the smell of the dung.

Henri left his mother where he had found her, sitting wrapped in a blanket by the fire. He went out into the street thinking about Elizabeth. He wondered in the middle of the street not paying any attention to his surroundings. But he had done what Tom said couldn't be done, and later he will meet Elizabeth at the lonely tree and ask her hand in marriage. He was sure she would marry him especially as now he had the coin. Finally he would be able to better himself and maybe as the years passed the Richards would have more of a respectable name, and it was all down to his actions this night.

As Henri walked along daydreaming of a better future, soldiers burst from the dark passageways and surrounded him. With swords drawn and levelled at Henri, escape was impossible. They shoved Henri face down onto the mucky ground and shackled his hands. A soldier twice the size of Henri roughly searched him and found the purse of coins hidden in his boot. They pulled him back to his feet and back handed him across his face.

"Enough." A voice said.

Henri looked up at the person who had spoken. He wasn't dressed the same as the other soldiers but as a Knight in the Order of the Star. Henri spat blood from his mouth on to the ground and tried to speak, but no words could he find in the confusion. People came out of their homes to see what the commotion was. Then a voice Henri recognised screamed at the soldiers.

"Leave him alone!" Henri's mother shouted rushing over to Henri. She had heard the commotion and fearing the worst came rushing out.

Two of the soldiers intercepted her, holding her arms to restrain her. The Star Knight went over to her and said, "This boy is under arrest in the name of the Lord of Heath Hollow."

"Why, what has he done?" She angrily asked.

"Theft, I believe he'll hang in the morning." He said turning and signalling for the soldiers to move.

Henri's mother broke down and fell to her knees shouting, pleading at the leaving soldiers to let her son go. Helpless she felt, and helpless she watched as her son was led away in chains.

For tomorrow Henri would hang.

Chapter 2

Tom was roughly shaken awake from a deep drunken sleep. He groggily sat up and swung his legs off the small wooden bed. His eyes were blurry and his stomach felt as if rolling waves were crashing around inside of him. He rubbed at his red ringed eyes to clear them, and standing in front of him was Sally, his favourite whore.

She was beautiful, short with a slender figure that pleased many men; she wore a plain woollen red dress that emphasized her womanly figure. Her long dark hair was tied in to a ball at the back of her head and she had painted her eyes green, giving her an exotic look that would attract more custom.

"You know you're not supposed to stay the whole night." She said with a stern look upon her face.

Tom said nothing for a moment and just stared into her deep sky blue eyes. He could see she was angry, but her eyes told him it was all pretence. "Why didn't you wake me then?" he said with a broad grin across his face.

"I tried, but you were so drunk that even the heavens collapsing would not have woken you."

"Well I've awoken now." He reached out, grabbed her waist and pulled her on to his knee. He stroked at her breasts then began pulling up her dress, stroking her inner thigh.

She cheekily slapped his face and stood back up. "You have no money left, and besides, I'm not working until

51

tonight." She said walking over to a small table and pouring a small wooden beaker of water. She took a sip and went back over to Tom, handing him the beaker. "You had better get dressed and be on your way."

"Why what's the rush?" Tom said before he greedily gulped down the water.

"You know the rules; if Degros finds out you've spent the night again, he'll rip your arms off for sure this time."

Tom thought of the tavern keeper's massive hands grabbing his arms and slowly pulling them out of their sockets. He shuddered at the thought, nobody but an idiot would dare get on the wrong side of Degros.

"Quickly, get dressed." Sally said throwing Tom his clothes, seeing that he was looking suddenly very pale.

Tom tossed the empty beaker onto the bed and pulled on his trousers. "Did Henri come back last night?" He asked suddenly remembering that he was supposed to meet him here last night.

"I haven't seen him, though last night was a busy night."

Tom pulled on his boots and his thick green woollen tunic. "I had better go and find him then." He said fastening his belt around his waist. "I'll be back with more coin later Sal." He said with a grin.

"I'll look forward to it; now go before Degros finds you here." She said with a grin.

Tom turned and left Sally shaking her head. He liked Sally and had visited her whenever he had enough coin. She was older than him, though by how much he didn't know. He could find a comfort with her that no one else could offer him. Sometimes he would pay just to sit and talk with her, and once when he was drunk, he had asked her hand in marriage. Though he had been drunk, he could remember her laughing at the offer, and the memory still hurt.

He quietly opened the door and left the room. All was quiet; he crept to the edge of the balcony that overlooked the tavern below. Looking over the wooden railings below, he could see no one. The place had been cleaned and made ready for another day's business. He crept along as quietly as he could, passing several closed doors until he came to the stairs. He stopped at the top and stooped down for a better look. No sign of Degros. Rising back up, he rushed down the stairs, making enough noise to have woken the whole town, and across to the entrance and slipped out of the door, into the street.

It was a dull, overcast morning. The snow that had fallen the day before had now melted away leaving muddy puddles dotted around. People were busy clearing the streets of last night's festivities. The letter of the law also meant Tom was supposed to help, but he had other concerns and had no intention of helping. The marketplace was busy with merchants setting up their wares on the stalls that lined the edges of the cobbled square. Tom decided the first person he would go and see was Elizabeth. Maybe she had seen Henri? Maybe he was with her now?

Tom strode off avoiding the mucky puddles as best he could. He had to quickly weave around a merchant carrying an armful of silk, narrowly just avoiding knocking in to him. The merchant called out a curse and carried on with his business. Then from the corner of his eye he saw Degros, a giant colossus of a man carrying an ale cask over each shoulder.

A shudder ran down Tom's spine at the thought of being caught by him; if he had stopped in Sally's bed a little longer he would have been caught, and would have lost his arms to this man. Tom rubbed his arms as if he felt the pain of Degros grabbing his wrists and pulling his arms out of their sockets with an unimaginable strength. He stopped in his tracks, wondering if the tavern keeper could really have the strength to pull his arms off. He looked over at Degros's arms. They were as thick as tree trunks and longer than his body. Whispers amongst the common folk said that his ancestors were Lords of the Gigantes, and one couldn't gaze upon him and wonder. Everything about him was unwelcoming and tough; his squared head even looked as though it had been made of bricks. Tom decided that Degros could have ripped his arms off only using one hand, and that he wouldn't risk getting caught again.

He walked over to Elizabeth's father's stall in the far corner of the market place, only to find she wasn't there. Two of her household servants helped Elizabeth's sister Catharine set up. She wore an elegant green dress with white and yellow flowers stitched in to it. He kept a distance, waited a little while and watched, hoping that Elizabeth might turn up at any moment. She never did and after a while he gave up. He went over to Catharine and asked, "Where is your sister?"

Catharine stopped what she was doing and shot Tom a look of disgust, as if his very presence near her was an unbelievable outrage within society. "What business does one so lowly born have with my sister?" She said in a polite but mocking way.

"I wondered if she has seen Henri." Tom asked ignoring Catharine's mocking tone. "I think your sister may have seen him."

"My sister returned late last night in tears, and I know that no good fieldworker had something to do with it. I swear if he has tried to dishonour her," she paused to regain control of her temper "Then my father shall see him swing."

"That's not what he wanted her for!" Tom blurted out, surprised by the accusation made.

Catharine suddenly stopped what she was doing and gave Tom her full attention. "So what did that fieldworker want with my sister?" She asked, as her interest in the matter was suddenly tickled.

"Nothing, I don't know." Tom said looking away from Catharine's inquisitive gaze.

"Tom you will tell me what you know, or I will inform my father that Henri has insulted her honour as a fair maiden."

"You can't do that; Henri would never do such a thing."

"All I know is that nobody of any worth will take the word of a Richards over that of a De'lacy; now I would tell me if I were you."

Tom felt trapped, he couldn't think properly, his stomach was churning and his head hurt. "He was going to ask her hand in marriage." He said, feeling defeated and weak.

Catharine shot a burst of laughter at Tom, causing the merchants on the stalls next to them to stop and look. "My father would never agree to such a thing!" She snapped. "Besides she didn't sound very happy last night, or this morning, she refuses even to leave her room. Then I'd be the same if one so low asked my hand in marriage." She giggled and shook her head. "Stupid boy, how was he even supposed to pay for the wedding, with soil from the fields perhaps?" She added, giggling the whole time.

"I've told him as much myself, but he wouldn't listen." Tom said, hearing how pathetic he must have sounded.

Catharine was about to speak when the marketplace was interrupted by the ringing of a bell. It was the Town Crier, a monstrously fat man dressed in long crimson robe with little brass bells hanging all over it. He waddled into the centre of the marketplace ringing his bell, which made his fat wobble in motion with the ringing. People stopped what they were doing and drew in closer to the Crier. Once he had the attention of the marketplace he raised his hands in to the air and spoke out in a clear booming voice.

"Hear ye, hear ye! Good people of Heath Hollow, his lordship bids thee all a happy summer's end. He now commands that provisions be stowed in the granaries ready for the coming of winter. His Lordship shall then ration them accordingly, so that none may starve during the cold winter. Any found to have undeclared produce shall face the full justice of the lord's law. Those who are by law the lord's property are hereby commanded to make clear the streets, and then back to the fields to be about your lord's work.

Lastly and darkest of all, that during the night upon the hill road, the most despicable crime of murder took place. The bodies of twelve men lay slain upon the cold ground."

The crowd began to fidget and mutter with disbelief, who they wondered would commit such an evil thing on such a night? The muttering became so loud that the Town Crier had to ring his bell in order to regain their attention once more.

"His lordship offers a reward of five silver crowns to any with information that will bring the murders to justice. Should any have information they should seek out the Lord Aide immediately."

With the mornings announcements finished, the Town Crier waddled off to another place in the town to make the announcements, ringing his bell as he went. He would spend the morning waddling around the town ringing and shouting the Lord's news as he went.

Tom watched the Crier waddle off, thinking of what he just heard. That's where Henri must be, at the hill road. His father would make him go and scavenge the bodies for anything of value. He felt suddenly more confident of finding Henri. To the hill road he thought.

"Well Tom you heard the lord's orders, now go clean the streets and leave your betters to their business." Catharine scornfully said breaking Toms thoughts.

Tom said nothing, not wanting to speak anymore with Catharine. He decided she was stupid and mindless. Everything she said was a mirror of how society viewed things and how they wanted it to be. As long as those higher up in society were alright, what did it matter about those below? He walked away heading for the hill road to find Henri, maybe he had stolen enough coin to buy his freedom from the lord as well. When he had found Henri he would ask him he told himself.

Catharine stood watching Tom walk away. She had managed to find out from him that Henri had asked her sister's hand in marriage. But why was she crying? She couldn't think why and decided she must go see her sister. She called to one of her servant and asked them to fetch her father's steward to mind the stall.

Tom walked the narrow streets heading north. The streets were a mess, but they always were. He tried to keep as close to the middle of the street as possible, many of times he had been in the wrong place at the wrong time and a chamber pot had been emptied from a window above, covering him in muck, but it was impossible not to tread in any of it. The rich had special shoes that lifted them above the muck, but not Tom, he was lucky to have shoes at all. He passed people sweeping rubbish in the streets and an old man called out to him. "You come to give us a hand young Thomas?"

"No, I'm wanted back in the fields." Tom lied, not stopping to talk and walked on.

"Well you're going the wrong way then." The old man shouted at Tom's back.

Tom began to jog, slipping in the muck as he went. He soon left the town behind him and took to the hill road. He came to the place of the murders and was met by a scene of chaos. Guards were everywhere and a crowd of peasants had gathered to gaze at the bloody horror.

There was an excitement to the crowd and much talk about who could have done this. Local thieves some said, wild beasts said others. "No this was the work of demons." Said an old woman.

"No, no, these were mercenaries, come to sack our town." An old man with one arm said. "It's why they have come that's worrying." A voice answered. The crowd excitedly spoke for hours after of a coming war that would end all things. But one thing was for sure, it had made people nervous. Last night was seen as a holy night and only possessed monsters could have done such a thing on such a night.

Tom pushed his way to the front of the crowd; he could see the bloody, motionless bodies of soldiers littering the ground. Their leather jerkins bore no sigil of any lord, but they were big men that looked terrifying even in death. Guards moved from body to body, lifting and placing them on the backs of carts, along with their weapons that were lying alongside the bodies. But where was Henri?

The guards weren't letting anybody near the bodies and Henri was not amongst the crowd. Tom started to get anxious over what could have happened to Henri. He walked away from the crowd, leaving them gossiping of the night's events. He leaned on a tree besides the road, fearing the worst his head started to spin. He fell on to his knees, squelching in the mud as he fell, and vomited.

But what had happened to Henri? He had never let him down before. Images of Henri hanging began to form in his head. Perhaps he had been captured and had spent the night in a small dirty cell, to be hung later this morning. Despair took hold of him. He began to shake and once more vomited on to the ground.

Then he heard the ringing of a bell that regained his senses. The Town Crier he thought, suddenly standing up and realising. There was no mention of a hanging to take place. Henri couldn't have been caught, he must be at home, and if not, then he would have been at some point, and his mother must have seen him. He would have been home at some point, he said out loud to reassure himself.

Tom, suddenly very confident, turned back down the hill road and ran to the Richards family home, leaving the chaos on the hill road behind him.

*   *   *

Elizabeth had spent most of the night crying, and now she sat on the edge of her four-poster bed, staring at herself in a silver hand mirror that she held out in front of her. Her eyes were red, puffy, her hair un-brushed and she was still dressed in her blue dress from the night before.

Late last night after the market had closed, she had gone to the lonely tree to wait for Henri, wondering what it was he had wanted to ask her. Deep down she thought she knew, he would ask her to be his mistress. Secret lovers like in the stories. There by the tree she waited in the snow and cold, with the sound of the nearby river running through the air. He never came.

She waited for as long as she dared before it finely got too cold and she ran all the way home, bursting into tears as she collapsed onto her bed. Now she wondered why he hadn't shown up. She thought Henri had liked her, she was sure of it, so why? Then anger entered her thoughts. She was too good for him; anyway he is only a fieldworker she told herself. She would never speak to him ever again, she decided.

She threw her hand mirror at her pillow in anger and flung herself back on the bed, looking up at the carvings of knights rescuing fair maidens on the roof of her bed. She wished life was like the old stories, where knights in shining armour would sweep maidens off their feet and onto the back of their noble steeds, riding off into the sunset together to marry, and live happily ever after. But true life was not like that. Instead men were liars and women didn't marry for love, but for position and power. She was not like that she told herself, and decided that

61

one day she would marry an honest man, a man who would never let her wait alone in the cold for half the night. She would marry for love. She closed her eyes to relieve the dull ach in her head, and fell into a light sleep only to be awaken an hour later by a loud knocking at her bedroom door.

"Elizabeth, are you awake?" Came the familiar voice of her sister through the door.

"Go away Catharine."

"Let me in. I need to talk with you."

"Well I don't want to talk to you." Elizabeth snapped back.

"I know why you spent the night crying. It was because Henri asked your hand in marriage wasn't it."

Elizabeth shot up off the bed and rushed over to open the door. She pulled the locking bolt back and opened the door to find her sister smiling on the other side. "Quick come in." She said, pulling her sister in by her arm.

"Elizabeth stop you're hurting me."

"What did you just say about Henri?" Elizabeth sharply asked, shutting the door behind her.

"Did he try and force himself on you?" Catharine asked. "It's ok you can tell me."

"What! No. what did you say about Henri asking for my hand in marriage?" Elizabeth asked back with a look of confusion across her face.

"Last night Henri asked for your hand in marriage, and I assume you said no, so he tried to force himself on you didn't he?"

Elizabeth stood shocked at what Catharine had just said. "No he never tried to force himself on me! And he never asked my hand in marriage either, so where did you hear this?"

Catharine paused as if she was unsure if she should say anything. "Tom came to the stall and was asking for you. He said that Henri was going to ask for your hand in marriage. But don't worry I set him straight, and told him what folly it is. He even thought you might be with Henri now. Is that why you spent the night crying?"

Elizabeth was confused. "No, last night after the market had closed I went to the lonely tree to meet Henri there, but he never showed. He told me at the marketplace that he wanted to ask me something, but I didn't see him after that." Tears began to fill her eyes. She turned away from Catharine to try and hide them.

But Catharine had already seen them; along with the look on her face as she had told her that Henri was going to ask her hand in marriage. "You couldn't accept such an offer. Elizabeth you're the oldest daughter of the richest merchant in the town. You're supposed to marry up, not down."

"I know that, I'm not stupid. But I must find Henri and speak with him." Elizabeth said wiping away her tears.

"I don't think you should see him anymore, if father finds out, he'll lock you away in a tower, just like in them stories you like so much."

Elizabeth turned abruptly on Catharine, "You had better not tell him or I'll......" A sharp knock on the door interrupted her before she could finish. She snatched opened the door to her mother's handmaiden's old, stern face. "What do you want?" Elizabeth asked in anger.

The old handmaiden had been in her mother's service for many years and had known the two sisters since they had been born. She wore a white dress with a matching cowl on her head that shown that she was a fair maiden, untouched by the hand any man.

"That is no way for a young lady to speak!" Her mother's handmaiden sharply reproofed. "Your Lady mother says that you are summoned before your father, he awaits your presence in his private chambers."

"Well I must bathe and change first." Elizabeth said going over to her bed and slumping on it.

"Your mother said I'm to escort you to your father forthwith; and a young lady should be bathed and ready before the sun even rises." Her mother's handmaiden gave Elizabeth a look as if it was pointless to try and argue otherwise.

Elizabeth knew better than to argue with the old handmaiden. She stood brushing at her crumpled dress with her hands. "We'll speak later." She said looking at her sister.

"Very well," Catharine could see the look of concern on Elizabeth's face "I haven't told him anything." She added as Elizabeth left her bedchamber.

Elizabeth was escorted across the hallway and down the stairs in silence. She disliked her mother's handmaiden; she seemed to see everything, even before it had even happened.

"Is there anything you wish to tell me my young lady?" The old handmaiden asked Elizabeth, sensing that Elizabeth was hiding something.

"No, I haven't slept very well, that's all."

"No one would sleep well still wearing the dress they walked the streets in last night." The old handmaiden said in a suspicious tone.

Elizabeth avoided answering the implied question and carried on across to the hall in silence. The other servants were busy cleaning the squared hall of last night's feast that her father had held for the wealthiest merchants of the town. She walked around the large polished table and through a double door that led to a long corridor.

The corridor was dimly lit by large candles fixed in fancy glass candle sticks placed on small well-polished tables. Old paintings of ancestors hung on the walls all the way to her father's private chambers. The old handmaiden escorted her to the large door at the opposite end and knocked. "Whoever he is you had best forget him." She said as she turned and left Elizabeth at her father's door alone.

Elizabeth began to fear the worst, did her father know about Henri? How had he found out? Trouble was waiting for her just behind the door she thought.

"Enter!" Shouted her father's voice. Elizabeth opened the door to find her father standing before his desk. He was dressed in his finest clothes of dark green velvet edged with golden lace. He was short, plump with a bold head and a close clipped beard. He was a self-driven man, driven by the need for money and advancement. But behind her father's desk sat another and He didn't look friendly.

The man had a thin, pale hawk like face that betrayed his age. His small, beady black ringed eyes seemed to be everywhere, but you couldn't see what he was looking at. His long robes were colourless, all black apart from a gold chain of office with a key hanging in the middle that hung around his shoulders. Despite him being indoors, he wore a tricorne hat with a long red feather pinned at the back.

"My Lord Aide I present my eldest daughter Elizabeth." Elizabeth's father stood aside and gestured for her to step forward.

"My Lord Aide." She said stepping forward and giving a clumsy curtsy.

The Lord Aide rose from the high backed chair behind her father's desk and walked over to her, casting his beady eyes over her womanly figure. "Does she yet bleed?" He asked Elizabeth's father, his face betraying no emotion.

Elizabeth could smell wine on his breath and a hint of sweat coming from his body as he walked around her, inspecting the goods he was being offered. She wondered what was going on and why she had been summoned.

"She is now sixteen years and bleeds as a grown woman, my Lord Aide."

"Good, then we have an agreement." The Lord Aide said as he rubbed his cold hands together.

Elizabeth began to feel angry, how they dare to speak of her in such a manner, and as though she was not even in the room to hear. "What was I summoned for father?" She asked, unable to hide the anger in her voice.

"You are to marry John Kinge, the son of the Lord Aide." Her father announced.

An arrow of shock struck Elizabeth deep inside her stomach. "I can't marry him father." She quickly blurted out, not being able to think properly.

"You will do as I bid!" Her father shouted at her, with his face reddening in anger.

Elizabeth stood looking sullen. "I'm not one of your meat pies you can sell off at a whim." She said, trying to think how she could stop this from happening, and then she remembered Henri. "I can't marry John, as I am promised to another." She said in a more polite manner.

Her father shot her an angry look. "I haven't given my permission for you to marry any other, too whom have you been promised?"

"I'm promised to Henri Richards." She answered, looking away from her father to avoid his angry gaze.

The Lord Aide's emotionless face suddenly betrayed an interest at the mention of the name. Elizabeth's father however was furious.

"You will not marry one so low, and will marry whom I have chosen for you!" Her father said rushing to her and grabbing her arms. "Do I make myself clear? You marry who I choose! And I choose John Kinge."

Elizabeth fought back tears and nodded. Her father released her arms and she quickly spun round and ran out of the room, weeping as she went.

"Forgive me my Lord Aide, but she shall do as commanded. Rest assured that no other proposals have been made." Elizabeth's father said fearing that the arrangement could have been compromised.

"Very well, I shall draw up the contract and be back on the morrow for you and your daughter to sign." The Lord Aide said. As he left the room a sly smile crept across his face. "Time to deal with that small problem". He said softly to himself.

*   *   *

Henri no longer had any sense of time. His ribs were hurting and bruised, making breathing a painful experience. He was tired, hungry and had severe aching in his back and legs. Every time he tried to stretch out he was met by a cold, wet stone wall of his cell, and his aching went on.

The night before he had been roughly taken back to the castle and beaten by a jailer who was heavily muscled. He had been hit until his ribs were bruised and he could no longer stay on his feet. He had given his name and then he was thrown down into a cell cut into the ground, with just enough room for him to sit curled up in. He had drifted in and out of consciousness like a lost soul falling in an eternal darkness. Whenever he woke, all he could hear was the whistling of the guard as he paced up and down above him. He had once tried to force open the metal bared door above his head; only to be hit with a whip for his troubles.

Henri was ready to die, wanting all the pain to stop. He imaged the crowds that would gather to watch him do the gallows dance, their shouting as his bladder gave and his body jerked; a good end for a Richards. Tears began to well in his eyes, no, better to face death as a man and not a crying baby he told himself.

Henri fell back into an uneasy sleep and the next thing he knew he was being pulled out from of the small cell and dragged down a long dark passageway. He struggled to find his strength to use his legs and was bundled along and up a small stairway into the daylight of the courtyard. It was a dull, grey day, but the light hurt his eyes and he had to close them to calm the pain. He was dragged across the courtyard, stumbling on the cobbled stones as he went. Then the light went darker from behind his eyes and Henri smelt a familiar smell. He opened his eyes to see the room he was in last night. It was piled high with weapons, even more then Henri had seen the night before. He was then taken and shoved up the spiral stairs, to the back of room on the next floor and up that set of stairs to the room where he had stolen the gold.

The guard holding Henri's right arm banged on the thick oak metal studded door with his armoured gloved fist. The door was opened by a small, slender, finely dressed man who gestured for the guards to bring him in. The guards walked through the door, dragging Henri with them and threw him to the floor before a large desk.

"Stand the filth up." Henri had heard that voice the night before when he had hidden in an empty box.

Henri was roughly picked up from the floor and placed on his feet. His legs were wobbly and he felt suddenly very sick, but he forced himself to stay upright on his feet. He recognised the old man sat in a high back chair behind a well-polished desk. The Lord Aide's cold grey eyes stared straight into Henri's. Beside the Lord Aide stood a grim looking, weather worn man dressed in the garb of a Star Knight, all black with a white eight pointed star upon his chest.

"Do you go by the name of Henri Richards?" The Lord Aide said in a voice that commanded obedience.

Henri tried to speak but his mouth was too dry and all that came out was a choke. The grim man came forward and pulled a small water skin from his belt. He unstopped the skin and offered Henri to drink. Henri took the offered skin and greedily drank his fill. He looked around the room at the many chests that must have been filled with silver and gold. The two guards stood either side of the door, close at hand should they be needed. To his right was a fireplace with a lively fire burning brightly, filling the room with its heat. By the fire stood the small finely dressed man who had opened the door to them. Henri had never seen him before, he knew who the Lord's officials were, and he was not one of them. Henri had the sickening feeling the man was an executioner come to measure him up for a rope.

"Well are you Henri Richards or not?" The Lord Aide said regaining Henri's attention.

"Yes I am." Henri woodenly answered.

The Lord Aide pulled open a draw and tossed the purse Henri had stolen onto his desk. "Do you deny that on the night of summer's end in the first year of King Henry, the fourth to bear the name, which you did transgress to steal a purse containing ten gold crowns?"

Henri could see no point in denying it; after all they had found the purse on him. "I deny nothing and ask for the lord's undeserved mercy."

The Lord Aide put his hands together and leaned menacingly forward on his desk. "This purse contains nine gold crowns, where is the other one?"

"Don't know." Henri coolly replied.

A guard stepped forward and kicked Henri at the back of his knee, sending him crashing to the ground.

"I shall ask you again, where is the other golden crown?"

Henri struggled back to his feet "I lost it somewhere in the streets." He said, not wanting them to know that he had given it to his mother.

The Lord Aide's face betrayed nothing of what he might do. Instead his long bony fingers picked up a parchment from off his desk. He looked at Henri with his hard, cold eyes and said in a harsh tone. "The penalty for stealing from your lord is death, and death is what you deserve for your crimes. However, the lord in his mercy has granted you a chance of redemption. He recognises your skill of robbery and has released you to the command of Captain Ulric, who is in need of a person of such skill." The Captain besides the Lord Aide nodded his agreement with what was being said. "Do your job to his satisfaction and his lordship shall grant you a full pardon along with your independence." He then held up the parchment for Henri to see.

Henri looked at the written pardon in disbelief; he felt for sure he would be hung and left for the birds to peck away his rotting flesh. Do this one thing and he could earn his freedom in an honest way and then ask Elizabeth's hand in marriage he thought, but what was he expected to do?

The Lord Aide placed the parchment back onto his desk and waved his hand as a sign that the meeting was at an end. The finely dressed man by the fire stepped forward, bowed and grabbed Henri by the arm, leading him out of the door. A guard closed the door behind them, leaving the Lord Aide and Captain Ulric alone.

"I would rather see him hang, but instead you force my hand to let him live." The Lord Aide sharply said.

"Forgive me my Lord Aide, but my skilled thief was killed during the attack on the hill road and I am in need of a skilled thief."

"Bah." The Lord Aide spat "He's a simple, no good for anything other than working in the fields."

"A simple who managed to sneak past your guards, steal your gold and slither back out without being detected. If it wasn't for my man he would have gotten clean away." Captain Ulric said as he went over to a small side table by the fire and poured himself a goblet of watered down wine.

The Lord Aide gave a grunt of irritation; he disliked the crude captain's familiarity and wanted to dismiss him as soon as he could. He picked up Henri's pardon along with the purse filled with gold crowns and went over and stood beside the fire. "Henri must not return. Use him as you will, but he must not return." He said tossing the purse to Ulric.

Ulric opened the purse and smiled. "Very well, but why is it that he must not return?"

"He could cause me problems should he live, now do we have an agreement?"

"We have." Ulric grinned.

"Good, then you may leave as soon as you're ready." The Lord Aide said as he threw the letter of pardon on to the fire.

Henri was taken back down from the treasury tower and back across the courtyard. He thought he was being taken back to the small cramped cell in the underground dungeons, but he was led towards the building next to the dungeons instead. He was ushered inside to a white plastered room with a wooded planked floor. A small fire crackled away at the far end and sat before the fire were six other men dressed in the same way as the captain he had seen in the treasury tower. They turned and looked at him, then turned back to the fire and began muttering amongst themselves. The finely dressed man who had escorted Henri turned and left without saying anything.

Henri felt uncomfortable, he had just been passed on to a new master with no explanation of what he was expected to do; he had been traded, like cattle is traded at the market he thought to himself. But he knew why he had to do it, he wanted to earn that pardon with his freedom and marry the woman he loved. The only other choice was to hang as the thief he was.

One of the men broke away from the others by the fire and approached Henri. "So you're the rat that avoids detection in the night." He said, coming to stand before Henri.

Henri recognised the handsome face that was staring at him; it was the same person who had arrested him the night before. Henri stood with a look of scorn across his bruised face.

"What, no thanks for saving your life rat boy." The handsome man said, to Henri's disbelief.

"Thanks for having me beaten you mean." Henri replied sarcastically.

"Was it my hands that beat you?" He paused, letting Henri think, and when no response came forth he carried on. "Nor was it my command to have you beaten, so do not thank me for things I have not done. You're a stealthy thief my young rat, but not to stealthy for me it would seem."

Henri noticed a strange accent in his voice and the slight darker tinge of his skin. "Where are you from?" Henri asked.

"What a cleaver rat to have noticed that so quickly."

"I'm no rat, and my name is Henri." He said getting irritated by being called a rat.

"I am Symond, born in the city of Elon-Dor." He said, holding out his hands and inclining his head. "Now we are friends."

"Why am I here?" Henri asked."

Symond sighed and placed his hand on Henri's shoulder. "First you should clean yourself up, if one could not see you, they would be able to smell you. Then we had better get you fed."

Henri stomach growled at the thought of food as he nodded his agreement.

Symond went and fetched a pail of water while the others began cooking, sharpening their swords and packing their things into packs. He soon returned with the water and placed it in the corner where Henri had stayed out the way of the others, watching them.

Henri stripped down and began to wash away the dry dung. The water was icy cold and seemed to revive the muscles in his body; he washed away the blood on his face and padded his body dry with the cloth Symond had brought with the pail of water.

"Here take these." Symond said, handing Henri a bundle of clothes.

Henri took the new garments and put them on. He now looked like the others, dressed in all black; the only difference was his garb had no white star upon his chest. Another knight came over holding a pair of boots and a pack with a rolled up blanket strapped on top.

He was lean with a big red bushy beard that matched his hair and a hard face that had seen too many cold winters. "I'm Garret, the long-sighted as I'm called by some."

"And I'm Henri, the rat boy."

Garret chuckled and passed Henri the boots and pack. "Well even a rat will need good boots where we are going."

"Where are we going?" Henri asked him. But before any answer was given the door opened, and Captain Ulric entered.

"Are we all packed and ready to leave?" He asked to no one in particular.

"Yes Captain, all provisions have been made ready for us to leave as soon as we've eaten." Garret answered.

"Good, then let us eat our fill and be on our way." He looked at Henri. "You to boy, you're one of us now."

All eight of the company sat in a circle, each with a platter filled with thick bacon, eggs, bread and cheese. Henri greedily ate his share and then sat silently watching his fellow companions. They were not what he expected Star Knights to be. They seemed crude, rough and unfriendly. They were nothing like what he had been told Star Knights were like, but what he wondered the most was why they were here, and not at the Star Perceptory in the town?

Ulric finished his platter and wiped his greasy fingers on the tail of his long black surcoat. He fished out an old map from the pouch strapped on to his belt. He cleared some room and unfolded it out in the centre of their made circle. "The village of Raven Wood is about six or so miles south of here; we shall head for the inn there and spend the night. Then early on the morrow we shall pass through the woods and on to the Plains of Pendor." He said tapping at a dot near a small wood. This news was met with utter silence.

Henri looked at the faces of his new companions and saw fear. But fear of what he didn't know. The company sat in silence letting the news sink in, and then Symond finally spoke. "Tales of the evil in that wood have travelled far, would it not be better to take the road to Market Barton and then east."

Ulric shook his head, "The dogs snap on our heels, we must throw them of our scent."

"Well they won't follow us in there!" Garret snapped, trying to sound as if he were not unnerved.

Henri had had-enough; he had plenty of questions and no answers. "Who is chasing you and what do you want me for?" He blurted out, unable to stay silent anymore.

The group of knights looked surprised at one another as if they were unsure of what they should tell him. "In time I shall tell you young one, but not here, where the walls have eyes and ears." Ulric said, to Henri's disappointment. "Now let us leave this place, by night fall I want to be at the inn at Raven Wood." He said, clapping his hands together. "Gather your packs and fill your water skins."

The knights dispersed around the room and made ready to leave. Within the hour the company set out leaving the castle behind them. But instead of using the road that led through the town they turned right at the gatehouse and stumbled down the overgrown hill, and across into the fields, avoiding the town altogether.

The sun had broken out from behind the clouds, making it feel warm, as though summer had never ended, but a cold breeze gently blew reminding the town that winter was on its way. The ground was still wet from the early snow that had melted away, making the fields' boggy and hard going.

Henri could see people bustling around in the fields, stock piling produce onto carts. A light breeze carried their muffled voices along with it. He decided that all wasn't that bad, despite being ankle deep in mud and being led off on an unknown adventure. His good luck had shone through once again he thought; he should have been hung for his crime, but instead he had been given a chance to redeem his honour.

The company then passed by the lonely tree and thoughts of Elizabeth began to whorl around Henri's head. He felt guilty about not being able to meet her last night, but what could he have done? Visions of her standing alone in the cold night waiting, expecting him at any moment, made his guilt worse. He stuck his thumbs into the straps of his pack that Garret had given to him, and carried on in an attempt to block the visions out; but they kept on forming in his mind.

They soon came to the banks of the river Tostig. Ulric stopped the company and looked at distant wooden bridge about a mile or so to the southeast. He pulled out a telescope from his pouch and cast an eye over the bridge ahead. "All quiet." He said snapping shut his telescope.

"Are you looking for the troll?" Henri asked, suddenly feeling excited but afraid at the same time.

"What?" Ulric said confused.

"I heard a story once off a troll called Anselm who lives under the bridge; he charges one piece of silver to pass, any unable to pay the fee he eats, bones and all."

The knights laughed and shook their heads. Ulric shot them an angry glance that ended the laughter. "Save your wet nurse's stories for later boy." He said as he signalled for them to move on.

The company moved on once more and Symond came and walked besides a worried looking Henri. "Have no fear my young friend, I have travelled the kingdoms many times, and I have yet to see any troll." He said smiling, showing his white teeth.

"It's not that." Henri felt comfortable with Symond, more so then with the others, but he was unsure why. "I've never left the town before." He admitted. "And the men that have come back telling tales of monsters and other sorts of evil I do not wish to see."

"How old are you boy?"

"This will be my fifteenth winter."

"A little too old for believing such stories, is it not?" They strode side by side in a moments silence, before Symond spoke again. "Evil comes in many different forms, not all things monstrous are evil, and not all things of beauty are good."

Henri thought on what Symond had said and replied. "Nothing is what it seems."

"Very good, you learn fast my young friend. But one lesson we should all learn is that our eyes see most things, but it is our heart that sees the truth."

Henri was puzzled and was unsure what that meant. "I don't understand." He said feeling foolish.

"You will in time. But always remember, our eyes see, but our heart sees the truth. Now repeat it to me."

Henri stopped and looked into Symonds hazel brown eyes. "Our eyes see, but our heart sees the truth."

"Very good, my young friend, and never may you forget it." Symond said, as he slapped Henri on his back.

The small company of Star Knights and Henri crossed the bridge and headed south, leaving the town of Heath Hollow behind them.

Chapter 3

The village of Raven Wood was odd. Its buildings were odd, its people were odd, and it even smelt odd. Every morning the village Elder would walk twice around the outskirts of the village naked, whipping bloody stripes across his already scared back. A wailing woman would follow behind him dancing and crying out, asking for another day's protection against the mischievous woodland spirits that the villagers believed to be ever present.

The people of Raven Wood were suspicious of everything and lived in fear of the woods that lay on the doorstep of their village, which they simply called the haunted woods, and no one in the village would enter those woods. Many would not even look upon them, through fear of being cursed.

Stories of elves sallying forth from the woods and snatching children from their beds as they slept had been told for generations. One such story told of a mother who went into the woods to save her son, only to be shot with a cursed arrow. She went mad, believing that a spirit had possessed her. For weeks she was tormented and twisted until she was no longer herself. Then the Elder had her taken to the sacred grove, and sacrificed her to appease the woodland spirits. Some say that her spirit still haunts the sacred grove, and that one day she will take revenge upon the village that had sacrificed her.

The village itself was in need of repairs. The wooden buildings were rotten and falling down and Henri's first impression was that the village looked like the aftermath of a siege. Not that he had seen what the aftermath of a siege looked like. The village was dirty, smelly and had a disturbing atmosphere that unsettled Henri. He looked to his companions who seemed steadfast and ready for any event. They seemed unworried by the place, as if they had experienced much worse than this strange village.

As they walked down the main dirt road towards an inn at the far end of the village, a group of children followed their every move. They pointed and giggled at the strange men dressed in black. Twice Garret turned on them, scattering them, but they always came back, like flies around dung. People peered out of their doorways, staring with suspicious eyes at the strange men who had entered their small, quiet village.

They reached a drab looking inn, which was by far the best kept building in the village. Ulric turned to his small company and said in a hushed tone. "Do nothing to upset the locals." He paused a moment before he pushed open the door, and one by one the company entered.

The inn fell silent.

The few people inside stopped dead and glared at the Star Knights. Few visitors ever came to Raven Wood, and it had been many years since Star Knights had passed this way, it made the locals nervous and they sat silently, watching the new comers with both wonder and fear.

Time seemed to have stopped with only the crackling of the fire as proof that it still passed. Finally Ulric stepped forward and spoke. "We need a room for the night." He said loudly. "We have coin to pay."

A middle-aged, thin, scruffy, dirty looking man with wispy straw hair stood up from behind a table and walked over to greet them. "I'm Ghent, keeper of this Inn." He said, smiling and showing his broken, black rotten teeth.

"I am Captain Ulric of the Order of the Star, and these are my men." He said, jerking his head to the men behind him. "We are in need of a room big enough to accommodate us all."

Ghent spread out his thin arms and laughed. "We have rooms a plenty, yes, but a room big enough for you all, I have none."

"We don't need beds, just enough floor space to roll out our blankets."

"Well in that case, I give you my biggest room." He fished a large key from a pocket on the front of his dirty apron and handed it to Ulric. "Up the stairs, last door on your right."

"My thanks, but first my men and I are in need of food and a few jugs of you fine ale."

Ghent shook his head. "Forgive me sir, but we have little enough food for ourselves, and with winter coming."

Ulric pulled out a thick gold coin from his purse and held it up for Ghent to see. "House and feed us for the night, and you shall be well paid for your trouble." He said as he rolled the coin between his finger and thumb, seeing the gold shine brightly in Ghent's eyes.

"Very well, good sir, I shall tend to your needs." He said bowing low.

The tavern keeper went over to an empty corner, pulled two tables together and placed eight chairs around it. "Come now my sirs, sit and I shall fetch a couple of jars of my fine ale." He said bowing and scuttling off to fetch the ale.

Ulric walked over to the table, closely followed by his companions, with their every move being watched by the locals.

Henri could feel the eyes of the locals hard at his back. He quickly walked over to take a seat on the far side of the table, with Symond pulling out a chair next to him. Henri sat with his back to the wall, nervously looking around the inn.

Things just didn't look right, everything seemed dull and strange. The walls were unpainted plaster that was crumbling away, leaving holes as big as a man's fist. The wooden floor was beginning to rot and was soft enough in some places to put your foot through. The low ceiling was lined with thick wooden beams that gave the inn a closed in oppressive feel. There were a few local people in the inn and they just sat staring at the company of outsiders, which made Henri feel all the more uncomfortable.

"Why do they stare?" Henri whispered to Symond.

"They are a strange people, suspicious of everything and everyone. Most have probably never seen Star Knights before." Symond answered.

"But why are they strange, is it something to do with the woods?" The room seemed to darken at the mention of the woods.

"You had best keep quiet my young friend; we wish not to upset our hosts. All I will say is that the old stories tell of evil things that dwell in those woods."

Henri had a surge of annoyance. "Why does no one tell me anything?" He said a little too loudly that an old man dressed in rags, stood up and pointed at Henri without saying a word. A wave of terror swept down Henri's spine that forced him to look down at the table.

Ulric, who had heard Henri, said, "What is it you want to know?"

"What do you want me for?" Henri asked, lifting his head and looking Ulric straight in the eye.

"We are in need of your skill…." Ulric paused as the tavern keeper came back carrying a wooden tray with eight beakers and two large jugs of ale.

"I've ordered four fat chickens killed for you sirs, if that's alright." Ghent said as he placed the beakers and jugs on to the table.

"My thanks," Ulric said, "Have it served with eggs, cheese and fresh bread."

The tavern keeper smiled and gave a bow, "As you wish, my sirs."

The company passed the clay jugs and poured themselves a measure of brown ale. Ulric took a deep swig from his beaker and said to Henri in a hushed tone. "We need you to steal an ancient artefact for us."

"What from here?" Henri asked, surprised by the fact that a Star Knight had wanted him to steal. He had always been led to believe that Star Knights were men of honour, and that stealing was beneath them, but he was not a Star Knight, and that must be why they needed him to steal for them he reasoned with himself.

"No not from here; here we do nothing to upset our hosts." Ulric said, giving Henri a stern look.

"So where, and what is it you want me to steal?" Henri asked, suddenly feeling worried of what was expected of him.

Ulric paused as if he was still unsure whether he should say anything or not. He took another swig from his beaker and gave Henri his answer. "Have you ever heard of the Chalice of Knowledge?"

Henri thought for a moment. "There was once an old woman back home who spoke of a magic chalice that glowed blue when filled with water."

Ulric nodded, "The very one. Back before the founding of the kingdom by Elnar the Great, the ancient kingdoms had become tainted by what they called the Darkness. The kings of old summoned a star from the sky and from it forged a chalice. A powerful spell of knowledge was then placed onto the chalice, and all kings drank from it." Ulric paused to take another swig of ale and then he looked around the inn to make sure no one was eavesdropping. "It was done with the best intentions, but alas they grew greedy for more knowledge. The ancient kingdoms warred for possession of the chalice until they crumbled and fell, taking many secrets with them.

The great king Elnar was able to claim the chalice and end the war; he then founded the Order of the Star and charged it with the keeping of the chalice. They did so until the death of King Edward the Fifth in the year 611 Ac. From then on kings were no longer the Grandmaster of the order. The then new king Philippe the Third demanded that the order give up the chalice, but instead Grandmaster Everard of Beolog had the chalice hidden, fearing that the king would use it for himself.

Two weeks ago thieves broke into the Star Temple vaults at Baleford and stole a map that pointed to the whereabouts of the chalice. We need to get there first, if we don't then the kingdom will once more fall to war and ruin."

Henri was startled to find out that he was expected to steal a magical chalice, which could mean life or death for the kingdom, and it all rested on him, a peasant, being able to steal it. "Where is the chalice being hidden?" He asked.

Ulric paused and shifted in his seat as if the question had unnerved him. "That is for another time and not for the here and now." Ulric stood and paced over to the fire, and stared aimlessly into the flames.

Symond placed his hand on Henri's arm. "He wishes not to scare you, that's all my young friend. It is a place best not spoken of in a place as suspicious as this." He said looking over to the locals who still sat staring at the company.

Henri looked over at them and once more the old man dressed in rags stood and pointed at him without saying a word. Henri shuddered with discomfort. "Who is that man pointing at me?"

"He is an old seer, and for a small fee shall tell you your destiny." Symond answered, picking up his beaker and gulping down his warm ale.

"Why is he pointing at me though?"

"I do not know, though maybe it's because you're dressed as a sergeant and he believes he will find custom with you later."

"What do you mean?"

"Star Knights do not seek out seers for fear of the dark powers, but sergeants have a yearning to hear that one day they shall be great warriors and achieve Knighthood. They believe it too, and then in battle they become reckless, and are killed. So heed my advice and stay clear of all seers."

Henri wondered what his destiny would be, steal a magical chalice and what, go home, and marry Elizabeth?

He began to doubt whether he was up to the task forced on to him. Perhaps he would be killed by the thieves that were also trying to steal the chalice. A quick dagger across his throat in the dark, he thought. "I'm going out for a piss." Henri said, wanting to clear his head of such dark thoughts.

"Be careful my young friend." Symond said as he stood to allow Henri past.

Henri, alone, went outside. The sun was fading to the west and soon it would be night. It was going to be a cold night; the sky above was clear and later the stars would be out in force. A cool breeze swept down from the north that made Henri shudder. He pulled his cloak tightly around his body and stared at the nearby woods.

They were a lush green and brown with elegantly shaped trunks, a contrast to the dull village that stood before it. Henri thought they looked peaceful and pleasant; nothing like as if anything evil dwelt there, but he felt strange as if they were alluring him. He felt a strong temptation to run over to them and go to see if anything did dwell there, but he managed to resist the temptation. Tomorrow he would find out he told himself.

He gave another shudder and walked around to the side of the inn and unbuttoned his trousers. The comforting, muffled sound of Symond and the others voices filtered through the thin walls as Henri urinated up the side of the inn. He finished, buttoning back up his trousers and turned. Standing in front of him was the old seer.

Henri tried to hide the surprise from his voice. "I don't want my destiny told."

The old seer said nothing for the moment and stood rooted to the spot where he stood, staring at Henri with empty eyes.

"Leave me be old man, I don't want any trouble." Henri said taking a step forward to pass the old seer.

The seer's eyes suddenly turned black, and his face turned to the colour of ash. He stretched out his frail arm and pointed straight at Henri with a long bony finger. "There shall come one, and never again shall there be another." His voice boomed mightily.

Henri took a step back in terror. He wished he had a sword, a dagger or anything so that he could strike down the old seer before him, but he had nothing and instead just stood frozen in terror.

The old seer stood silently pointing at Henri for a moment longer before he lowered his arm, turned and faded away before Henri's eyes.

Henri could not believe what he had seen. He had never seen or heard of such a thing before. The tiny hairs on the back of his neck stood as a cold shudder ran down his spine. He was frozen for the moment, unable to move or think properly. He told himself to move, to get inside to the safety of Symond and the others, but his legs would not move. He had wanted to scream for help, but nothing came out. Suddenly as if released from a spell he found his movement and ran back inside the inn to find his companions still sitting around their tables. He rushed over to them still in a haze at what had just happened.

"What is it my young friend?" Symond said concerned. "You look as though you have just seen a ghost."

"I......I.......I....." Henri stuttered.

"Come sit and have a drink." Symond grasped a jug and poured out a beaker of dark ale.

Henri went and slumped on to his chair next to Symond and drank deeply. "I saw......I saw....the seer......he came to me, outside." Henri paused to take another long drink. It tasted bitter and warm, but it seemed to calm him. "Outside, he crept up behind me, I turned and there he was."

Symond poured more of the dark liquid into Henri's beaker and then watched as Henri drained it in one.

"He stood pointing at me, then his face went grey and his eyes, his eyes turned as black as night, and he said......, he said there shall come one, and never again shall there be another. But what does that mean?"

Symond sat thinking, but he couldn't make sense of it. "I do not know, but one thing is for sure, we are in a strange place and stranger places are yet to come."

Henri shuddered once more and looked around the inn. Everyone seemed to be looking at him.

"Henri, are you all right?" It was Symond that had spoken, and it was the last thing Henri heard as his vision blurred and he fell from his chair.

Tom had run all the way from the hill road to Henri's small hovel to find Mary standing outside the doorway shouting and slapping at Bill.

"Why did you let him do it? Just so you could have more coin to spend in the tavern!" She screamed at him. "For once could you not think of others instead of yourself……? You could have stopped him Bill!" she added as she slapped Bill across his face.

Bill instinctively struck her back, knocking her to the ground. "Bloody stupid woman, you should know better." He said standing over her with clenched fists, ready to strike her again.

"Stop, Bill!" Tom shouted.

Bill seemed to calm with Tom's arrival, he muttered something Tom didn't quiet hear and strode off, red-faced in search of drink.

"Are you alright?" Tom asked Mary, helping to her feet.

"He's given me worse." She said, brushing the dirt off her dress.

"Let's get you inside and clean your face up."

Then without another word she slapped Tom across his face. "No Tom, I have to try to save Henri, and since you let him do it too, you can help me." She said as she began to walk off.

Tom rubbed at his reddening cheek and rushed beside her. "Save Henri from what? Was he caught last night?"

Mary rounded on Tom. "So you do know of it then?" She said in a stern voice that made Tom take a step back.

"I tried to talk him out of it, but he wouldn't listen. I even offered to go with him but he refused."

"Good, for if you had gone too, you would have been strung up next to him."

"What, I don't understand?" Tom said confused.

Mary stopped and looked Tom straight in his eyes. "You know he was arrested last night for stealing gold from the lord? A Star Knight said he would be hung for his crimes."

"No, I left him at the foot of the castle. I waited for him at the Wheel, but he never came." Tom suddenly felt ashamed for letting Henri go through with his plan. He should have never let him do it. "Wait, the Town Crier never said there was to be a hanging." He said, suddenly remembering the announcements.

"Then he must be being held by the Star Knights." Mary said as she rushed off once more.

"Wait, why would Star Knights be involved in the lord's problems?" Tom asked.

"I don't know Tom, but we will ask them."

Tom hurried along with Mary towards the Star Perceptory. They passed gangs of other peasants sweeping the narrow streets, with one young boy with dark curly hair calling out to him. "Where you going Tom, you're supposed to be cleaning the streets?" Tom ignored the boy, but felt uneasy about it.

"He's right, I should have checked in with the Foreman by now; he'll notice I'm not there." Tom said feeling worried that the Foreman would send guards for him.

"Never mind, they won't hang you for that!" Mary snapped back at him.

Tom could see she was deeply upset, but he couldn't think of any words that might comfort her, so he said nothing. They walked on in silence with neither Tom nor Mary wanting to admit that perhaps there was nothing they could do for Henri and that they would have to accept his fate.

The Star Perceptory lay to the north on the outskirts of the town. An easy walk, but by the time they had reached the Star Perceptory Tom was sweating as though he had done a hard day's labour.

Mary had already been to the Star Perceptory twice in the night, only for the Sergeants guarding the gates to turn her away both times. The last time they had even threatened to arrest her, but still she had pleaded to speak with the Marshal, and had only left when the Sergeants had guaranteed her an audience with the Marshal in the morning.

The sun had broken through the grey clouds and gave a little warmth to the day and Tom cuffed away the sweat on his forehead with the back of his hand.

"You should stop drinking so much." Mary said as they walked towards the two Sergeants guarding the open gates.

"I will when I find me a nice wife." He replied.

The Star Perceptory was itself a mini castle. High, thick stonewalls with tall round towers built regularly along the wall, which surrounded a cloister of buildings that the few Knights and Sergeants worked and lived in. A tall, mighty keep stood at the heart of the mini castle. Thick, blackened oak gates, studded with metal stars, barred the only entrance, which was guarded day and night by two Sergeants.

The gate was now guarded by two different Sergeants since Mary had last been here. They stood and watched as Mary and Tom walked towards the open gates. The elder of them raised his hand and spoke. "What business do you have here then?"

Tom hated confrontations and had wanted to turn around to go home, but before Tom could say anything Mary answered in a clear confident voice that betrayed none of her emotions. "We're here to speak with the Marshal."

The two Sergeants looked at each other in confusion. "We weren't told the Marshal was expecting anyone." The older of the two Sergeants said.

"I was here last night, a Sergeant told me to come back in the morning." Mary said, feeling her anger starting to rise.

"Well more fool you then, since when has a Sergeant had the authority to hand out an audience with the Marshal."

97

He said with a smug look across his face. "Am sorry but the Marshal is too busy to see you, he has more pressing matters to attend to. So turn around and be off with you."

Mary's anger exploded "I know you have my son, now let me in to speak with the Marshal!" She shoved the Sergeants aside and rushed through the gates, screaming. "Where is my son?! Where is my son?!" Tom tried to pull her back, but she shook him off. "I want to speak with the Marshal!"

The two Sergeants raced towards them and drew their swords. "You two are under arrest." They closed in on Mary and Tom to restrain them, when a knight who had seen the commotion rushed over and took control of the situation.

"Lower your swords!" He said waving his hand. The two Sergeants sheaved their swords and quickly grabbed Tom and Mary by the arms. "I am Commander Frey." He said bowing to Mary.

"I'm Mary Richards and this is Tom." She said in a more polite manner.

"Now that we are acquainted, what is the meaning of all this?" The Commander asked in a more serious tone.

The Commander was dressed in a dirty, long black surcoat with a white eight pointed star on his chest that marked his rank as a knight in the Order of the Star. He was as tall as Tom, and looked battle hardened. His shoulder length dark hair was unkempt and heavy stubble covered his jaw line. He looked as though he had been traveling for days.

His face tried to hide any emotion, but last night's sorrow, gave him an aura of heartache that seeped out of him.

"They were seeking an audience with the Marshal, Commander. We told them to leave, but they assaulted us and charged in." The elder of the Sergeants answered for them.

The Commander looked to Tom. "Is this true?"

Tom met the Commander's gaze and lamely answered. "Yes."

"I wish to beg the Marshal for the release of my son." Mary quickly added.

The Commander looked puzzled. "I do not understand my lady, do we hold your son here?"

"Yes, Last night a Star Knight came with the town guards and arrested him. He's not being kept in the lord's cells, so he must be here."

A flash of concern swept over the Commanders face. "Forgive me my Lady, but we don't tend to cross with the town guards. It's either our jurisdiction or not. We don't usually tread on each other's toes." He said as he rubbed at the stubble on his jaw. "Are you sure it was a knight in the Order of the Star?"

Mary felt her anger rise again. "I maybe a woman, but my eyes work as well as any mans, or knights!" She said sharply.

"Forgive me lady, I meant no offence. It's strange that's all."

"Commander, should we take them to the dungeon?" The elder of the two Sergeants asked.

The Commander shook his head and dismissed the two Sergeants. "No, be about your duty. I'll take care of this." The sergeants released Tom and Mary from their grip, and without saying another word, went back to guard the gate.

"Come; let us talk in more comfortable surroundings." He said, gesturing for them to follow him. He led them to a small room adjacent to the gatehouse. Inside it smelt musty and the walls were bare stone that were covered with many cobwebs. A fireplace filled with smouldering hot ashes was built into the back wall. Placed along the other walls were wooden benches, with small round tables placed between them.

"Come sit you down." The Commander gestured for them to sit on a bench in the left hand corner nearest to them. He them sat on the bench that faced them. "Now tell me all about this arrest last night."

Tom and Mary both spoke in turn, telling the Commander all they knew about Henri stealing a purse of gold from the lord. Mary spoke of him returning home and being arrested by a Star Knight who was accompanied by the town guard. She left out the part of Henri giving her one of the thick golden coins, as she had hidden that away and had no intention of giving it back, for in winter it would be much needed.

The Commander listened intently, nodding his head and rubbing at the heavily stubble on his chin as the story unfolded. Once Mary had finished the tale the room fell silent as the Commander collected his thoughts.

"Both of you are too remain here, as our guests. I'll have Sergeants bring you some water." The Commander said as he stood.

"He's a good lad sir, please let me petition the Marshal for the life of my son." Mary pleaded as tears began to roll down her cheeks.

The Commander filled with sorrow knelt down and looked into Mary's crying eyes. "There may come a time in all our lives when we must do a little bad, to gain a greater good." He said with a warm sincere face. With that he stood back up. "I need to make a few inquiries into this matter, but to my knowledge no prisoners are being kept here." He walked over to the door, and before he left he said, "I shall return shortly with my findings."

Mary wiped away the tears on her cheeks with the edges of her apron. "He knows something Tom."

"He said he's going to look into it. Mary you need to calm down. All we can do now is wait and see what he finds out."

"No Tom, did you see the way he was listening, something made sense to him." She stood and paced the room. "Something's wrong Tom, I can feel it. I feel as though Henri's in great danger."

*   *   *

"HENRI." The voice came from the woods.

"HENRI." The voices said again.

"Who's there?" Henri called out. He was standing at the edge of the woods, not daring to enter.

"COME QUICKLY HENRI." The voice sounded like a loud whisper. It seemed near but far away at the same time.

Henri was barefoot, dressed only in a pair of black trousers that were torn off just below the knee. He looked around, but saw nothing but mist and the woods before him. Above him dark clouds gathered, threatening rain. He took a few steps closer and shouted into the woods. "Who's there?" He was answered only with the silence of the dark, gloomy woods.

Spots of rain began to fall. Henri took a deep breath to calm his racing heart and stepped into the woods. He leaned against a tree trunk, waiting for his eyes to adjust to the gloom. He could hear the rain beating against the leaves above his head. There was a clatter of thunder followed by a flash of lightning that momentarily broke the darkness of the woods. He felt uncomfortable, as if there was someone hidden in the gloom watching him. He looked around but saw nothing but tall grey trees towering over him.

"Come out, I know someone's there!" He shouted.

"COME, THIS WAY HENRI." The voice seemed to eco all around him.

"Who are you, and what do you want?" Henri could sense eyes watching him; an uncontrollable fear began to swell deep inside of him.

"QUICK HENRI, THEY'RE COMING!" This time the voice sounded urgent.

Henri was about to shout out and ask who was coming, when a flash of lightning once more lit up the woods. A figure, hooded and black was lurking, watching Henri from a distance. He squinted to try and make sense of the figure, but he couldn't make out any features, only a dark shadow of a figure against the trees.

"Who are you?" Henri nervously asked.

The figure was silent.

Another flash of lightning broke the darkness. This time Henri noticed that the figure was closer.

"RUN HENRI!" The voice was panicked.

Henri filled with a sudden sense of terror, ran. He ran like he had never run before, until his lungs burned with the effort.

"QUICK HENRI THEY'RE COMING, RUN!" The voice was getting more frantic.

Henri kept looking back as he ran, he couldn't see the dark figure giving chase, but he knew it was there, edging towards him, he could feel it. Onwards he ran, weaving around the trees not knowing where he was or where he was going. The sound of leaves and twigs crunching beneath his bare feet seemed to echo around the grey silent woods.

"QUICKLY HENRI, THEY'RE COMING!"

Henri tripped and fell. He lay on his back feeling as though his lungs would explode and his heart would burst out of his chest. He took a deep breath and tried to get up, but found he couldn't move.

A flash of lightning revealed four hooded black figures a short distance away from him, silently taunting him with their evil presence. He wanted to scream out, but his body was powerless. Another flash broke the gloom. One of the hooded figures was moving closer to him. It was silent; no footsteps or crunching of leaves and twigs, no breathing, nor were any words spoken. It seemed to float slowly towards him.

Powerless to move Henri lay paralyzed, watching as the dark figure slowly moved towards him. It seemed to take an age for the hooded figure to draw closer, and the closer it got the colder Henri became.

The dark figure came and stood over his motionless body. Henri looked upon the dark figure, no face or features, just a black mist that concealed it, hiding away its true form. Inside Henri was fighting, screaming. But his body lay motionless like a block of ice, cold, heavy and immobile.

The dark figure stooped down and knelt on his chest. He could feel the pressure of its weight, driving the air out from his lungs. Henri began gasping for air as two grey lifeless hands reached out and wrapped themselves around his neck. He began to choke.

"Henri……" This time the voice was familiar, but still seemed far away. "Henri!"

Henri awoke startled. He sat up off the floor and looked into Symond's worried face. "What happened to me?" Henri asked.

"Your face……it turned black……and then you…..you passed out." Symond said confused.

"I did?" Henri said sounding surprised.

"Yes my young friend, you have been out for a couple of hours now……, but more importantly can you stand?"

Henri nodded. "I think so." Symond helped him to his feet. It was then Henri noticed the blood on Symond's surcoat. "What's happened, are you hurt?"

"No it is not my blood. After you passed out, the locals said that you had been chosen as a sacrifice for the woodland spirits, and demanded that we hand you over to them. So then we had a bit of a disagreement." He said with a smile.

Henri looked around the room and could see a dozen bodies piled up in the corner of the room, their eyes were still open with blood oozing from the mortal wounds that had ended their lives. The other of his companions was crouching behind makeshift barricades, readying for another attack.

"They have attacked us twice now, and are even now massing for another attack. We were unsure how much longer we could have held out. "

Ulric came rushing over from the makeshift barricade that barred the entrance and grabbed Henri by the scruff of his neck. "What did you do?! I said do nothing to upset the locals." Ulric said angrily. "We have lost two men because of your stupidity."

"I didn't do anything." Henri said defencelessly.

"Forgive me Captain but we have no time for this. We must leave this place forthwith." Symond said stepping in to help Henri.

Ulric realising the merit in Symond's words reluctantly released Henri. "We go out the back way and run straight for the woods. We'll be safe there."

"From this angry mob at least." Garret said implying that they would face even worse in the woods.

Ulric ignored Garret's remark, but it was true, who knew what dangers they would face in there. "Gather your packs and let us leave this cursed place." He ordered.

What remained of the small company gathered their packs and made ready by the back door for the mad dash to the woods. They knew the back door would be being watched and that the locals would pursue them all the way, but it mattered little as they were peasants armed with whatever they could find, no match for well-trained soldiers that were properly armed.

Ulric pushed aside a table they had used as a barricade and opened the door. He took out his telescope and cast his eye over what lay ahead. The woods were a short distance away, about half a mile away Ulric reckoned, but between the woods and the inn were empty boggy fields, that would slow them down. He snapped shut his telescope and placed it back into his pouch.

"Half mile of bog land to cross, so nobody fall, we all run as fast as we can straight for the woods. If anyone falls, you're on your own, everybody keeps moving. Is that understood?" He said looking around the faces of his companions. They all silently nodded their agreement. "Good then, let's go."

One by one the company burst out of the door. They had all barely gotten out, when an angry roar from around the inn alerted them to the locals that had hidden around the side. They rushed straight for the company wielding axes, clubs and pitch forks, full of bloodlust and ready to kill.

Henri stayed close behind Symond, tailing his every step. It started off easy as the ground was solid, but soon the ground became soft, and the pace became a slow struggle for safety. The mud stuck to his boots making every step heavier and heavier until his right foot sunk deep into the mud. He tried to free himself by wiggling his foot, but it wouldn't move. He looked behind and could see that the angry mob of locals was closing in on him. He began to panic and started to dig his foot out with his hands. Quickly he removed the mud and pulled with all the strength he could muster, and fell down, face first into the mud as his foot came free.

He tried to scramble forward on his stomach, but a hand had grabbed hold of his leg and started to pull him back towards the village. "Symond, help me!" Henri shouted in desperation. He rolled on to his back and kicked out at the person holding his leg.

A feeling of utter despair griped Henri as Ghent the tavern keeper stood over him, hefting a large club above his head. "It's nothing personal lad." He said as he was about to deliver a blow that would have knocked him unconscious. Then Symond from out of nowhere, crashed into him, knocking him to the ground. A pair of strong hands pulled Henri to his feet.

"It's not a good place to die." Garret said as he pushed Henri and pointed to the woods. "Go laddie, we'll hold them back."

Henri looked on as Symond and Garret fought with the locals. They were surrounded and outnumbered, fighting back to back with confident swings of the sword that cut down many of the locals. He could see that the locals never stood a chance against the two well-trained Knights, so he turned and trudged on across the bog as quickly as he could.

Ulric and the two other knights were crouching down at the woods edge waiting for the others to catch up. Henri went and crouched besides Ulric, panting to catch his breath. "Symond………… and Garret……….are……." But before Henri could finish Ulric pointed across the bog and spoke.

"They are coming now." He looked straight into Henri's eyes and added, "luckily for you."

Symond and Garret caught up with the others, blooded and tired. "Henri, are you alright?" Symond asked, catching his breath.

"Yes, thanks to you and Garret." Henri answered, feeling ashamed that he had needed rescuing.

"Enough! The next time we'll leave you to your fate." Ulric snapped, looking hard at Henri.

The light of many torches lit up the sky above the village and the sound of angry shouts drifted along with the night air.

"Now let's move out, before them pack of dogs find some courage and come at us again." Ulric said as he turned and stepped off into the woods.

Henri paused looking at the woods before him. They seemed strange now he was closer to them, unlike any other woods he had seen before. He felt as if someone or something was watching him, waiting for him to enter.

"Come, my young friend, we must leave here." Symond said as he placed a hand upon Henri's shoulder.

"Symond, what is in these woods?"

"Truly I do not know, but the stories say that Elves used to inhabit these woods, others say they still do, so stay close to me."

"It's just I had a dream………."

"Forget it and keep your mind clear."

With that the company stepped into, what was locally known as the haunted woods.

*   *   *

Hours passed, and day had slowly turned into night.

Mary and Tom had waited anxiously for Commander Frey to return. Three times Mary had gone to the doorway where a Sergeant stood guard over them, and asked how long the Commander would be. Each time she was given the same reply of a silent shrug. Two other Sergeants had brought bread, cheese and a jug of water at mid-afternoon. Marry had begged them for any news, but they also knew nothing.

Mary had paced around the room, sitting on one bench then pacing over to another. She had been through all sorts of evil perils in her mind, and was beginning to think that she may never be allowed to leave this place. When Commander Frey returned, he looked tired, even his voice sounded tired. "Come with me, the Marshal shall see you now."

He led them out across the training yard, which in the day had been busy with Sergeants and knights training for battle, and through the double doorway of the keep. They silently climbed a spiral staircase that came out at a long corridor that was brightly lit with many torches. They walked along the corridor, passing a few small doors until they came to a richly decorated double door that was guarded by two Star Knights who opened the doors for them. They went through into the Marshal's chamber.

The chamber was kept clean and tidy and the walls were covered with colourful tapestries depicting old battles. The roof was domed and painted black with white stars scattered across it. Below, the Marshal sat behind a large desk littered with parchments.

He looked to be in his sixties and his hair was the colour of snow. His face was heavily wrinkled which betrayed his age, while his body shown no sign of weakness. He looked fit and capable enough of using the two handed broad sword that was hung on the wall behind him.

He looked at Mary and Tom with hard eyes. "Come sit you down." He said in a voice that demanded immediate obedience. Tom and Mary quickly sat on the two chairs before the Marshal's desk. "Commander Frey informs me you're looking for your son." He said looking at Mary.

"Yes, he was arrested last night by a Star Knight accompanied by the town guards. I was told he would hang today, but Tom here, says that the crier never made any announcement of a hanging." Tears once more fell down her cheeks. "I beg you sir, please spare the life of my son, though he's not perfect, his heart is good."

The Marshal felt Mary's pity. "My dear Lady, it is with the saddest news that I must now speak. Last night no Star Knight made any arrest; all was accounted for here, and never left till the morning."

"Are you calling me a liar!?" She snapped back at him. "I know what I saw, and I saw a Star Knight!"

"You saw what you thought to be a Star Knight." Commander Frey said stepping in to calm Mary.

"What, I don't understand? Where is my son?" Mary said helplessly.

The Commander looked to the Marshal for his permission to continue. The Marshal sat back in his chair and nodded his approval.

Commander Frey begun, "Two weeks ago thieves disguised as Star Knights infiltrated our Perceptory at Baleford and stole a map."

"What has this to do with my son?" Mary interrupted.

"The Commander will get to that, so please do not interrupt him again."   The Marshal said, gesturing for the commander to continue.

"It was no ordinary map, but one that revealed the location of an important artefact. I was ordered to take a small company to pursue the thieves and retrieve the map. Then last night my small company was ambushed upon the hill road. I lost two of my company.

The thieves were seen heading for this town, but we had been unable to locate them, until earlier. An informant has told us of a party of Star Knights with one Sergeant crossing the fields and heading south towards the village of Raven Wood. If what you have told me is true, then your son must be with them."

"But why would the lord allow this? Surely he would have kept Henri in the dungeon of his own keep." Tom said, unable to make sense of any of it.

The Marshal placed his hands together on his desk and leaned forward. "Earlier today I sat in council with the lord, I queried him on the matter, but alas, he knew nothing of any arrest. The lord then summoned his Aide, a man burning with ambition and greed. The lord asked him of any arrests during the festival, he denied any knowledge and assured the lord that it was a peaceful night, but I could tell he knew something, his beady eyes told me that somehow he is involved, but why, I do not know. We must find out."

Mary shook her head, "sorry, but if the Lord Aide knows something about my Henri, then I'd better go speak with him."

"I would advise against that my lady. It could endanger you."

"Endanger me how?"

"I know little about the Lord Aide, but I do know that he is a dangerous man and that he's planning something. If he feels you're on to him, he won't fret to have you............ removed shall we say."

"Then what am I to do?" She said, feeling weak and helpless.

"Nothing, we will handle this. I have gained the lord's permission for Tom to be released to Commander Frey's company. They will continue their pursuit to apprehend the thieves at first light. Your son, we would like to question about these thieves, maybe he could shed some light as to who they are, and are working for."

"Why me," Tom burst out. "Why do I have to go, I can't fight or have any experience with this sort of thing, I'd be no good and….."

"But what you can do is identify Henri." Commander Frey said interrupting Tom's doubtful words. "We need you to identify him, so that we can protect him."

"Tom you must help Henri, if you don't go Henri could be mistakenly killed. Tom please go and help save Henri." Mary pleaded, as tears rolled off her cheeks and fell to the floor.

Tom paused, realising the truth in Mary's words, and nodded his agreement. "Alright, I'll go."

"Good, it's settled then. Brother Humphrey!" The Marshal called. One of the doors opened and a short stocky Star Knight strode up before the Marshal. "Marshal" He said as he stood rigged, ready to receive his orders. "See this good Lady gets safely home." He ordered.

"Yes marshal." He turned to Mary, "Please follow me lady."

Mary remained still for a moment, unsure if she should just go home and carry on as normal. She felt as though she should do something, but what? Realising that there was nothing she could do but trust the Star Knights, stood and let the Star Knight escort her out of the marshal's chamber.

Tom nervously remained where he was. He felt as if the weight of the kingdom had been placed on his shoulders, and he didn't like it.

"Thomas you will go with Commander Frey, he will instruct you further. Now go get some rest, you leave at first light."

With the meeting at an end, Tom was led away to ready himself for the adventure that was yet to come.

Mary had walked towards home in silence and disbelief, with only the sound of Humphrey's boots clapping against the cobbled streets echoing in the cold night. How had Henri managed to get himself into such a mess? For the first time she wished he was like his brothers, then he wouldn't have got into this mess. They would never have tried anything so reckless. He had always dreamed of greater things, never wanting to accept who he was. Only now those dreams had put him in great danger.

She walked into the dirty narrow street close to her hovel. "You can go now." She said to Humphrey who walked by her side.

"Is this your home?" He asked, already knowing the answer.

"No, but its close by, I'll be quiet safe from here."

"You heard the Marshal's orders; I am to escort you home." Humphrey said in a tone that ended any attempt to argue otherwise.

They walked on silently until they reached her home, a small squalor with a thatched roof that looked as though it could fall down at any moment. At the entrance of the door, was a figure sitting with its back to the wall, knees drawn up to its chest with its arms wrapped around them. Its head was buried in its arms, sobbing.

"Who's there?" Mary called out.

The figure stopped sobbing and looked up. It was a face Mary recognised.

"Elizabeth, what are you doing here?"

"Is Henri here? I must speak with him."

"Oh my poor child," Mary said helping Elizabeth to her feet and looking into her tear filled eyes she added, "You had better come inside and sit down."

Chapter 4

From a distance the woods had looked welcoming and friendly. A pleasant place where one could take a leisurely stroll; but it was all a façade. Once inside it felt anything but friendly, or welcoming. A heavy atmosphere of paranoia clung to the woods, as a mist clings to a river on a cold winter's morning.

Long ago before men had inhabited the land, elves had lived peacefully in the woods. They had a great affection for the woods and for the things that grew in them. They had spent many unhindered years tending the forests of the land, and as a result the woods and forests flourished.

As the years passed, other races came from across the great waters, bringing with them axes to fell the woods and build mighty castles in their place. The elves were grief-stricken, too small and weak to fight back to reclaim their land, they turned instead to the Imps and their lore of magic, to defend the woods.

The Imps, who also had a love for the woods, had lived alongside the elves for many years. They gifted them with a powerful spell that would attract anyone who would gaze upon the woods, alluring them in, like a flower attracts a bee. Then once deep in the woods the magic would send them paranoid; elves would then shoot them with cursed arrows, sending the trespasser mad for the rest of their lives.

As time passed the woodland elves became known as a menacing folk and people learned not to enter the woods they inhabited, for fear of their cursed arrows. Even though the elves had long departed from the land, the magic they had placed on the woods remained strong, as if it were only placed yesterday.

Now Henri and the company were in the woods, and from the very moment they had stepped into them, the paranoia had begun to seep in. They had felt as though they were being watched, as if eyes and ears were everywhere, watching and listening to their every move. Sometimes they thought they had heard whispers calling out to them, but each time they turned to look, nothing was there.

A wispy mist clung to the ground, giving the woods a menacing atmosphere that would terrify even the bravest of men. Ulric had ordered that no torches be lit for fear of what they might attract. So with only a little moonlight seeping in through the treetops to light their way, they moved on nervously keeping a constant lookout for anything that might be lurking in the darkness of the woods.

Henri was sure he could see shadows following them in the treetops. He had spoken out, pointing to the top of a tall tree, but nothing was there. Ulric told him that it was his eyes playing tricks, and all it was, was the wind, but Henri was not convinced. He was certain someone or something was following them, but what? Maybe there was more than one, he didn't know, and that thought frightened him.

They came across an ancient stone pathway that twisted and turned its way south through the trees. It was badly broken in parts with weeds growing between the cobbles. They followed the pathway with caution, constantly looking behind them.

"Symond I can hear something." Henri said, unable to hide the fear from his voice.

"What is it you hear?" Symond said turning to look at Henri.

"Clicking, like a herdsman would click his tongue to move his herd."

Symond stood still and listened. "I hear nothing but our own footsteps."

Just then a loud rustling forced Henri and the company to sharply turn to their left where the noise had come from. The company had drawn their swords and were ready for whatever evil might be lurking for them.

Ulric carefully crept over and stabbed his sword into the bush. A small wild cat shot out, startling Ulric. He sighed in relief and sheaved his sword. He looked back at his company who looked as equally relieved as him and said, "Let's move on, the sooner we leave this place the better."

They moved off in silence with only the sound of their heavy boots banging and crunching on dead leaves that had fallen onto the stone pathway. Soon Henri could hear the clicking noise again, this time all the company heard it.

"What was that?" Ulric said looking around, trying to identify where the noise had come from.

The company stopped and fell silent, not even daring to breathe too loudly. They listened but heard nothing but silence. "Maybe it's the elves." A knight called Laurence said.

"What a load of shite, it's just Stories to frighten children." Ulric said sensing Laurence's fear.

"Where I come from stories are often true." Laurence took a deep breath to steady his nerves before he said what he was truly thinking. "Maybe we should turn back, before it's too late."

Ulric snapped, "You coward, you want us to run because of children's tales!" He exhaled deeply to calm himself. "Garret, do you see anything?"

Garret who by far had the best eyesight in the company took a moment to cast his eyes around the woods. "No," He said shaking his head. "Nothing but trees and bushes, though anything could hiding out there with this mist."

"Then let's move on." Ulric waved his hand, signalling for the others to follow, but another member of the company spoke out.

"No, Laurence is right, we should turn back and take our chances with the village folk." It was Bard that had spoken, a small slender man who normally kept his thoughts to himself; though this time he felt the need to speak out. Ulric walked up to him and looked him straight in his green eyes.

"We go on and continue our mission." Ulric sharply said, ending any further outbursts from anybody else. He looked around at the others and added, "We move on, and we don't stop until we're clear of the woods." He spun around and strode off, heading south along the overgrown pathway. The company reluctantly followed on; though they agreed with Laurence and Bard, they never voiced their concerns. Ulric they knew was a violent man, and would not tolerate anybody questioning his orders. They hadn't wanted to enter these woods, but they knew the real Star Knights would not enter them; they would go around them, giving Ulric and his company a head start. It was a shortcut they needed and must risk.

Hours passed by and still the pathway went endlessly on towards the south. The company walked in single file with Garret taking the lead. The pathway had narrowed and was becoming badly broken up, it begun to steadily climb up hill towards an ancient overgrown stone circle. Once the company had reached the stone circle they naturally stopped to rest, but Ulric urged them on. "No stopping until we're clears of these woods." They reluctantly climbed back to their tired feet and walked on leaving Henri and Symond behind.

Henri looked in wonder at the tall stones; he stood gazing up at a wide pillar of stone that reached above the treetops, he had never seen such a thing before. "What is this?" He asked aloud to no one in particular.

"It is the work of the Gigantes." Symond said coming to stand beside Henri.

"What was it for?"

"Wise men say they used stone circles like this to plot the movement of the stars."

Henri rubbed at the moss that was growing over the cold stone. "What are these strange markings?"

"They are the runes of the Gigantes, the earliest form of writing known to man."

Henri looked at the strange markings scratched into the stone; they were straight line markings that Henri couldn't make any sense of. "What do they say?"

"I know not, but they were a great people renowned for their craftwork."

Henri looked up at the stone pillar didn't doubt it; even now after centuries of weathering one could still cut their finger running it along its edges. "So where are they now?"

"No one knows for sure, but it is said that they crossed the great waters shortly after the war for the chalice, and some say that one day they shall return to claim the land they had once ruled."

"I remember an old woman who once told a story about a giant; she claimed that her grandmother had been friends with one and had visited its cave many times. She used to finish the story by showing a silver flower that never seemed to die; she said the giant had grown it for her grandmother." Henri smiled at memory. "I never believed it until now." He said.

Symond placed a hand on Henri's shoulder. "Come now; let us catch up with the others."

"The others?" Henri said as the reality of where he was shook him from out of his childhood memory.

"While you've been daydreaming about giants the others have continued on without us."

Looking around Henri suddenly realised that the others had left him and Symond behind. "Yes we'd better move on, Ulric won't be happy with me holding us up; besides this place is starting to give me the creeps."

They began to walk away from the stone circle when the clicking noise sounded once more. Henri turned to look back and saw a shadow quickly move behind a stone pillar at the far side of the circle. He stood still nervously watching the stone pillar. "There's something following us." He said in a panicked voice.

Symond glanced back and saw nothing, but he could feel the presence of something, something evil. "Run as fast as you can until you catch up with the others."

"What about you?" Henri asked, fearing for Symond.

"I'll be right behind you, now go!" Symond said drawing his sword.

Henri ran, suddenly filled with a terrible fear. He kept looking back expecting to see a monster giving chase, but no monster did he see. Symond was about thirty paces behind him, running with sword in hand. The sound of his chainmail chinking kept Henri running at a quick pace. He looked back again and again thinking he had heard Symond shout him, but he hadn't. He was so busy looking back that he never seen the patch of broken path in front of him. Tripping on a root of a tree that had surfaced up through the broken pathway, he went crashing off the pathway and rolling down the hill, not stopping until he was at the bottom.

Henri slowly got to his feet, brushing away dirt and leaves that clung to him. His right sleeve was torn open revealing a cut on his forearm that hurt as if his arm were on fire. He held his forearm tightly to stop the bleeding and looked around. He had fallen into a clearing with the remnants of a fire in the middle. First he thought that he had stumbled into the camp of whatever inhabited the woods, but as he inspected the remnants of the fire and seen the dense cobwebs, he realised that the clearing hadn't been used in a long time.

"Henri!" It was Symond's voice.

"I'm down here; I think I've found something." Henri said as his eyes set upon a wooden chest that was part buried with decaying leaves and cobwebs. He went and knelt down by the chest, eager to see what was inside.

The lock was broken and the wood was rotten, soft enough to push a finger straight through it. Henri eagerly opened the lid, and inside was a pile of damp mouldy clothes. The smell made Henri gag; he quickly removed them, tossing them aside, and at the bottom of the chest was a sheaved dagger. It was twelve inches long with a black handle bound with silver wire. He pulled it out of his scabbard; the blade looked new and was still sharp, written along the blade were the same runes he had seen back at the stone circle.

Symond climbed down the hill and knelt beside Henri. He saw the dagger in his hand and took it from him. "In all my days I have never seen such a fine blade." He said looking at the blade in wonder.

"I found it, it's mine." Henri said, fearing that Symond would keep it for himself.

"Forgive me my young friend, I wish only to look. I have never seen a blade forged by the Gigantes before."

"The Gigantes made this dagger?" Henri said amazed by his find.

"Yes, they made the finest blades in all the kingdoms. Now keep it safe and secret."

"Secret, why must I keep it a secret?" Henri asked, puzzled. He wanted to show-off his find to all his companions, and boast on how he had the finest blade in the company, if not the kingdom.

"A blade like this has great value and many should want it for themselves." Symond said handing the dagger back to Henri. "Keep it hidden away and tell no one of it. Now we had better catch up with the others."

Henri pushed the dagger back into its scabbard and tucked it inside his right boot.

They both rose to their feet and Symond noticed the blood dripping down Henri's arm. "You're hurt." He said as he ripped off a strip of cloth from the bottom of his surcoat. He tied it tightly around the small wound, "Here this should stop the bleeding." With Henri's wound bound they climbed back on to the pathway and hurried along until they had caught up with the others.

They were sitting by a narrow stream that gently flowed west, with Ulric impatiently pacing up and down the near bank. He saw Henri and Symond approach and angrily strode over to them. "Where have you two been? You are holding us up; we must stick together if we're to get out of this cursed place!" He said, red-faced with anger.

"We were separated at the stone circle; something is following us, I could not see it but I feel it is close by, watching us, waiting for a chance to take us." Symond answered.

Ulric glanced back up the pathway, he was sure he could see distant shadows moving from tree to tree edging closer towards them. "We stick together; whatever is following us is trying to separate us and pick us off one by one."

"We won't ever get out of here!" A pale Laurence burst out, unable to hide his fear any longer his thoughts formed words and poured out of his mouth. "It's coming for us; I can feel its evil eyes staring right at us. We shouldn't have entered these woods. It will kill us all."

Ulric had heard enough. He abruptly turned and ran at Laurence, pulling him to his feet and back handing him across his thin face before shoving him back onto the ground. "Shut your stupid mouth; what do you know about it!"

"I know we should never have entered these woods!" He shouted back, spitting blood from his mouth. Ulric kicked out hitting Laurence in his head and breaking his nose.

Henri was shocked to see the sudden ferocity of Ulric's anger. He never thought Star Knights would do such things to each other. He stood silent besides Symond unsure if he should do or say something to help Laurence. He took a step forward and was about to speak out, but Symond pulled him back, stopping him.

"We keep on moving; whatever is following us won't attack if we stay together." Ulric said and gave Henri a long hard stare. "You have yet to prove your worth, and can start by filling the water skins. Ulric tossed Henri his empty water skin. "We leave as soon as the water skins are filled."

Henri collected the skins together and walked down to the stream's edge. He knelt down and unstopped a skin, plunging it in to the stream to collect the water. The water felt cold and refreshing. It seemed to revive his strength and send his tiredness fleeing from his body. He untied the cloth that bound his wound and washed it in the cold water and then tied it back around his wound; where the water quickly healed the cut.

Laurence came and knelt down near Henri; he cupped some of the cold water in his hands and splashed it onto his face. He winced in pain as he washed away the blood, but instead of feeling revived as Henri did, he felt like his face was on fire. Screaming in agony at the pain, he began to wildly thrash about, slapping at his body as if he were on fire.

127

Ulric and the others came rushing over. "Laurence what's wrong?" Garret said grasping hold of him.

"It burns, make it stop, please just make it stop!" He screamed back. Then as suddenly as the burning had come on, it stopped and Laurence fell silent.

"Is he dead?" Ulric asked.

"No his heart still beats." Garret said feeling the pulse in Laurence's neck.

"I have heard of this before," Symond interjected, "long ago the Imps placed spells upon some streams, so that only one of true heart may drink from it, to any lesser man it would be their doom."

Just then the clicking sounded again, only this time it was followed by loud bangs and a deafening screech that could have shattered glass. The trees began to waver and the ground shook. Ulric's face turned to the colour of snow, "A woodland demon!" He yelled. "We must leave here now while we still can."

"Wait what about Laurence? We can't just leave him here." Henri said horrified by the thought of leaving him to such a cruel fate.

"Laurence has just volunteered to give us a head start." Ulric said as if he felt no guilt about leaving him.

Henri looked to Symond for support, but surprisingly found none. "If we carry him, it will slow us down, and we shall all share his fate." Symond said, knowing that they needed Laurence as a sacrifice to escape the woodland demon.

Through the trees came a shadow wraith so vile that whatever it touched would shrivel up and die. Its true form was concealed by a black mist that surrounded it. From the paranoia of the woods it fed and grew strong. The elves were able to keep it from growing stronger, but ever since they had departed from the land, the wraith had grown into a power no man could yet tame. Its gaze fell upon the company and it once more screamed a deafening screech that sent fear into the hearts of the company.

The company fled the wrath of the wraith, leaving Laurence helplessly lying beside the stream. They ran as fast as their legs would carry them along the pathway. Henri could feel Symond's hand pushing him on, urging him to move faster. Twice He had nearly tripped, but both times Symond's strong hands had reached out and stopped him from falling.

The wraith was not giving chase; it had seen Laurence's unconscious body and had dragged him off deep into the dark woods to devour his soul, sending it to an eternal darkness of torment.

A few miles on and the company had come to the end of the woods; they were puffing and panting for breath, falling to their knees with exhaustion.

The morning had dawned and Henri squinted against the bright sun looking out across vast grasslands with bulging hills that went as far as his eyes could see. The ground was wet with dew and the land seemed to sparkle in the morning sun.

"Where are we now?" Henri asked Symond.

Symond took a moment to catch his breath before he answered. "The land before us is the great Plains of Pendor."

The company took a few moments to rest in the peaceful morning sun, and then a terrible scream shattered their peace. They all recognised Laurence's voice and felt the guilt for having left him, but what else could they have done. Had they of tried to save him, they too would be screaming their last scream.

His scream was suddenly cut off and Ulric stood. "We can't rest here; it's not safe; we must move on and find a safer place." They all got to their tired feet and exhaustedly walked on, leaving the woods and its evils behind them.

*　　　*　　　*

The marketplace of Heath Hollow was as busy as always, with people bustling and bartering from stall to stall in search of the best prices. The excitement of the festival of summer's end had long ended, and life had fallen back into their normal patterns.

The murder on the hill road was still being talked about, with many believing that the town was going to be pillaged and burned, but nothing more had happened, no more murders, or a rampaging army coming to sack the town. So the town returned to their normal talk of the rising cost of bread, but for Elizabeth it couldn't have felt more different from any normal day.

She had yet another restless night of tossing and turning in her bed, tormented by thoughts of having to marry John Kinge, a man she had never met before. He was rumoured to be a fine handsome man with prospects of a high position at the lord's court, a fine marriage for the daughter of a merchant, but Henri was a fine man also and she already knew him, but did she love him?

Now sitting in a daze on an upturned wooden box at the back of her father's stall, she began to think of Henri. She endlessly stared at the white plastered buildings with thick black beams opposite, thinking. She was feeling so tired that her body felt as though it were made of stone and at any moment she would fall into an eternal slumber.

The night before she had spent hours with Mary, sobbing with disbelief as Mary had told her about Henri, but still she struggled to believe it. She had told Mary about her father's proposal for her to marry the Lord Aide's son and that she had refused saying that she had promised her hand to Henri.

Mary had assured Elizabeth that her father couldn't force her to marry if she was promised elsewhere. She had then urged Elizabeth to remind her father of that law, and stick to what she had said. I will act as a witness to you being betrothed to Henri, she had told Elizabeth. But her father would never listen, or accept the marriage. He would force her to marry a man she didn't know, or love, all to aggrandise the family name, and there was nothing she could do about it.

She was deep in troubled thought when her sister Catharine came and sat on the box next to her. "My dear sister, what terrible affliction troubles you so on such a fine morning?"

Elizabeth snapped out of her daze. "It's nothing; anyway shouldn't you be minding the stall?"

"Yes, and you are supposed to be helping me remember, but all you have done is sit here staring into space."

"Sorry, it's just this marriage father has arranged; it's shocked me that's all."

"It's ok; two of father's creatures are minding the stall anyway. So you're worried about the betrothal to John Kinge?" Catharine sympathetically asked.

"Yes of cause I am, I don't even know him."

"You just need to get used to the idea, that's all." Catharine said sensing the anxiety from her sister.

Their conversation was interrupted by an old man dressed in a fine green tunic with small yellow leaves stitched into it. It was one of their father's stewards. He looked down his long nose tipped with small round spectacles and said, "Ladies." As he bowed down his wig fell from the crown of his head. He quickly grabbed it and placed it back onto his head. "Lady Elizabeth, your father requests your presence."

A wave of anger rolled down Elizabeth's body. "Well he can summon all he wants, I'm not going!"

"Forgive me my lady, but your father commanded that you are to make for his private chamber immediately."

Elizabeth stubbornly looked away as if the conversation was at an end.

"She shall join our father presently." Catharine interjected. "Now I wish to speak to my sister alone."

The steward for a brief moment was unsure if he should leave without Elizabeth. "Very well, I shall check all is well with your father's stall." He bowed low once more, this time holding his wig in place, and went about his business.

Once he was out of sight Catharine stood and pulled Elizabeth up by her arms. "I do not understand, father has arranged you a good marriage, a very good marriage, and you sit here sulking? Think about it, your husband will have a place at the lord's court, and you'll be there also, dining with the upmost people in the town. You will be dressed in the most fashionable dresses and know all the latest gossip."

The lord's court was not where Elizabeth wanted to go. The court was said to be full of dashing knights and rich men, the high eagles of society, but Elizabeth knew it to be full of serpents only serving themselves. Not eagles she thought to herself, more like pigeons that shit on everything else.

"I can't marry a man I don't know or love." Elizabeth said weakly.

"You shall meet him soon enough and you will learn to love him, in time." Catharine said trying to comfort her sister. "Many young ladies would like to be in your situation." She added with a smile.

"I wish it would have happened to anybody but me." Elizabeth said with scorn.

Catharine hugged her sister. "One day you shall look back at this and laugh, wondering why you were hesitant to marry such a fine man, who will in time grow to love you, and you shall learn to love him also."

"What of Henri? I know he loves me."

"What of him, he's a fieldworker and not worthy of the affections of a merchants daughter." Catharine said harshly. "Besides, how is he supposed to keep you or a family home? He hasn't even got the means to buy his independence from the lord."

Elizabeth thought for a moment, Catharine was right Henri couldn't keep her; he had no wealth or prospects of gaining any, but he did love her and she liked him, or at least she thought she did. Even though Catharine was younger then Elizabeth, she was quiet often the wiser of the two when it came to the prospects of marriage.

"I need to think." Elizabeth said pulling away from Catharine.

"Think, what's to think about? It's an easy choice, either you want wealth and position this marriage will bring, or the pain of poverty that Henri has to offer." Catharine said with disbelief that Elizabeth was even considering marrying a lowborn peasant.

"I don't have much of a choice do I." Elizabeth said feeling trapped.

Catharine shook her head. "Father knows what's best for you; you just have to trust him, in time you will see he was right."

Elizabeth nodded her agreement. "I had better go then, best not to keep father waiting too long."

"Everything will be alright, you'll see." Catharine said smiling at her sister.

Elizabeth walked away from her sister and the busy marketplace. Her mind was mixed up about what she should do. She knew deep down inside herself that she couldn't marry Henri. He was a good man, but a man who had no means of supporting her, and she had grown accustomed to the finer things in life. Whenever she had imagined having a family of her own, it was always to a wealthy gentleman with a big house and a garden full of colourful flowers, and Henri couldn't make them dreams a reality, and John Kinge could.

She walked up the main road that went uphill towards the richer quarter of the town. It was a cleaner, wider road then all the others, and had proper drainage ditches on both sides, where waste would flow down into the poorer part of the town, there it was collected and taken to a dung heap outside of the town.

Elizabeth was so deep in thought that she never noticed the horse galloping down towards her. The rider wore the plain black surcoat, the attire of a Sergeant of the Star Knights. He looked uncomfortable and was barely able to control his steed; he hurriedly pulled on the reins to avoid hitting her, and barely managed to bring it to a stop a few inches away from her.

"Sorry, I haven't quite got the hang of it yet."

Elizabeth smiled, "It's alright." She said, not recognising the familiar face. She began to walk off when the Sergeant called out to her.

"Wait, Elizabeth!"

Elizabeth turned and looked up into the Sergeant's face, and recognised it. "Tom." She said, surprised by the fact that he looked so different, almost manly. "I'm sorry, I didn't recognise you, and you look so………."

"Handsome." Tom cut in with a smile.

Elizabeth blushed. "Different." She finished.

There was an awkward moments silence before either of them spoke. "Are you alright?" Tom asked. "It's just you don't look yourself."

"I'm fine; I just haven't slept very well."

"Nor me, I've been up trying to get the basics of this." He said patting his horse's neck. "I'll get the hang of it though."

"Mary told me about you going with the Star Knights to find Henri; I thought you would have left by now."

"We should have left at first light, but we had to wait for supplies to be readied, and me to learn how to ride this thing."

The sound of horses' hooves beating against the cobbled street interrupted their awkward conversation. A band of four Star Knights cantered towards them, coming to a stop a few feet away from them. One walked his horse, reining in alongside Tom. He looked down at Elizabeth with his hard, but friendly eyes. "My lady." He said bowing his head to show his respect. "Tom we must be on our way, enough time has been lost already this day; and try to maintain control of your horse."

"I am trying; I've never ridden a horse before, well not until last night anyway."

"A horse can sense your emotions, so try not to panic." The Knight looked back to Elizabeth and bowed his head once more. "My lady I bid you a good day." He tugged on his reins and lightly squeezed his horse with the inside of his knees to walk it on. The other knights followed his lead, leaving Tom alone with Elizabeth.

"I had better get going." Tom said, feeling more awkward then he ever had before. Normally he was never short on anything to say, but today he just couldn't find the words.

He clumsily urged his horse on and it began to walk away when Elizabeth called out to him.

"Wait!"

Tom stopped as Elizabeth walked up beside him.

"Is it true Henri was going to ask my hand in marriage?"

Tom nodded. "Yes, he planned to buy his independence and ask you for your hand."

Undoing a green ribbon that kept her hair tied back. She handed it to Tom and said. "Give this to Henri." Tears formed in the corners of her eyes. "Find him Tom, tell him………tell him……… that I'm sorry."

Before Tom could ask what she was sorry for, she had turned and rushed off up the road towards the rich quarter of the town. Tom stuffed the ribbon into a small pouch on his belt and rode on feeling uncomfortable about the brief conversation, unsure of what she had meant by *sorry*.

Elizabeth walked home, fighting back her tears as she went. She felt helpless, worthless, a mere puppet that moved to the puppeteer's jerk of the string. She walked halfway up the wide road and took the second right down a joining street that led towards her family home.

Outside her home stood two of the town's guard, dressed in red and yellow quartered surcoats with two black stags locking horns. She could feel their eyes gazing at her as she strode past them. One gave her a toothless smile and a mocking bow. "My lady," He said as she passed by. Both burst into laughter. "Sorry girl, it's a private joke, that's all."

Elizabeth ignored the guards, and entered her home through the grand doorway that led into a richly decorated hallway with a polished black and white tiled floor. She walked through the dining hall and down the familiar passageway lined with painting of ancestors until she came before the doorway to her father's private chamber. The door was slightly ajar. She heard voices coming from inside, and instead of entering, listened in on the conversation.

"Why would the Star Knights be interested in him? This could be a big problem if he comes back." The familiar voice of her father said.

"As I have said he shall not return, I have seen to that. The Arcani shall dispose of him once they no longer need him." This voice was one Elizabeth had heard before, and even behind a door, the Lord Aide's voice made her shudder.

"Yes, but can you trust the Arcani?"

"We came to an agreement to help each other; I would support their mission for the King, and in return they would ensure that I am made Lord of Heath Hollow, but I have a safety net in place should they fail their task."

"What safety net?" Her father asked.

"This morning I will issue a warrant for Henri's arrest as a runaway, so even if he does return, he shall be hanged for desertion from the lord. So even if the Arcani fail, my son shall still marry your daughter. You shall be made the new Lord Aide, and in turn you will pay a wealthy dowry, that I will use to raise more men for the King and the coming war. Then he shall make me lord, making your daughter the future Lord's Lady."

Elizabeth couldn't believe what she had heard. Had she endangered Henri's life? If she had never said she was promised to him, he would have been safe. Things were already in motion, things that she couldn't change; and that made her feel useless, and above all, guilty.

She was now set against the marriage that would help in their cause, and would try whatever she could do to stop them. Then part of her deep down only heard that she would become the High Lady of the town, and that thought seemed pleasing to her. A sudden sense of power momentarily took hold of her. She quickly swallowed it back down; no one would force her to marry, she would be the master of her own fate, she told herself.

Elizabeth knocked on the door, and without waiting to be beckoned in, entered. She could feel the anger rising inside of her; clenching her fists, wanting to lash out at her father's face that gave her a shrewd smile as she entered his chamber. "You wanted me father." She said unable to hide the scorn from her voice.

Her father was stood before his desk with his hands behind his back, watching as his daughter came and stood next to him. The Lord Aide was sat in her father's high backed chair behind his desk, watching her as an eagle watches its prey.

"Have you forgotten your manners girl; curtsy, you're standing before the Lord Aide." Her father said sharply.

Elizabeth offered a quick defiant curtsy. She hated the Lord Aide and promised herself that she'd try and spoil his plans, but how she was unsure.

The Lord Aide grabbed a rolled up parchment on the table and unrolled it. "This is a contract of marriage between our two houses, my son shall return any day now and you shall marry soon after. All you need do is to sign your agreement." He said weighing down the corners to stop it from rolling back up.

Elizabeth could see that her father and the Lord Aide had already signed the marriage contract. "That is something I cannot do." She said with a confidence that even surprised her.

Her father shot her a look of disbelief. "You will do as I command!" He snapped. "I have already agreed to this marriage so your refusal is pointless."

"I will remind you father, of the law of King James the second, which forced marriage, is now treason against justness and righteousness, punishable by banishment. I now invoke that right to refuse as I have promised my hand elsewhere."

The Lord Aide rose from the high backed chair and slammed his fist onto the desk. "Stupid girl, perhaps you are in need of a little reminder of your place!" He glanced hard at her father. "Keep her locked away until she sees the error of her ways. She shall change her mind once my son returns, he can be very persuasive." He said with a sinister grin spreading across his face.

Her father called out for one of his stewards. A thin man smartly dressed in a green tunic came in and bowed. "Yes master."

"My daughter is confined to her bedchamber until I say otherwise; now remove her from my sight." He said, unable to look her in the eyes, he turned his back on her.

"Come on now my lady." The steward said taking hold of her arm.

As he led her away she turned and pled. "Please father, you can't do this to me." Her words fell on death ears.

Elizabeth's father watched on as she was escorted out of his chamber, he felt a sudden pang of guilt and said, "Perhaps my other daughter would be more welcoming for the offer of marriage."

The Lord Aide looked at Elizabeth's father sternly. "The King is a weak man with no male heir. His first daughter the princess Aliena died of the plague six years ago, leaving the princess Acacia as the sole heir to the kingdom. Every nobleman up and down the kingdom has their own opinion on who should rule next, and have tried to marry their sons to her, though she has rejected every one of them. The nobles gather like vast rain clouds, and come spring the clouds of war shall burst, washing the kingdom in the blood of war. I need to be ready for the coming chaos, for in times of chaos, the ambitious shall climb the ladder of power. So waiting another year till your other daughter comes of age is not an option. We stick to our plan, and by this time a year from now I shall be Lord of Heath Hollow."

"And I shall be the new Lord Aide." Elizabeth's father said with a greedy smile spreading across his face, suddenly forgetting his guilt he picked up the jug on his desk and filled two goblets with wine.

"Indeed you shall, but first your daughter must marry my son." The Lord Aide said sternly to emphasize the need for the marriage.

"She will do as instructed, have no fear on that, my Lord Aide, or should I be saying my lord." Elizabeth's father handed him a goblet and bowed before the future Lord of Heath Hollow.

"Indeed," the Lord Aide said before taking a sip of wine. "Indeed I shall." Both of them laughed with pleasure at the thought of a better future, and continued making plans for the marriage.

Elizabeth heard the laughter behind her as she was led away. The sound seemed to mock her, render her useless. She decided she wasn't useless, and was going to do something to help herself out of this situation, but what she didn't know. She was ushered into her bedchamber where she collapsed onto the bed, sobbing until she had fallen asleep.

Later that day she awoke fresh from a deep sleep. An idea had begun to form in her head. She lay on her bed going over the idea again and again until she had convinced herself that it could work. In the morning she would run away, far away so she couldn't be forced to marry. That would hinder their plans. She packed a few of her clothes and personal belongings into a leather case then slid it under her bed. Later she would pick the lock on her door with the pin of her broach, like she had many times before. Then she would steal some food from the kitchen and sneak out of the front door and go, go somewhere her father wouldn't find her.

But first Elizabeth would have to escape.

Chapter 5

The short journey to Raven Wood was tougher then Tom had imagined it would be. The road was well maintained and suited for horses, but Tom was not. Twice his horse had bolted away because he had panicked and squeezed it too hard with his knees. Each time a Star Knight would quickly ride after him and regain control of his horse. To Tom's surprise they never reproofed or laughed at him, and just gave him advice and words of encouragement.

The motion of his horse made him wobble and bump around on his saddle. His Inner thighs were beginning to rub sore where he had gripped the horse in an effort to stay in the saddle. What made it worse was that he couldn't concentrate, he kept thinking of Elizabeth and what she had said.

Their brief conversation back in the Town had unsettled him. What had she meant by sorry? It was not her fault that Henri was in danger, Tom thought to himself. Did she know something he didn't? The thoughts kept on whirling around in his head, over and over until he was angry at himself for not being able to understand it. It's a stupid idea anyway; a fieldworker marrying a merchant's daughter was unheard of. Then it suddenly dawned on him, she was saying sorry because she couldn't marry Henri.

Tom thought of how upset Henri would be when he told him, but he should have seen it coming, he had told him as much many times before. Henri was a dreamer and would never settle for what he was, a lowborn fieldworker that was just expected to work until he died. It wasn't going to be easy telling him, but first he would have to find him, and that was not going to be easy either. He uncomfortably rode on with the image of a heartbroken Henri clouding his mind, when the smell of smoke nerved the horses. They began to whimper and sidestep.

Jerking on his reins to maintain control of his steed, Tom looked ahead towards the village and saw a thick pillar of black smoke rising up high into the sky.

"Halt!" Commander Frey called as he raised a hand.

The three other Star Knights with Tom came to a stop behind their Commander. He twisted in his saddle and said, "Brother William, scout ahead and report back."

"Yes Commander." William nudged his horse on and rode on up the road towards the smoking village.

They waited for what Tom thought was too long for William to return. When he did the news he came back with was disturbing.

"I rode right up to the edge of the village unhindered; I wasn't seen by anybody as the people there have gathered around a funeral pyre in the centre of the village."

Commander Frey rubbed at the heavy stubble on his jaw and nodded his head. "Are you sure no one saw you?" He asked.

"Yes Commander, they are too busy with their rituals for honouring the dead."

"Thomas." Commander Frey summoned.

Tom tried to nudge his horse forward, but it wouldn't move. "Forward you stupid bloody thing."

A Star Knight called Edward came alongside him and grabbed his reins, leading Tom's steed forward and stopping it once he was alongside Commander Frey. "Yes Commander." A red-faced Tom said.

Commander Frey looked at Tom and pointed towards the village. "Thomas I want you to go into the village alone; find out if the thieves are still there, if they are do nothing but come back and report to us. If they are not there, try and discover where they were heading."

Tom was shocked by the fact that he was expected to go alone. "Sorry Commander, but I don't think that I should go alone; I mean why can't someone come with me, I won't know what to do." He lamely added.

Commander Frey exhaled deeply as if he was tired of Tom's company, though he never said as much. "That village is tainted with dark powers," he said pointing once more to the village, "Dark powers we wish not to expose ourselves to unless necessary."

Tom shook his head. "What dark powers?" He said disbelievingly.

Commander Frey shifted in his saddle as if he was irritated by Tom's disbelief. "At the south edge of this village is a wood that long ago the elves placed an enchantment upon. The power of that enchantment still remains and the people who live in the village next to it have fallen to its power and trust no one. It is because of that power that our horses are reluctant to go on." Just as he had said it the horses started to whimper and stamp their hooves, as if sensing something evil in the air.

"So what makes you think anybody will tell me anything? Besides if it's that powerful of a spell I don't think I should go there." Tom said trying to change the Commander's mind.

"Thomas," Commander Frey sighed, "we are the Knights of the Order of the Star; baptized in the light of hope. We must abstain from any dark powers that could corrupt our hearts. You however are not and most likely already corrupted by the darkness that plagues' us all."

Tom didn't understand what he meant; no darkness plagued him, none that he knew of anyway. "Nothing plagues me, and I don't believe in all this darkness rubbish." He said, sounding very sure of himself.

Commander Frey looked at Tom with his hard, cold eyes, as if he could read his soul. "Have you fallen ill to strong drink?"

The expression on Tom's faced said it all. He quickly looked away to try to hide it. "Sometimes," He said knowing it was a regular occurrence.

"And have you lain with a woman, as a man would lay with his wife?" Commander Frey asked already knowing the answer.

148

Tom reddened at the question and avoided answering it by staying silent and looking at the ground. He began to think that maybe some sort of dark evil thing had corrupted him and wondered what his life would have been like without that corruption.

"You see young Thomas; the darkness does exist, and does plague your soul. Its greatest trick is to blind us and make us disbelieve it even exists."

Tom shook the thoughts of darkness corrupting him from his head, "Ok I will do it." He said to change the subject back to the task at hand, not wanting to hear of how evil he was.

"Good," Commander Frey paused and twisted in his saddle to look to William. "Take Thomas to the edge of the village," he turned back to look at Tom, "From there you will walk towards the village's centre and make the inquiries with the first person you come across. Once you have acquired the information we seek, come straight back to us, is that clear, you come straight back." Commander Frey's voice was harsh, but he had wanted Tom to understand that he was only to make inquiries about the thieves and not try and apprehend them on his own, should they still be in the village.

"I understand." Tom said. He felt anxious about the task, it seemed simple enough, but deep down he had a bad feeling, as if something bad was waiting to happen to him there.

William took hold of Tom's reins and led him up the road towards the village, and the closer they got to it, the duller the morning became. By the time they reached the edge of the village grey clouds had covered the sky, blocking out the sun and plunging the world below into coldness that chilled the bones.

Tom clumsily dismounted; as his legs hit the ground a lightning bolt of pain shot up his legs making him whimper with the pain.

"You shall get used to that soon enough." William said as he reached into his saddle bag and pulled out an old thread bare brown woollen cape. He tossed it down to Tom, "Here replace your cape with this one."

"Why?" Tom asked confused.

"Remember the locals don't trust outsiders, and right now you look like an outsider."

Tom unclasped his plain black cape, letting it fall to the ground, and fastened the grubby brown one around his shoulders. He picked up his black one and tossed it up to William and nodded that he was ready.

"Gather the information we need and come straight back, nothing more, is that clear?"

"Yes I understand." Tom said to reassure himself, as well as William.

"May the light of the stars guide you and keep you safe." William turned with the horses and trotted off back down the road.

Tom watched him go and exhaled deeply to calm his nerves. He pulled his cape tightly around him, covering his plain black tunic, then turned and walked on into the village.

As Tom walked into the village the stone road gave way to a wide dirt road with broken wooden buildings flanking it on either side. He could see a mass of people crowded around a pyre further on down the road, and the smell of burning flesh clung heavy in the air, making him gag.

The local people were so engrossed with their funeral rituals that none noticed Tom as he nervously walked closer towards them. Now he was getting closer he could feel the heat of the pyre prickling at his skin, and the stench of the bodies burning went right up his nose, causing him to retch.

He went over to a narrow alleyway to the right of him and leaned against a wooden house, spitting. Regaining control of his stomach he looked over to the pyre with both wonder and horror. It was hard to make anything out because of the dense crowd and smoke, but as the villagers began to dance gaps appeared and Tom could see through. What he saw disturbed him.

A man covered in grey mud wearing a loin cloth and a grey eyeless mask that covered the top half of his face, danced around the pyre, twirling a wooden staff as he went. He was not alone, on either side of him were two wailing women chanting and dancing in long dresses that brushed along with the breeze.

Tom watched on wondering how the grey man could see. Mesmerised by the twirling and chanting he couldn't tear his gaze away. It was terrifying and yet beautiful at the same time and he could feel the passion radiating from the crowd. He reminded himself of why he was here and with a huge effort, tore his gaze away from the pyre.

Looking around he noticed an old woman dressed in a dirty dress coming out of a door and sitting on a stool outside of a house opposite him. Perfect he thought. He walked over to her and asked, "What's happened here?"

The old woman jumped, startled as she never noticed Tom approach. She looked up squinting with her pale eyes, "Who are you?" She asked in a suspicious tone.

"Sorry, I've been away on business and have only just got back." Tom said avoiding the question.

"Oh, you must be Jacobs's boy." The old woman said.

"Yes that's right," Tom lied, "Now what's happened?"

"I'm so sorry to have to tell you that your father was killed last night."

"He was, how?" Tom said trying to sound both upset and angry.

A small child with red curly hair and a freckled face had seen Tom talking with his grandmother. He had never seen the strange man before and came running over from the crowd by the pyre to stand next to her. He stared at Tom with suspicious eyes.

"It happened yesterday," she hugged her grandson and kissed his forehead, "In the evening, they came."

"Who came?"

"Star Knights. They came seeking shelter for the night, but it ended with the spilling of blood after they wouldn't give up a chosen one among them."

Tom looked over at the pyre, its flames flickering high into the sky, and worried that he might be too late. "Did you kill them all?"

"Sadly no, we attacked them many times, but they escaped into the woods. They killed many of us, hence all the mourning." She said gesturing with her hand at the pyre. "We managed to kill two of them; their bodies are to be taken to the sacred grove and given to the waters to appease the spirits.

"Where are their bodies now?" Tom asked fearing that Henri could have been killed.

Her grandson walked around to Tom and pulled at his cape, suspecting something was odd with the stranger.

"Leave him be." The old woman said.

Tom held his cape tightly, clutching it around him, but the child wouldn't give up. He was pulling so hard that it tore open and revealed Tom's plain black tunic underneath.

The old woman saw his tunic and screamed out. "It's a Star Knight!" She screamed. "It's a Star Knight!"

The people at the back of the crowd heard the scream and turned around. They saw the plain black tunic and recognised it instantly and began to rush over in a blind fury.

Tom quickly turned to run, but the child had grabbed hold of his arm. "Let go!" He snatched his arm out of the child's weaker grip and ran back the way he had come; but it was too late. The child had delayed him just long enough for the mob of angry locals to catch up with him.

They roughly grabbed hold of Tom and shoved him down on the ground, encircling him. They grabbed his arms and forced him up onto his knees. They were like a pack of wolves, snarling and taunting around their prey.

Tom could sense their anger and thought that at any moment they would rip him apart, ripping his flesh away from bone to end his life. Instead they fell silent, parting to let the grey man wearing the mask into the centre. He stood in front of Tom and jabbed him with the end of his staff, forcing Tom to look up at him. He noticed that the mask wasn't plain; it had two pale yellow eyes painted on it where eyes should be. The grey man then knelt down to Tom's level, looking him straight in the eyes and began hooting like an owl.

Tom was terrified. He didn't know what the grey man was doing, it seemed like childlike taunting, but it was far more sinister then that. Tom closed his eyes in fear, not wanting to see any more of the grey man's taunting.

He could still hear the hooting as the crowd began to chant drowning out the hooting; and then a thud, followed by a sharp pain in his head.

Then all fell silent.

*   *   *

The wind that blew across the Plains of Pendor was bitterly cold. It whirled and whistled around the distant burial mounds and into a small cave where the company of thieves were now resting. Ulric had forbidden any fire to be lit, for fear the smoke would attract unwelcome attention. So the company had slept next to each other, rolled up in blankets they had carried on their packs, to keep warm, each taking a turn to keep watch at the mouth of the cave.

Henri though tired, had slept little. He kept on thinking about what had happened in the woods, the sound of the demon's screech still rang in his ears, but the worse of all was the guilt of leaving Laurence. Giving up his attempt to sleep, he rolled out of his blanket and walked out the mouth of the cave; and there sat Symond, staring out over the plains.

"You should be resting." Symond said, seeing Henri walking over towards him.

"I can't sleep. The sound of the demon's scream haunts me, and every time I close my eyes I see it." Henri looked back to the nearby woods and shuddered at the memory of the demon.

"Fear it no more; it cannot leave the woods. You are quite safe my young friend."

"It's what else that's out there that is worrying me." Henri said looking out across the plains.

"You are right, greater perils are yet before us. That is why you must try and rest."

Henri ignored Symond's hint for him to go and rest, sitting silently instead, watching the wind swishing against the tall grass.

There was a long silence between them as they both thought about what dangers could be lying ahead. Symond knew, he had heard the stories, but he stayed silent.

A yawning Ulric came out from the cave and stood in front of them. "You see anything?" He asked Symond.

Symond shook his head. "Only nature." He replied.

Ulric pulled out his telescope from a pouch on his belt and unsnapped it, casting an eye southeast. He saw nothing but endless grassland that led all the way to the burial mounds; even though they were miles away, they sat like a colossal mountain that dwarfed the land around it. He lingered his glass on the mounds for a few moments before snapping it shut with a sigh. He turned back to Symond and said, "We need to take stock of what provisions we have left, and make plans accordingly." Without another word he strode off back into the cave to rouse the others.

"What I don't get?" Henri said thinking out aloud. "Why are we looking behind us for the thieves and trying to keep ahead of them? I mean, why don't we set an ambush for them and take them by surprise?"

Symond sat silent, thinking of how he should answer. He had never been comfortable with the lie, but they had to know if Henri could be trusted and wouldn't just run away at the first opportunity. He hadn't, so he decided on telling Henri the truth. "We are the thieves." He said avoiding eye contact with Henri.

Henri deep-down had known it, but it still surprised him. "What?"

"Do not worry my young friend we wish you no harm; and know that our quest is still one of great importance."

"So if you're not Star Knights, who are you?" Henri asked.

Symond seemed reluctant to say anymore, as if he had said too much already; but decided that the truth was the only way forward. "We are the Arcani." He finally said in a hushed tone.

"I've never heard of the Arcani before."

"We were founded by King Philippe the third in 615Ac as a counterforce to the Star Knights. Since then we have worked in the shadows of secrecy and answer only to the King himself." Symond said looking straight at Henri.

"So is this quest for the King then?" Henri asked.

Symond nodded. "Yes, the King is now fifty two and sickening with age. His grip on the crown weakens and he has no male heir to succeed him. The nobles are raising men to claim the throne for themselves, and come the spring the kingdom will be at war with itself. The King has charged us with the task of finding the Chalice of

Knowledge. Only then with the power of the chalice, will the King be able to keep the noblemen in their place. "

Henri sat silent for a moment, letting the true reality of the situation sink in. "Is it Star Knights who are after us?" He asked.

"Yes, the map we stole was one of great importance to them; many powerful men would pay a King's ransom to have it."

"Why is the map so important?"

"It reveals the location on the chalice."

"I don't understand; if the King finds the chalice and stops a war, why would the Star Knights want to keep it hidden away?" Henri asked confused. He had been led to believe that Star Knights were the promoters of peace, not war.

"That I do not know, maybe they wish to keep the power for themselves. Maybe it is because all the nobles would still make war anyway, only this time for the chalice and its power; and if it fell into the wrong hands...." Symond left his final words unsaid, obvious of what would happen.

Henri thought that maybe the Star Knights were greedy for the chalice's power and wanted to keep it for themselves. "So where is the chalice being kept?" He asked expecting to hear that it was being kept in a stronghold guarded by an elite core of Star Knights.

Before Symond could answer Ulric came back out of the cave and beckoned them in. "You two."

"Come my young friend Ulric wishes to make plans, and it is best not to keep him waiting."

Henri and Symond rose to their feet, walking back into the cave they saw Ulric, Bard and Garret packing what little provisions they had left into the packs.

"We have enough food for another day, so from now on we're on half rations; that gives us two days, at a pinch three, to find a safe place and gain fresh supplies." Ulric announced.

He pulled a map out from his pouch and unfolded it on the cold stone ground. "Stratton Manor House is a three day journey from here, but if we go through the burial mounds we could make it in two."

Garret nodded his agreement. "Aye tis true, it would save us time; but would it not be best to go round? After all, the mound is a place where the bones of the fallen now rest. It would not be wise to upset the spirits that dwell there."

There was a moments silence while they considered what was being said. Ulric knew they were nervous, especially after the events in the woods, but in order for a quicker route, risks needed to be taken.

"I think we should go through the mound." Henri said, breaking the silence. "After all, we don't want the Star Knight catching up with us do we?" He added.

Ulric stood shocked, "You know?"

"Yes I know," Henri said defiantly, "But what I want to know is if my pardon is real?"

"You saw it yourself; once your task is complete a full pardon along with your independence from the lord is granted." A sly smile crept across Ulric's face, "I shall take good care of you, no need to fear."

"Forgive me Captain, but it was I who told him the truth. I felt he could be trusted." Symond interjected.

"That was not your decision to make." Ulric reproved.

"I'm not going to run off, if that's what's bothering you." Henri said. "I will help you as long as you keep your word and ensure I get my pardon."

"Of course, it's all been arranged." Ulric snapped, "Now is it settled; are we to go through the mound and make for Stratton Manor House?"

The others agreed, knowing that they needed to reach a safe place and gather some more supplies as quickly as possible.

"Good, the Strattons have always been friendly to the king's men; we shall find food and shelter there." Ulric said. "Now what water do we have left?"

Garret tossed a water skin over to Ulric, "That's the only one we have left, so we need to take it easy."

Henri had another skin filled with the water from the stream in the woods, but he had kept it hidden away from the others at the bottom of his pack. It had revived his tired body and he wanted to keep it for himself for when he was exhausted. Though he tried to convince himself it was because of what happened to Laurence when he had drunk the water.

Ulric unplugged the skin and took a quick sip. "Everyone take a sip." He said passing the skin to Bard. "We drink nothing more until nightfall."

The others took their turn with a quick sip until the skin was passed to Henri. He pressed the lip to his mouth and slightly tilted it, pretending to take a swig, not wanting to drink their water as he had hidden a skin in his pack.

With everyone having drunk some water, they rolled up their blankets and made ready to leave. Henri shouldered his pack and left the cave, walking in silence alongside Symond. They walked on for hours heading straight for the burial mounds, and by the time they reached them Henri's feet were blistered and sore.

The mounds had been built in the aftermath of the Battle of Pendor Field, as a resting place for the slain. They had been built with huge stone blocks that had once dominated the plains, but now hundreds of years' later, moss and grass had covered them, making them look like odd shaped hills. The biggest was the centre mound which was encircled by eight smaller mounds that seemed to dimly glow green in the dull light.

The company stood before the centre mound looking at the huge stone doorway that bared the entrance.

"This is the biggest thing I've ever seen." Henri said amazed by the size of the mound. It was only now he understood why it would take another day to go around it.

"It is the burial place where the battle's dead were placed." Symond told him.

"There must have been thousands of them."

"It was a big battle." Bard interjected. "A battle the songs say, where arrows fell like rain and the clash of steel was like thunder, the screams of the dying lingered on the wind and could be heard many miles away."

Henri shuddered at the thought. "How are we going to open that?" He asked pointing to the huge stone doorway, bringing his mind back on the task at hand.

"We don't." Ulric answered. "Grave robbers must have been here before; we look for the entrance they made."

Bard and Garret went in search for an opening and it didn't take long for them to find one. They came back with news of an overgrown opening a quarter of the way up directly above the main entrance. The rest of the company followed them to the opening and prepared to enter the mound.

Ulric pulled two lanterns from out of his pack and lit them. He then picked up a stone and wrapped it in a piece of oil soaked cloth. Leaning over the opening he set the wrapped stone alight and dropped it down the dark opening. It fell down a long shaft hitting the bottom, *chink chink chink*. Ulric couldn't see the glow of the light and guessed that the shaft must fall all the way to the ground level below. "Who has the rope?" He asked, turning back to face the others.

Garret had already fished the rope out of this pack. He tied one end around the base of a small tree that grew out from between the stones and threw the other end down the shaft.

"How far down do you think it goes?" Ulric asked Garret.

Garret shook his head, "I don't know, at least a hundred feet or more I should think."

Ulric thought for a moment, and then turned to Henri. "You go first."

"What? Why me? Surely it would be better if someone with experience went first." Henri said shocked by the request.

"It was you who snuck into the lord's castle were it not." Ulric said with a grin. "I can't think of anyone with more experience then you."

Henri knew it was pointless to try and persuade Ulric otherwise. He took a deep breath to calm himself down and stepped over to the opening. He sat down on the ledge with his legs hanging over edge and grabbed hold of the rope, peering down the long, dark shaft below. He began to lower himself down when he suddenly realised that he wouldn't be able to see. "Wait how am I supposed to see down there?"

Ulric knelt down by Henri and placed the handle of a lantern into his mouth. "Don't drop it." He said as he patted Henri on his head.

Henri began to climb down into the darkness, placing one hand below the other and letting his feet find footholds. The light above slowly began to dim and he was left with only the glow from the lantern to light his way. He kept looking down hoping to see the ground, but all he could see was what seemed to be endless darkness. After what seemed hours he came to the end of the rope. He just stopped there thinking that he failed and that he ought to climb back up. Instead he stretched out with his feet to see if the ground was just below his feet, but all he felt was empty air.

Henri was about to give up and climb back up to the others when a sense of pride swept through him. He wouldn't give up, and decided that he would continue on down the shaft to prove his worth to the others.

Slowly he begun to climb down finding foot and hand holds with ease, until at last he came to the ground. He crouched down and placed the lantern on the ground by his feet. Looking around he could see that he was in a small dugout chamber with just enough room for two people to stand in. He looked back up and shouted, "Ok I'm at the bottom!"

The sound of Symond's voice came echoing down the shaft. "Stay where you are, I'm coming down."

Henri could hear the sound of Symond scraping on the stones as he climbed down, he suddenly remembered that the rope wasn't long enough and called out a warning to Symond. Waiting for Symond he picked up the lantern and looked around. He found a small tunnel that had just enough room for a person to crawl through; it was the only way to get in deeper to the mound.

Symond reached the ground and called up to for another to start the climb down. He crouched by Henri and patted his back, "Go on." He said gesturing for Henri to crawl through the tunnel.

Henri once more took a deep breath to steady his nerves and began to crawl along the narrow tunnel, pushing the lantern along with him. It was much worse than the climb down. Thick cobwebs covered the tunnel; many times Henri had to brush them off his face. Then the tunnel suddenly got narrower and he was forced on to the flat of his stomach, pulling himself forward with his hands. He began to panic as he could feel the tunnel closing in all around him, fighting back his temptation to scream out, he franticly wiggled along until at last there was space.

The tunnel led out into the side of a grand passageway lined with huge carved stone columns that held up an elaborately decorated stone roof depicting the Battle of Pendor Field. Everywhere there were thick cobwebs that looked like they had been there for centuries.

Henri looked around in wonder at the elegant stonework, it was truly amazing, a wonder of the world that was hidden away in the dark. There was a foul smell that lingered in the heavy air, and the humidity made it stifling.

Symond was the next out of the tunnel. He was covered in cobwebs and dust; walking to Henri he said, "There is a foul smell of something evil here."

Henri held up the lantern and peered into the gloom. "I can't see anything other than cobweb covered stonework."

Garret came coughing and spitting out of the tunnel. "What is that smell?" He said as he stood next to Symond.

Symond shook his head, "I don't know, but I dare say we shall find out."

"I smell a spider." Garret said as he brushed off cobwebs from his surcoat.

Henri felt a shudder roll down his spine at the mention of a spider. "I recon there must be thousands of them looking at the amount of cobwebs."

"No not thousands, but maybe one big one." Garret said.

The sound of scuttling and scraping echoed down the long passageway, sending shivers down their spines.

Ulric came out of the tunnel closely followed by Bard who carried the other lantern. They went over to the others, brushing off the cobwebs that covered them.

"Smells like a giant spider." Ulric said sniffing the air.

"Perhaps we should go back." Henri said fearful of what might be lurking in the dark.

"We can't, the rope snapped on me." Bard said. "I fell down the last quarter, lucky I didn't break something."

"Lucky I was there to break your fall you mean." Ulric said rubbing his ribs. "We have no choice but to go on." He added. "These mounds were built on a simple plan; this passageway will lead into the burial chamber. From there we will find a similar passage that leads to the backdoor. We go quietly and swiftly, and hope that the spider is not at home." He took the lantern from Henri and led the company down the dark passage towards the burial chamber.

The giant spider they feared was at home, and had already heard the noise they had made. It scuttled off to hide in a large crack, with its many dark eyes peering out from the shadows, waiting for a chance to spring forth and capture its next meal.

Ulric led the company swiftly on. They passed many small chambers filled with the skeletons of the fallen. After two hours of an endless gloom the passageway led out into the main burial chamber.

It was a massive stone built dome, with elaborate statues to honour the dead ringing the outer wall. A huge mound of weapons and gold treasure was piled in the centre. The company rushed over on seeing it and began to inspect the cups, coins and the many other fine things that were piled there.

"To think of all this gold just lying around doing nothing would be a crime." Bard said with a hint of greed in his eyes.

"Best we take some then." Garret said agreeing with Bard. He pulled off his pack and went to scoop some of the coins into his pack.

"No." Ulric said fearful of the dangers. "Let's get out of here before it's too late."

As Ulric tried to stop Garret and Bard the giant spider sprang from the shadows with great speed and voracity.

The giant spider was hundreds of years old, but moved with the speed of a young spider. Its body and legs were covered in sticky, thick black hairs. A distinctive skull-white stripe ran the length of its body.

Symond was the first to see it, calling out a warning to the others as he grabbed Henri's arm. "Go, find the way out."

Henri, who hated spiders, turned and ran towards the other passageway without even thinking of the others. Bard and Garret without hesitation dropped the gold in their hands and drew their swords.

Ulric put down the lantern and grabbed an old spear from the pile of treasure, waving it at the spider to keep it away. The others stood beside him wafting their weapons desperately, they tried to step back towards the passageway, but they were caught between the spider and the pile of gold.

Henri found the passageway that led to the backdoor; he stopped running and knelt down behind one of the massive stone pillars. Looking back he couldn't see the others, but he could see their elongated shadows locked in mortal combat with the giant spider. He was frozen with fear that this was the end; he would die here in this dark place alone without knowing some of the joys of life he had yet to taste. No he decided, he would not die here, today he would swallow his fears, today he would begin to earn the respect of others, but how? Then he had an idea.

Getting to his feet, he ran back over to the others. They were still in fierce combat with the giant spider and never noticed Henri as he came and rummaged through the treasure. He found some old cloth and rolled it up, tying a knot at one end. He scooped up a handful of cobwebs and wrapped them around the knot.

"Henri what are you doing?" Symond yelled as he noticed Henri. "Get out of here why you still can."

"I know what I'm doing!" Henri shouted back as he opened the lantern and lit the knotted end of the cloth. It set alight with a fierce flame and Henri dashed off to the right to flank the spider. He came up behind its fat body and swung the rolled up cloth as hard as he could. It hit and stuck to the thick hairs on its fat body, setting it alight. It shrieked and scuttled off in a panic back into the crack where it had sprung from.

There it burned and met its end. Its burning body gave off a green smoke that lingered around the burial mound for hundreds of years after. Some would say that its evil spirit still dwelt in the mound and on the anniversary of its death its shrieks could still be heard.

"Well done Henri." An exhausted Ulric said. "Perhaps there is more to you then I thought."

Henri was still shaking with fear and couldn't think of anything to say, so he stayed quiet.

"Right let's get away from here, gather your things." Ulric said pulling Bard back to his feet.

The company picked up their packs and left the main burial chamber. It took hours before they reached the backdoor, but when they did they found it open.

"This must be how the spider got in and out." Symond said.

"Luckily for us it was left it open." Ulric replied.

They left the burial mounds behind them, wandering further along the Plains of Pendor. The day had turned to a drizzly cold night with a chilly breeze blowing from the east. They walked on for a couple of hours more before they stopped for the night.

Henri wrapped himself in his blanket and lay down on the wet, cold ground. He fell into a deep sleep; once more dark dreams haunted his sleep.

*   *   *

Tom regained consciousness. He tried to move but found he couldn't. His hands had been tied around a stake that had been driven upright into the ground before a small, dark watered lake. The sound of chanting surrounded him, but he couldn't see anything even though he knew his eyes were open. He began to wonder what was going on, and then it all came back to him.

He remembered talking to the old woman with the little red haired boy, the crowd that had rushed him, and then the memory of the strange masked man flooded his memory. He began to fear, what was going to happen to him? He struggled against the rope that bound his hands in the hope that he might free himself, when the sounds of owl like hooting made him stop immediately.

The blindfold was ripped away from his eyes and standing in front of him was the strange man covered in grey mud, sinisterly grinning. Tom noticed he was on the edge of a small lake surrounded by trees and bushes. Wicked looking knives and an axe was on the ground before him. The local people stood in a semi-circle around him hooting like owls.

The masked man held up his staff and they fell silent. Two other men also covered in grey mud stepped forth carrying two bodies. Tom could see that they were dressed as Star Knights; it must be the thieves they were looking for.

The strange masked man placed his staff on the ground and picked up a double handed axe with a broad, sharp head. He gave a command for one of the bodies to be brought before him. A body was dragged in front of Tom where all could see. He lifted the axe into the air above his head, and with one mighty blow struck the head off the lifeless body. He bent down and picked up the head, holding it up for all to see, as clotted blood dribbled down his arm.

The crowd began to hoot like owls, and the strange masked man tossed the severed head into the dark waters of the lake. As the crowd fell silent the other body was dragged forward and shared the same fate as the other.

With the two bodies beheaded the rest of their remains were taken away and tossed onto the pyre. The strange masked man then turned his attention to Tom. He picked up a small wooden dish filled with blue paint and painted a strange symbol on Tom's forehead with his finger. Next he picked up another dish, this one filled with a white powder. He held it up in front of Tom's face and blew it.

Tom shook his head as the powder was blown in his face. "Let me go!" He spat. He could feel his face tingling and numbing. His body quickly became paralyzed, but he was still fully conscious, fearing that he would share the same fate as the two other bodies. There was a flash of light as the strange man pulled a knife from a purple and gold case that was on the ground. He held the ceremonial dagger up for all to see, chanting some strange words in a language Tom had never heard before. The crowd also began chanting the strange words, filling the twilight with a sinister sound.

The chanting ended and the strange man removed his mask. Where his eyes should have been there was just skin, an eyeless horror that seemed to see everything. A sinister grin once more spread across his face as he pulled the dagger back ready to plunge it into Tom's heart.

Then before the final blow could be struck, a long arrow with black feathers struck the strange man straight where his right eye should have been. It was followed by more arrows that struck into the ground near the crowd of locals. Afraid, they quickly dispersed back off into the village.

Commander Frey came from behind the nearby bushes and ran over to Tom. William followed on with bow in hand, ready for any sudden attack that might happen at any moment.

"Thomas can you hear me." Commander Frey said as he cut Tom free.

Tom feebly flopped onto the ground, unable to do anything else. Commander Frey knelt down beside him and turned him over to face him.

"Thomas it's me, remember me?" Commander Frey said looking for any response, but finding none.

"Wait look." William said. "The white powder, it's a sedative; he'll be paralyzed for hours."

"We need to get him out of here quick." Commander Frey said pulling out a long whistle from his pouch. He blew three long blasts to summon the others.

They came with the horses, swords drawn at the ready.

"Quickly get Thomas onto a horse." Commander Frey ordered.

William picked Tom up and bundled him onto a horse. They all mounted their horses and rode off speedily, escaping the village of Raven wood.

They rode on until night fell and they were forced to stop, making a camp for the night so that they could rest and regain their strength. Tom's arms and legs began to tingle as the effect of the sedative powder wore off. He felt like he was a piece of ice thawing out beside a fire, and after a few hours he was able to talk again.

"What happened to me?" Tom asked.

Commander Frey heard Tom and came and sat beside him. "You were paralyzed in preparation for sacrifice. It seems as though the effects are diminishing. Are you well enough to talk?"

Tom nodded his head, "I think so."

"Good, then what did you learn? Are the thieves still in the village?"

"No, last night they were attacked by the villagers. One of them, like me, was chosen as a sacrifice, but they resisted. I know two of them were killed in the fight."

"Was one of them Henri?" Commander Frey interrupted, thinking that he could send Tom home if it was.

"No." Tom answered shaking his head.

"Good." Commander Frey said glad that an innocent person hadn't been killed. "So which way did they go?"

"They went into the woods."

A flash of horror swept across Commander Frey's face. "What madness drove them in there?" He stood back up and stared towards the distant woods.

"Are we going to follow them?" Tom asked fearing that they too would enter the woods.

Commander Frey shook his head, "No, I will never willingly enter such a place." He stood silent; thinking of what might be their plans. After a short time he decided that if they had survived the woods they would be on the Plains of Pendor.

He spun around to face everyone and announced his thoughts. "By now they must be on the plains, come morning we shall ride around the woods and search the plains. They may have gained an advantage over us, but we have the horses."

"How do you know they don't?" Tom asked.

"Because no horse would ever enter that place, now get some sleep sunrise will be in a few hours."

Commander Frey took the first watch while the others slept. By sunrise they would continue their pursuit of the thieves on the vast Plains of Pendor.

Chapter 6

For the last two days Elizabeth had been trying to run away. Twice she had managed to pick open the lock on her bedroom door and sneak down to the backdoor, all to no avail. Each time she was seen and escorted back to her bedchamber by one of the household servants. Now her father had her mother's old handmaiden keep a constant watch on her. She sat outside of her door knitting all day, stopping at regular intervals to see if Elizabeth needed anything. At first she was met with hostility as Elizabeth was driven mad the constant clicking and clacking of the knitting needles, but now Elizabeth had seemed to calm down as if she had finally accepted her punishment.

Elizabeth however had not accepted her punishment. She was still determined to escape, but how? She kept walking over to her window pondering with the idea of jumping out of it, but she thought it more likely she would break a leg in the process. Maybe she could tie her bed sheets together and use it as a rope to climb down. For the last day she had pondered with the idea, even tying her sheets together ready to make her escape.

Late last night she made her move, but once she had lowered her makeshift rope and sat on her window ledge with her legs dangling over the edge, she had second thoughts. What if the sheets tore, sending her falling down onto the cold, cobbled ground below? What if she fell on her head? They were thoughts she didn't like to think of, and Instead of trying to escape she climbed back inside her bedchamber window, pulled up her bed sheets and went and slumped back on her bed, falling asleep in moments.

By the morning Elizabeth was woken to the news of a banquet to announce the betrothal between her and the Lord Aide's son. It was not something she was looking forward to. She planned to make herself look as unappealing as possible to put off her intended marriage mate, but her mother's old handmaiden was prepared for such an attempt. She came in and laid a white elegant dress on the bed with the instructions to rise out of bed and prepare herself for her betrothal to the Lord Aide's son.

Elizabeth had exploded with anger saying that she was not betrothed to the Lord Aide's son and that she had no intention of being so. She would never agree to such a thing she had screamed out as loudly as she could. It was all to no avail and her plan to make herself look unappealing went where she didn't, out the window.

Her mother's handmaiden had summoned for two other female servants to bring in warm water so that Elizabeth could wash. She refused at first until the old handmaiden ordered the two other servants to hold her while she roughly scrubbed at Elizabeth's pale skin. Elizabeth stopped resisting knowing it to be futile and it wouldn't have got her anywhere anyway. She let herself be washed and made presentable for her betrothal later that day.

Her mother's handmaiden then spent hours brushing and pinning up her hair until it looked exactly how a young lady's hair should on such an occasion. They had both remained silent throughout the passing hours as Elizabeth

178

was groomed to look her best. Elizabeth's silence was through defiance, but the old handmaiden's was through guilt.

When she herself was a young girl she had been promised to an ugly cattle farmer who smelt worse than his livestock. She had acted in the same way as Elizabeth by trying to argue and change her father's mind, but that too had come to no good. She had been formally betrothed at a family feast like the one that would take place later today, but before she was wed she had run off, changing her name and appearance. She had never told anybody and had kept her secret deep down within herself. Maybe Elizabeth could find a happier road in life, like the one she had found for herself she told herself. No, this was different; Elizabeth was not expected to marry a cattle farmer, but a highborn, she would have a fine life, unlike the one she would have had with the cattle farmer, but the guilt would not disperse and looking down at Elizabeth she could see her former self, and the guilt persisted.

Hours later, when Elizabeth was almost ready, Catharine knocked and entered. "The guests are starting to arrive." She said expecting Elizabeth to be ready. She was dressed in a red silk dress with golden lace. "Father requests that you bless us with your presence."

"He was that polite was he?" Elizabeth replied sarcastically.

"N........I'm to escort you down." She said instead. "Let me help you in to your dress."

Elizabeth let Catharine and the old handmaiden help her in to the white dress that the old handmaiden had brought in earlier. It was a long elegant dress, a dress that some women could only dream of having. For Elizabeth it was ugly and felt heavy as if there were invisible chains stitched in to the seams.

With Elizabeth fully dressed and ready for the betrothal banquet the two sisters linked arms and walked down to their father's hall where the banquet was taking place.

"Don't worry sister, all shall turn out for the good." Catharine said seeing the worried look on Elizabeth's face. "Who knows, maybe I'll attract the attention of a rich merchant and gain an advantageous marriage myself."

"There is more to all this then just gaining an advantageous marriage!" Elizabeth snapped back.

"What do you mean?"

"I mean father would probably gain, but what about me? I'm forced to marry a man I don't love and he doesn't love me. He most likely will treat me bad, and I'm expected to like it." Elizabeth said more thinking out aloud to herself.

"Hush now sister, life isn't one of them stories you read about. It will be hard at first, I'm sure of that, but love will grow, you just need to give it time, that's all."

They came before a double doorway that was the entrance to their father's dining hall. It was flanked by two servants wearing green tunics embroidered with golden leaves. They saw the two sisters and opened the doors for them.

"Just smile and be polite, for the sake of the family."
Catharine said fearing Elizabeth might make a scene.

"Don't worry sister, I'll behave myself." Elizabeth replied
with a forced smile.

As the doors were opened a blast of hot air mixed with
the sound of many different conversations greeted them.
The hall was brightly lit by hundreds of candles that had
cooled molten wax around their bases. Richly coloured
tapestries hung on the walls, trapping in the heat of a
roaring fire that blazed in the huge marble fireplace. A
servant called out announcing their presence and
everyone sat around their father's long, wide table stood
in recognition of the two young ladies that entered.

A place had been made for them besides their mother
who was sat at the right hand side of their father at the
head of the table. They both watched like hawks as their
two daughters came and took their place beside their
mother. They both looked beautiful, and would do the
family proud their mother decided.

Elizabeth took her seat beside her mother, who gave her
a reassuring smile, and looked around the table as the
other guests sat back down. Like the feast her father had
held a few days ago, the hall was full of the wealthy
merchants who were evermore greedy for more money.
They were all dressed finely with their wives beside them
dripping with jewels and flattery, the cream of the town.
But despite all their finery they couldn't hide the common
smell of sweat that clung in the air around them. All
Elizabeth saw were greedy, fat men, willing to sell their
daughters as if they were mere pieces of property to be

bought and sold for a chance to gain an even greater fortune.

Beside her father, to his left, were two more empty chairs, they must be for the Lord Aide and his son she thought. She felt relieved they were not present and hoped that they wouldn't turn-up. Of course they would its John Kinge's betrothal, she thought to herself.

"Daughter, are you well?" Her mother asked breaking Elizabeth's thoughts. She was dressed in a pale green dress with fur trims and had her dark hair pulled back and pinned in a bun at the back of her head, emphasising her round face.

Elizabeth looked straight in to her mother's blue eyes. "I don't want to marry John Kinge mother, I can't, and I don't love him." She took a breath. "Besides why should I be forced to marry just so father can become a Lord Aide?"

"Careful you speak to loudly!" Her mother said sharply. "Many people here would like to see your father fall." She grabbed Elizabeth's hand, "You may not love him yet, but it will grow." She said with a smile. "Besides I have made a few inquiries about your betrothed."

Elizabeth was shocked to hear that her mother had been seeking information about her prospective husband.

"Don't look so surprised, you are my firstborn child, I would not let you marry a monster."

"I'm not ready for marriage, mother can you not change father's mind?" Elizabeth pleaded.

Elizabeth's mother let go of her hand and spoke sternly. "You are no longer a child Elizabeth; it's time you learnt that. John Kinge is a fine man, and can offer you position and wealth. He is admittedly ambitious like his father, but that is something we are all guilty of."

Elizabeth looked away from her mother feeling angry and weak. She wanted to scream and run out of the hall, but where could she go, feeling trapped she began to accept that there was nothing she could do to help herself.

"Take comfort in knowing that you will be able to influence important matters." Elizabeth's mother said regaining her attention.

"What do you mean? Women are not permitted to attend matters of business." Elizabeth said looking back at her mother.

"Your father maybe the head of this household, but it is I who pulls the strings."

Elizabeth once more looked shocked. She had learnt more about her mother in the past few minutes then she had in her lifetime.

"When I met your father," Elizabeth's mother went on, "he was an unambitious merchant with one small stall. Now he has many spread out over the kingdom, and soon if all goes well, he will be made Lord Aide."

The reality of that it was her mother who was behind all this struck Elizabeth like a hammer strikes a nail.

"Behind every successful man is a stronger and more calculated woman." Her mother added.

Elizabeth was sat thinking that the whole world was somehow against her, when the doors to the hall were opened and a servant announced the arrival of the Lord Aide and his son. The hall fell silent and all stood inclining their heads as they passed by to take their seats on the left hand of Elizabeth's father. They both stood tall, walking with the confidence of kings.

The Lord Aide was stone-faced and dressed in his usual attire, plain black robes with his chain of office hanging around his shoulders. He wore atop of his head his usual tricorne hat with a long red feather sticking out at the back. He greeted no one and went straight to his place that was set out for him at the head of the table.

His son couldn't have looked more different. He was dressed in a pale blue outfit with darker blue flowers embroidered on it, with a pure white silk shirt underneath that's frilly sleeves edged out from under the tunic's sleeves. He smiled and even stopped to shake the hand of some of the other merchants as he passed.

Elizabeth's first impression was that he was handsome and well groomed with a pleasant smile. He seemed more humble then his father and more at ease with the surroundings. She watched him as he cheerfully went and sat at his place beside his father. She felt a pang of guilt for thinking the Lord Aide's son was handsome, quickly reminding herself that she opposed this marriage, she tore her gaze away.

With all of the guests having now arrived Elizabeth's father toasted the Lord Aide and ordered his servants to bring in the feast. Silver platters of meats, spiced pies, fruit, bread and cheeses surrounded with red berries were placed on the table for the guests to help themselves. Elegant silver jugs filled with the finest red wine followed the platters of food.

The guests ate and drank their fill whilst making polite conversation as minstrels played soft pleasing music in the background. Elizabeth had barely eaten, just picking at a piece of bread and taking a few sips of her watered-down wine.

Now that the guests were content with food and drink Elizabeth's father stood, gaining their attention. "Distinguished brothers," He spoke in a clear voice so that those sat at the far end of the table could hear him, "We gather here tonight for the most noblest of reasons; but first let us once more raise our glasses to our esteemed guest of honour." All raised their glass goblets and inclined their heads to show their respect to the Lord Aide. "Noble brothers," Elizabeth's father went on, "it gives me great pleasure to announce that our two houses are to be united in matrimony. My eldest daughter," he gestured for Elizabeth to stand.

Elizabeth at first was reluctant, but one stern look from her mother forced her onto her feet.

Now that his daughter was standing Elizabeth's father continued on. "The son of our esteemed Lord Aide," He turned to John Kinge, who without being needed to be beckoned, stood. "They shall be wed within a few weeks from now as soon as may be arranged."

There were a few murmurs from around the table as the news of the marriage sunk in. Elizabeth's father made a toast to the betrothal that in his opinion would be for the betterment of all.

Once the announcement was finished Elizabeth's father beckoned his servants to bring in the cakes and more wine. The minstrels took up a jaunty tune and the guests began to dance and mill about, gossiping about the forthcoming marriage.

Elizabeth stayed in her seat, feeling helpless. She could sense the eyes of the other women in the room glaring at her, measuring her up, talking about her. It got to a point where she couldn't take it anymore. She stood and walked out of another double door that led to an open promenade lined with white stone pillars. Leaning against a cold pillar and looking out over the gardens she began to try and think of a way she could get out of this marriage, but no plan other than to simply just run away came to mind.

Elizabeth closed her eyes, feeling the cold breeze blowing against her face when a voice she didn't recognise broke her peace. "Beautiful night is it not."

Not expecting anybody to have followed her out, she was startled by the voice that spoke out to her. She stood upright, quickly opening her eyes. Standing before her was John Kinge, her betrothed. "Yes." She said, not knowing what else to say.

There was an awkward moment's silence between them before John spoke again. "You have a well-kept garden." He said to break the silence.

Elizabeth looked at the garden and thought it looked bare. The day before servants had ripped up the flowers that had died back, leaving only a few bushes that would grow back come the spring. In a way Elizabeth felt like one of her father's bushes, allowed to bloom and grow, but always cut back to give the image her father wanted the world to see.

"I'm sorry." John said, leaning up against a pillar next to Elizabeth.

"Sorry, what for?" Elizabeth asked, intrigued why such a man should be sorry to her.

John blew out a long breath, as if he was calming his nerves. "This marriage," he paused to think of how best to say it, "I'm not sure I can go through with it."

Elizabeth was stunned. "I don't understand." She felt a flash of anger sweep through her; why didn't he want to marry her?

"Forgive me, I put that badly. What I mean my lady, is that, and please forgive me for saying as much, but I do not love you."

Elizabeth was shocked by his confession; did he feel the same as her? There was another awkward silence before she spoke. "I forgive you if you can find the same kindness to forgive me; for I too am guilty of the same thing." She could see John smile, his white teeth shone in the moonlight, a contrast to his tunic that looked almost black in the pale moonlight.

"With all my heart, I forgive you. It seems we are both victims of our fathers' ambitions." He stopped leaning on a pillar, took Elizabeth's hand and kissed it. "May I be so bold as to gain an agreement from you?"

"If what you seek is within my power to give." Elizabeth said blushing.

"When we're together, let us both be honest with each other and speak only the truth."

Elizabeth felt comfortable with John. She began to wonder what she had been so worried about. Here in front of her was a man who wanted only to speak the truth with her; maybe he would make a fine husband after all she began to think. "Yes, but you must promise never to talk to anyone about what we say." She said seeking the assurance she needed to hear.

"I so promise my lady. Now let us walk the garden in the moonlight together and talk." John offered his arm.

Elizabeth took his offered arm and let John escort her along the garden pathway. He made small talk about the public gardens in Baleford he'd walked through and of his school days at the military academy there. The conversation quickly turned back to the marriage and Elizabeth found that John felt the same way she did.

"My father tells me that you are promised to another." John said hoping to get Elizabeth to open up.

Elizabeth was at first unsure of what she should say. She was young, naive and had been made to feel at ease, so she began to tell John the truth. "Yes…… and no." she answered.

"How do you mean yes and no?" John asked puzzled.

"I mean yes I told my father that I promised my hand elsewhere, but I was never actually asked."

"So why say you have?"

"I didn't want to marry you; I still don't." She said blushing. "I said it hoping that my father would forget the whole thing. I found out that a boy I know was going to ask me the night of the festival of summer's end, but he never had the chance to ask me, but father never knew that so I told him he had."

John collected his thoughts and said, "So you're not promised elsewhere?"

Elizabeth shook her head. "No." As soon as she had said it she regretted it, fearing that John might tell her father she pleaded with him. "Please don't tell anyone, if father found out he would………"

"My lady have you forgot our agreement so quickly," John interrupted, "I intend on honouring it." He added with a smile.

Their conversation was interrupted by one of the household servants who came running up the path. "Forgive the intrusion sir, but your father has requested you join him at once." He said red-faced and sweaty.

"Very well I shall join him presently." John said dismissing the servant. He waited until the servant was out of earshot before he spoke again. "I must go and speak with my father, I'll try to change his mind, but I doubt any good shall come from it." He kissed Elizabeth's hand and said, "Know this though; I shall always treat you as a queen. Every day I'll bring you flowers, and know also that I shall not find it hard to love you." With that he turned and strode off.

Elizabeth called out to him, "Thank you."

He stopped, turned and bowed, "My lady."

Elizabeth watched him enter back into the feasting hall, fearing that she had said too much she began to cry. What had she done?

*   *   *

The past couple of days had been endless walking across grasslands that never seemed to change, mile after mile of empty wilderness, like an endless ocean of brown and green grass. Then one night, a fog so dense that you could have sewn a button on it had ascended from nowhere, covering the vast grasslands and dampening the company's spirits.

The Arcani and Henri had slept side by side, fearing that if they strayed too far from each other they would get lost. By the morning it was still just as thick. They were forced to wait a couple of hours hoping that the fog would clear, but it didn't. Ulric decided that they could wait no longer.

He lit his lantern, forcing it to burn as brightly as it could, and told the others to follow him in this order, Garret, Symond, Henri, and Bard. We'll take a roll-call every few minutes he told them.

They walked steadily on in complete silence unsure if they were even going in the right direction; they could barely see the person in front of them, never mind whether it was the right direction or not. Then every twenty minutes or so, they would stop and take a roll call, Ulric, Garret, Symond, Henri, Bard, it sounded as each of them in turn called out their names.

Hours passed by and the light of day began to dull into the twilight hours. Ulric once more called a stop and took a roll call, all were present. He asked Garret to lookout ahead to see if he could see anything. He looked out, squinting against the fog, and was sure he could see dim lights in the distance.

The news reassured Ulric that he had led them in the right direction. He let the others rest a little longer as they were both hungry and thirsty. They had finished off what little provisions they had left yesterday. He had hoped that by now they would have arrived at Stratton Manor House, but the thick fog had delayed them, forcing them slowly on with empty stomachs and dry throats.

Henri's head was throbbing with dehydration and his feet were blistered. He'd often tried to sneak a sip of the enchanted water that was hidden in the bottom of his pack, but each time he went to fish it out someone had disturbed him. He thought now of sneaking off into the fog and taking a sip. No, he told himself, he would get lost, but if he stayed close enough to see the light of the lantern and did it quickly. He didn't need to convince himself anymore and he slipped off into the fog.

"Henri, where are you going?" Symond called out after him.

"I'm just having a piss." Henri called back. He stopped a few feet away from the others, where he could still see the lantern's light, but not the others and he was sure they couldn't see him. He slipped off his pack and stooped down to take out his skin of enchanted water when a loud drawn-out howl pierced through the fog. He immediately pulled his pack onto his shoulders and ran back to the others.

"Wolves!" Ulric shouted out. "Wild wolves!"

The company quickly grouped together, standing back to back drawing their swords. Henri was standing beside Symond and went to draw his dagger that he had found back in the woods, but Symond put his hand on Henri's arm to stop him and shoved him back into the protection of the four man circle.

All went eerily quiet as if the wolves were gone, but Ulric knew they were out there, prowling around them in the fog, waiting for their chance to attack. Then once more from out of the fog came the howl of many wolves.

Moments later five wolves came snarling and snapping from out of the dense fog. They came close, growling and snapping out at their ankles in an attempt to scatter them. Ulric knew that if they did, they'd be picked of one by one and torn to pieces.

"No matter what," Ulric shouted out over the howling, "we stay together!" No sooner had he said it more wolves came rushing at them.

They waved their swords franticly, keeping the wolves back. After an hour or more the Arcani began to tire. One wolf saw its chance and jumped up biting hold of Bard's arm. Bard screamed out as the wolf pulled with all its strength.

Garret quickly stabbed at it, sending it yelping off. The other wolves simultaneously retreated back into the fog. Their haunting howls continued as the company drew their breath. Garret unclasped his cape and wrapped it around Bards bloody forearm.

Ulric unclasped his black cape, tossed it to the ground and smashed the lantern onto it. There was a burst of flames as the lantern glass shattered and set alight the cape. The others, including Henri, did the same, knowing that wolves' hatred of fire.

With Bard's sword arm now useless he swapped places with Henri, even handing him his sword to use. No sooner had they reorganized themselves the wolves came running from the fog once more, foaming from the mouth with anger.

The company used the tip of their swords to flick the burning capes at the wolves, hitting their intended targets. The wolves who were hit panicked as their fur caught fire. They franticly jumped and bumped into others, setting them alight. In a blind panic they fled off once more into the fog.

There was still plenty more of them out there, waiting, wanting revenge. They took up their discomforting howling once more, that sent shivers down Henri's spine. Then from out of nowhere, came a horn blast that sent the wolves scattering away.

A horseman approached them from out of the fog. He reined in close to them and asked, "What are four Star Knights and a Sergeant doing traveling this path?"

Ulric stepped forward. "We are making for Stratton Manor House, and our business there is our own."

"Well you've had a bit of luck then," The horseman said dismounting, "I am Lord Stratton, and had you continued on this path you would have missed my manor house altogether."

Ulric was shocked that he was out on such an evening, but was never less relived. "I'm Captain Ulric; this is Garret, Symond, Bard and Henri." He said pointing to each of them individually.

"Well now that we are acquainted perhaps you'll tell me why you're disguised as Star Knights."

His words took Ulric by surprise. "We are......."

"Let's not waste any more time on lies," He cut across Ulric. "Now it's getting dark and those wolves will be back soon, so let us retreat to better surroundings, and you can tell me your tale."

The wolves once more took up their haunting howl, only this time it sounded further away.

"Lead on my lord." Ulric said gesturing for him to take the lead.

Lord Stratton mounted his horse and led the small company to his manor house. The wolves followed their every step, howling, but never getting close enough to be seen. By the time they reached it the sun had sunk below the horizon to the west.

Stratton Manor House was an old stone built manor covered in ivy. An overgrown flagstone courtyard with statues of snarling wolves and bears filled the space between the stonewall that ringed around the manor house.

Lord Stratton gave Ulric and his company leave to rest and bathe in the manor's hot bath. It was large enough for all of them to get in, so they all stripped off their garments and jumped in and let the hot water drive the cold out of their tired bodies. For Henri it was a first, normally he would bathe in the cold river once or twice a year, but this he found much more pleasant.

Lord Stratton brought in large goblets filled with warm spiced wine and told them that once they had finished bathing to join him in the great hall for a small feast.

Henri thought it odd that the lord himself should bring them wine, and not a servant. He thought nothing about it at the time, but when they arrived no servant had greeted the return of their master, and now he thought about it, he hadn't seen any servants milling around either. He began to feel uneasy and suspicious. Something wasn't quite right about the place; it was musty and badly kept as if no one was ever in permanent residence.

The others never seemed to notice the strange atmosphere, and splashed jokingly around drinking the spiced wine. Henri climbed out of the hot bath and dressed himself. He picked up a goblet from the small table where Lord Stratton had placed them and went to take a swig, but the smell along with the bits of spice floating in it, made him change his mind. Something deep down inside himself told him to get away from the manor, far away, but instead he pushed the thought aside telling himself to swallow his fears.

Ulric came out of the bath and pulled his clothes back on. He saw Henri and went over to him. "You look tired." He said as he sat on a wooden stool beside the small table.

"I am," Henri admitted, "I feel as though I've been run over by a wagon."

"As do we all." Ulric saw Henri's goblet was still full, "Are you going to drink that?"

"No." Henri handed Ulric the goblet and watched as he downed it in one.

Ulric wiped his mouth with the back of his hand and belched. "We'll get some food and negotiate for more supplies, and then we can rest for the night. I want to be ready to leave at first light."

"Must we stay here?" Henri asked fearing the answer.

"There is a dense fog and prowling wolves out there," Ulric said pointing into space, "We would be mad to leave the safety of this place. By morning the fog will have cleared and those wolves will have buggered off."

"The fog will have cleared." Henri said to himself, Ulric had said that before, and it hadn't. What if the fog never cleared and the wolves never buggered off? They would be stuck here forever. He told himself he was being stupid, that the fog would lift at some point, and the wolves would soon give up finding easier prey elsewhere. Even after reassuring himself a part of him felt as though he would never leave this place. No longer able to keep his thoughts to himself He said, "There's something strange about this place, I can feel it...........it's all around us."

"What do you mean by strange?" Ulric asked. He had sensed the strange atmosphere but had dismissed it as he was in unfamiliar surroundings.

"I mean he's a lord, but look around us, this place is rundown and dusty, and I haven't seen a single servant; I mean what kind of lord has no servants?"

"A poor one." Ulric coolly replied. "Long ago his family fell from the king's favour, and the line of the Lords of Stratton diminished to poverty."

"If he's that poor how is he going to help us?"

"There is a vast difference between a poor lord and a poor peasant. A poor lord is still a powerful man with resources enough to give a king a sleepless night."

"Well why should he help us, we are after all on a mission for the king."

"Once I heard a duke at the king's court describe the king as a fire on a winter's night, stray too far and one will freeze to death, but get too close and one will burn."

Henri was unsure what that meant, but then he had never met a king before. "So we won't tell him we're on a mission for the king then."

"We'll tell him just that," Ulric said standing, "He probably expects as much. So to tell him anything other than the truth will be pointless. We need his help as much as he needs ours to regain the king's favour." He stood and slapped Henri on his shoulder then went over to the others, beckoning them out of the hot bath.

They climbed out of the bath and got dressed, then went to the dining hall, as Lord Stratton had instructed them to do. He had changed from his riding gear into plain red winter robes, and sat before his fireplace waiting for his guests to arrive. When they did he stood and greeted them, giving each in turn another goblet of spiced wine. He bid them to sit at his table, where platters of bread, cheese, salted fish and pork, had been laid out for them.

The company greedily ate their fill and sat back in their chairs gulping down the spiced wine. Henri however left his goblet untouched, still distrusting of the lord. The others knocked back goblet after goblet; and the more they drank, the more they needed. They began to feel content as if the kingdom's worries no longer existed.

Henri could tell that their senses were dulled, and that they were weakened by drink. So he decided to make an excuse to leave to go and drink some of his enchanted water to revive his tired body.

"May I, my lord, use your privy?" He said already standing and walking out of the hall. They were all so deep in conversation that no one noticed him leaving. It surprised him as he was certain Symond would have questioned him, it must be the wine he told himself. Henri left the others red-faced with glazed eyes to negotiate for the much needed supplies. He went and picked up his pack from a small storeroom where they had left them and walked out of a door that led out into the gardens.

The thick fog was mixed with a crisp coldness that made Henri shudder as he stepped out into the cold air. The bright moon gave the fog an eerie glow that made Henri evermore nervous. He opened his pack and took out his water skin. Sitting down on his pack he uncorked the skin and took a swig. To his surprise it still tasted fresh, as if it was just at that moment taken from the stream. He sat back against the cold wall of the manor and felt the aches and pains of the past few days fade away. He closed his eyes enjoying the moment, listening to the sound of howling wolves that echoed in the night. Then his peace was shattered by a loud scream followed by banging and the shattering of glass.

Henri shot to his feet and pulled out his dagger he had found in the woods. Still holding the skin of enchanted water, he rushed back to the hall and the scene that greeted him would remain with him forever.

The headless body of Bard lay jerking on the floor, blood pumping out from his severed veins. The others were lying around the floor unable to defend themselves. Across, on the far side of the hall stood what was not so long ago Lord Stratton; now there was a snarling wolf-like beast stood upright on two feet ready to pounce on Henri. Fear rendered him a frozen statue unable to move, he urged himself to move but his body would not listen.

The beast looked across the hall at Henri with its threatening yellow eyes. Seeing its next kill it leapt across the hall to his side. It grasped Henri and lifted him off his feet, throwing him into the wall with a force that should have knocked him unconscious. Instead it seemed to wake his body up. He quickly picked up his dagger and held it out as the beast leapt at him once more. It leapt straight onto his dagger, staggering back and howling with pain. It pulled the dagger out and licked its blood from the blade before tossing it back, daring Henri to do it again.

Henri suddenly remembered the water skin he was somehow still holding; remembering what it had done to Laurence he calmly stood, uncorked the skin and threw it straight at the beast. It hit the target, splashing the enchanted water over the beast. Its body began to smoke as it shrieked with torment. He seized his chance. Snatching up his dagger he leapt at the beast stabbing and slashing in a blind fury until it fell back onto the floor blooded and defeated.

Henri, covered in the beast's blood stood over it, blooded dagger in hand, listening to the beast's shallow breaths. He saw the water skin, picked it up and shook it. There was still a little left, so he poured the remainder on the beast's head, killing it.

Assured that the beast was dead he rushed over to Symond who was half conscious. "Symond are you alright?" He asked helping him sit up.

"Rest assured…… my young friend……., I still draw breath." He answered slowly.

"What happened?" Henri asked.

"The wine……the wine…….it was drugged."

"Lord Stratton…….how……what…." Henri stumbled with the words trying to find the question.

"He was a shape-shifter……now go tend the others, I must rest to regain my strength." Symond shut his eyes and instantly fell asleep.

Henri went and checked on the others; they were asleep, so he left them where they were to rest. He wiped the blood off his dagger and sheaved it back in its scabbard, which he now kept on his belt so it was close to hand. Then he dragged the body of the beast, which had now changed back to the form of Lord Stratton, onto a rug. He then rolled the body up and dragged it outside where he left it.

The sound of the wolves simultaneously howling in the distance sent shivers down his spine. Going back into the dining hall he saw Bard's headless body and decided to drag it into another room so he wouldn't have to keep on seeing it. He looked for Bard's head but he couldn't find it and gave up his search.

By morning Ulric had wanted to be away from this place, so too did Henri, so while the others slept he went around the manor looking for supplies. He would see to it, that by morning they were ready to leave.

*   *   *

John Kinge walked with the confidence of a conquering hero fresh from victory. He held his head high as he passed by the other guests, who stood in groups gossiping. They spoke of the marriage and what it would mean for them, and John Kinge liked that. He liked the fact that he had caused so much jealousy amongst the other merchants, and most of all their wives and daughters. He knew he had a face that women liked; he saw it every time one would glance at him and smile. He saw it now as one of the ladies nearby gave him that look he'd seen many times before; he smiled back and inclined his head, which made her blush and turn away to her father's angry face.

He knew also that husbands and fathers hated the fact that their women found him charming and would compare them to him. They would like nothing better than to knock him down to his knees, he thought to himself, and that gave him the most satisfaction of all, knowing that weakness of distrust between husband and wife, father and daughter. He could take his pick of them and there was nothing they could do to stop him.

202

The Lord Aide had remained in his seat, stone-faced with dignity. He disliked many here knowing them to be greedy and disloyal, but then they said the same about him. His years as Lord Aide had made many enemies, and one by one he had dealt with them so that now none would dare speak out against him. They knew he had an eye on gaining Lordship of the town and would like to stop it, but they were weak, lacking any real power. He saw heads turning as his son's arrogant stride cut a path through the throng of gossipers. He came and sat on the chair beside him, picking up a half full goblet and draining the remainder.

"So what have you found out?" The Lord Aide asked his son.

"What we suspected." He leaned over and grabbed a jug. "She never promised her hand." He said pouring himself a measure of wine. "She just said that hoping that her father wouldn't force her to marry."

The Lord Aide grinned with satisfaction. "And did you make an impression?"

"Father if there's one thing I know well, it is women. I was ever the gentlemen and spoke to her as one would with a frightened horse. I confided in her and she confided in me."

"What do you mean?" The Lord Aide asked puzzled and slightly alarmed by him confiding in her. "I hope you didn't tell her all of our plans."

"Of course not father; I merely told her what she wanted to hear." He took a sip of wine and smiled at the wife of a merchant who looked across the hall at him.

"And what did she want to hear?" The Lord Aide asked, regaining his son's attention.

"Only that I felt the same way as her; she just needed to hear that she was right for feeling the way she does."

The Lord Aide seemed to ease with the confidence of his son's words, but one thing still gnawed him. "Will she willingly marry you?"

The question seemed to linger in the air for a moment before John answered. "No, not yet; she's stubborn and knows this peasant Henri is somehow in danger, but even a stubborn horse can be broken." He said with a grin.

"You have a plan to sway her mind?"

John grinned from ear to ear. "Yes, I know just what to do; but we're going to need the help of her father."

The Lord Aide leaned back in his chair. "You shall have it, but what plan do you have in mind." He asked intrigued.

"She wants to marry for love," John said smiling, "and I can make her love me. I told her that I also could only marry one whom I loved." He added bursting into laughter.

For the first time that night the Lord Aide laughed, "Marry for love; it will be a dark day when one marries for love and not position."

The laughter had made those closes by turn to see what the laughter was all about.

"Let us retire to a more private place and discuss your plan." The Lord Aide said, not wanting their plan to be overheard.

The Lord Aide and his son found Elizabeth's father and withdrew to his private chamber, where John told them of his plan to fool Elizabeth into trusting him, and then to love him.

Chapter 7

The guests of the betrothal feast had long departed back to their homes. The household servants had begun the laborious task of tidying up the aftermath of the heavy drinking and feasting. Leftover bits of food needed to be thrown out to the dogs; the wine that had been left would be collected together in a cask and donated to the Star Oracle in favour of a good fortune. Then there was the mountain of dishes that needed to be washed, floors that needed to be swept and mopped, candles that needed to be replaced in the chandeliers; all needed to be done before they could retire to the servants' quarters and sleep.

Elizabeth lay on her bed listening to the muffled bangs and scraping of chairs against the floor, but it was not the sound of the servants tidying up that kept her awake; it was the thought of John Kinge.

Late last night he had returned to her with the bad news she feared he would tell her. He told her that he had spoken with his father, but was unable to change his mind. He feared that they had no choice but to go through with the arranged marriage. She had wept; John gave her his cotton handkerchief to wipe away her tears and had taken her in his arms, reassuring her that he shall treat her lovingly as she deserved. He had kissed her on her forehead and said that he wished he'd never come back from the king's Academy at Baleford, for doing so had only broken the heart of the fairest lady in all the kingdom. He stopped with her until she had calmed down and said that they were not yet married and there was still hope of one of their fathers changing their minds. Elizabeth had laughed and told him he was a fool for believing that.

Soon after he had left with his father, leaving Elizabeth feeling guilty about not wanting to marry him; he was handsome and had seemed to understand her, but most of all he had listened to her and had showed compassion.

What about Henri she asked herself? He was still in danger and she needed to help him, but how? She had been trying to run away but hadn't been able to get any further than the front door. Maybe John could help? No, he would need his father's help, and that was the one person she didn't want to find him. Then she thought of Tom and the Star Knights who were already out looking for him, but they didn't know that Henri was in danger. I've got to get to the Star Perceptory and tell someone there she said to herself.

Hours slowly slipped by before the servants had finished tidying and the house fell silent for the night. However one thing was different tonight; the old handmaiden hadn't been in to check on Elizabeth. every night since she had been confined to her bedchamber the old handmaiden had come in to see if all was well before locking the door; but not tonight.

Elizabeth crept over to her door and found that it was still unlocked. She carefully pulled it ajar and peered out into the dark hallway. Nobody, no servants patrolling, or her mother's old handmaiden sleeping outside of her door, all was quiet. She carefully closed the door and sat back on the edge of her bed wondering why the old handmaiden wasn't at her post. Run, came the sudden thought. Without needing to think furthermore of what she might need with her, she blew out her candle and quickly rushed across to the door, opened it and slipped out into the hallway.

She struggled to see at first, but her eyes soon adjusted to the dark, not that it mattered anyway she had walked this hallway many times before and could have walked it with her eyes shut. Walking as quickly and quietly as she could she came to the stairs, where she stopped and listened for anybody that might be milling around. Nothing but silence. Taking a deep breath to calm her rapidly beating heart she began to descend the stairs.

"Elizabeth?" The familiar voice of Catharine said breaking the silence. "What are you doing? Or should I ask where are you going?"

Elizabeth stopped halfway down the stairs and looked back up to see her sister stern face illuminated by her candlelight. "Nothing and nowhere." Elizabeth replied as she went back up the stairs and blew out her sister's candle.

"You were going to runaway weren't you?" Catharine said so softly it surprised Elizabeth.

Elizabeth unable to find the right words just nodded her head.

"Why Elizabeth, why do you want to run away?"

"You know why; I'm being forced to marry a man I don't love."

"Well you seemed to be getting on with him well enough earlier." She said referring to the betrothal banquet held earlier. "Anyway I know you like him; I could see it all over your face every time you looked at him. It was the first time I have seen you smile since you were told about the marriage." She added.

"He is a fine man," Elizabeth confessed, "and I know he feels the same way as me."

"So what's the problem?" Catharine asked.

"It's Henri."

"What's he got to do it? Elizabeth he is a no-good fieldworker with no prospects of being anything other than that. He doesn't deserve your affections."

"It's not that…..it's……..it's….." Elizabeth stuttered, unsure if she should say anything more.

"Elizabeth what is it?"

"He's in danger." She spat out. "I need to help him."

"Danger, from whom?" Catharine asked not understanding what her sister was trying to say.

"A couple of days ago I overheard father and the Lord Aide talking; they said that the Arcani could be trusted and they'll see to it that he never comes back."

"Who are the Arcani, I've never heard of them before."

"I don't know; but I need to tell someone at the Star Perceptory, maybe they can help."

Catharine thought for a moment, "Is that where you were going now?"

Elizabeth nodded. "I know Tom is with Star Knights now looking for him, but they didn't know who he was with; maybe if they did they would find him quicker."

A silence grew between them as Catharine decided on whether she should let Elizabeth go or to shout and wake their father up. "Go," she said turning away from Elizabeth, "Go quickly before I change my mind."

"Thank you." Elizabeth said shocked, and without needing anymore encouragement she quickly descended the stairs.

Before she could open the front door Catharine called down to her, "Do you love him?"

The question made Elizabeth stop dead. She thought about answering and decided that she couldn't. Instead she opened the door and slipped out into the night.

Catharine watched on as her sister left, feeling guilty that she had just let her go; but what else could she have done to stop her? She had a sudden sickening feeling that something bad would happen to her, so turned and sprinted to rouse her mother and father.

Elizabeth rushed across the courtyard and out of the front gates that had by chance been left open. She wished she had taken the time to pick up her overcoat, as the early hours were cold with a thin mist that clung to the dark cobbled streets that made her feel even colder. Nobody was around, the streets were still and quiet. She walked down the hill towards the poorer part of the town when the sound of a squeak pierced through the silence.

Seeing a statue of a sitting lion that guarded the entrance to another rich man's house, she dashed over and hid behind it. Her heart was beating so fast that she thought that at any moment it would burst out from her chest and go rolling down to the bottom of the street. Her imagination began to run wild about who it was coming down the street towards her. Images of drunken men out looking to ravish young women, or cut throats looking for plunder, whirled around in her head. Worst of all she thought, it could be the spirit of the Reaper of the Dead.

Years ago when she was a little girl, her mother's old handmaiden had told her of a terrible plague that had swept across the kingdom. She said that the plague had no respect for titles, age, or gender; all had suffered its merciless wrath. So bad did it become that bodies were piled high in the streets, where they began to stink and rot. Until one day a man took it upon himself to take away the rotting bodies. They say he was in league with demons that thirsted for souls; he became so tainted in dark powers that he would pray for the plague to linger on forever. After a time it came to pass and the people rejoiced. The Reaper as he became known did not rejoice; through fear of losing his union with the demons he began to murder any he would come across in the night. He was later caught and hung, his body burnt. Even now, years after his death some claimed to have seen his ghost pulling along a cart filled with the bodies of his victims; his squeaky wheel still heard echoing down the streets on a dark, quiet night, and all still feared the Reaper.

Elizabeth shook, fearing that the Reaper had come for her, and then she heard voices. They didn't sound horrible or threatening, so she peered around the statue to take a look. Coming down the road was not the Reaper, but three dirty men covered in excrement. They led a mule that pulled a cartload of dung that had a squeaky wheel. She breathed a sigh of relief; they were just gong farmers she said to herself.

She remained still as the gong farmers passed by grumbling and moaning about how the rich thought they were better than them, yet their shit smelt just as bad they said laughing. Once they were gone the street was quiet again and Elizabeth came out from behind the statue. She carried on walking down the street until she was at the end of the road. Here the streets were narrower and in places smelt awful; the houses here were so close together that one could lean out of their window and shake the hand of the person who lived on the opposite side of the street, here the streets were dark and claustrophobic. Twice Elizabeth's foot had squelched in something unsavoury, but she dare not stop to look, and feared what state the fringes of her dress must now look like.

Elizabeth made it to the empty marketplace with ease, she knew the way well enough, but from here to the Star Perceptory was a bit of a haze. She took a moment to think of a route she knew and was comfortable with.

"Well, well, well, what have we here then?" A deep voice that startled Elizabeth said.

"Looks like a bit of fun for us." A different voice said menacingly.

Elizabeth looked on as the two men walked from out of the shadows of an alleyway and came menacingly towards to her. She edged back until she hit a wooden shutter of a stall and couldn't edge back anymore. One of the men reached out and grabbed her arm to stop her running away.

They were scruffy, dirty and smelt of stale beer. Both had lost most of their teeth and had greasy unkempt hair. They eyed Elizabeth up and down with lust for the young bit of flesh before them, roughly tugging at her dress and ripping it.

She clutched at her torn dress. "Leave me alone!" She screamed out at them.

They just laughed. "Stop being a tease, you know you want it as much as we do lass." The older one of them said as he pulled her hands away from her dress.

"NO!" Elizabeth screamed.

"Come on now lass, there's only one kind of woman in the streets at this time of night." The man holding her arms grinned as one of her breasts fell out of her dress.

"NO!" Elizabeth screamed again.

They threw her to the cold ground and begun to unbutton their trousers in anticipation of taking their pleasure. "I'm going to enjoy this." The man standing over her said.

Then from out of nowhere a voice shouted, "Leave her alone!"

The two men turned towards the man that was now rushing towards them. He ran straight into the man standing over Elizabeth, shoulder barging him to the ground. He then turned his attention to the other man, quickly swinging a punch that hit him square on the jaw.

Elizabeth looked on in relief as she recognised her rescuer, it was John. He was battling the two men single handed, taking as many savage blows as he'd given, but somehow he had remained on his feet. All of a sudden the two men had enough and turned, running off into a dark alleyway. John gave chase as far as the alleyway before he stopped and went back to Elizabeth.

"John you're hurt." She said as tears rolled down her cheeks.

Blood was dripping from his nose and he had a deep cut above his right eye where blood poured down his face. "It's nothing," he said kneeling beside her, "It's just a cut."

There was silence between them as they both took in what had just happened.

"Did they hurt you?" John asked.

"A little, but they would have done much worse had you not turned up." She replied clutching up her torn dress. "Thank you." She then added.

John took off his grey overcoat and placed it around Elizabeth's shoulders, "Did you recognise either of them?"

Elizabeth shook her head. "No, I've never seen them before."

"What are you doing out at this time of night? This is no time for a lady like you to be walking the streets."

"I'm not a whore!" She angrily snapped.

"I know, I know," John said soothingly. "I wasn't implying that you were."

"Sorry." She said more calmly. "How did you find me, was it my sister who told you?"

John looked blank. "What do you mean?"

"My sister, was it her who told you that I had ran off?"

John still looking blank shook his head. "I didn't know you had until now."

"So what were you doing walking the streets at this time?" She asked puzzled by how he had been able to find her and what he was doing.

"The same as you." He replied with a smile. "Running off."

"You were running away." Elizabeth said with disbelief.

John nodded his head. "Yes, I thought that if I ran away they couldn't force you to marry me, so I ran. Then as I got near the marketplace I heard a scream so I came over, and the rest you know."

Elizabeth wiped away her tears with the sleeve of John's overcoat. "I think we have both been a little bit stupid." She said.

John took her hand and kissed it. "I think you are right." He said looking straight into her eyes. "Even now in this darkest hour your beauty shines through."

Elizabeth blushed and quickly changed the subject. "Let me have a look at that cut."

"No, no, its fine." He said as he stood up. "The sun will rise in a couple of hours; I had best get you home where it's safe."

"Father will be mad." She said wiping away more tears.

"I will speak with your father; I'll ask him to be considerate."

"You would do that for me?" She said both surprised and grateful that someone would do that for her.

"My dear lady, for you I would travel across the Great Sea just to pick you a single flower." John held out his hand.

Elizabeth blushed as she let John help her to her feet. "Then you truly are my knight in shining armour." She said softly.

John wrapped his arm around Elizabeth's shoulders and escorted her back home. They passed no one as they walked through the narrow streets and spoke little.

Once back, Elizabeth's family home was in a flap. Servants were busy lighting fires and preparing for breakfast; two were posted on the front gates and on seeing the return of Elizabeth turned to inform her father. She was ushered inside and was immediately swarmed by fussing servants.

Her mother's old handmaiden pushed to the front, crisply ordering the other servants back to their duties, and then turned her anger on Elizabeth. "Well never in all my days have I heard of such stupidity!" She said in such anger that it surprised Elizabeth, who had seen her angry many times before, but never like this. She took Elizabeth's arm from John's and led her upstairs back to her bedchamber.

John stood and watched as the old handmaiden ushered Elizabeth off; he was looking for something, something that would tell him his efforts were not in vain. Then as Elizabeth reached the top of the stairs, she looked back and smiled at him. It gave John every reassurance that he needed and felt confident that his plan had worked. He turned to a nearby servant and ordered him to take him to the master of the house.

He was led to Elizabeth's father's private chamber where he was waiting, sitting behind his desk still wearing his nightshirt and cap, beating a tattoo with his fingers on the edge of his desk. Behind him at either side were two scruffy, dirty men that smelt of stale beer. They were the same two men that had attacked Elizabeth in the marketplace.

"You were longer than planned." Elizabeth's father said with annoyance. "Has all happened as we arranged?"

John went over to a small table at the side of the room and poured himself a goblet of honey-water. "Yes, though I suffered more wounds then we intended." The cut above his right eye was now crusted with blood and swollen into an egg shape lump.

"You told us to make it look believable," The younger of scruffy men said stepping forward, "So we did."

"I hope my daughter wasn't harmed."

"No more than was needed; she'll be fine in a day or two. It will give us time to build on the foundations made tonight." John took a swig of the honey-water and continued on. "Then we shall begin the second part of the plan."

"Which is what?" Elizabeth's father asked as John had not yet confided that part of the plan in him.

"Pity." John said.

"Pity," Elizabeth's father repeated in puzzlement, "What do you mean by pity?"

"What I mean, is that in a day or so I shall be gravely ill due to this cut getting infected." He said pointing to his head. "Then you shall make sure Elizabeth hears of it and arrange for her to see me, I will take care of it from there." He drained the last of his honey-water and went to leave. "In the meantime you are to be more considerate towards her, she won't try and run off again." He said as he opened the door and walked out.

Elizabeth's father looked on as John confidently walked down the passageway. He hated the man; he was too smug and arrogant for his liking. Who does he think he is telling him to do this and that? After all he only rose with his father, and should he fall, then John would fall with him. He was only what others could make him he decided, what his money could make him. "You can go." He said realising that the two thugs were still standing behind him.

"We haven't been paid yet." The older one of them said.

Opening a draw Elizabeth's father took out a small purse filled with thirty silver tallons. "Here, now the balance has been paid, go."

"It's been a pleasure." The older one said as they left.

"Make sure no one sees you leaving." He called after them.

A panel opened from the wall and Elizabeth's mother stepped out from the hiding place. "It would seem all went well husband."

"If you call paying thugs to attack your own daughter, then yes all went well." He said feeling guilty. He had never wanted it like this; in fact now he thought about it, he was not sure he even wanted to be Lord Aide at all.

"You must stay strong, soon all our efforts will pay off, and you will be Lord Aide." Elizabeth's mother said as she placed a hand on his shoulder.

"Yes, but will you settle with being the wife of a Lord Aide, or have you ambitions for more, a queen perhaps?" He shook her hand off his shoulder and stood, storming out and leaving Elizabeth's mother alone.

*   *   *

Henri had slept little. His body ached with tiredness and his eyes were heavy, but still Henri would have little sleep. He had spent hours searching the manor's kitchen for supplies and had piled up the provisions he found back in the hall where the others were lying unconscious. Next he had found some water skins and had filled them in a barrel half full with fresh water. By the time he had finished the fire in the hall had burned low, he had seen logs piled outside the front door where he had dragged Lord Stratton's body, so he swallowed his fear and quickly crept out, gathering an armful of logs and rushed back inside without looking at the body. He placed the logs on the fire and poked at it until it came back to life. He sat in a chair that was by the fire and closed his eyes, drifting in and out of an uneasy sleep.

The sound of howling wolves gradually quietened as the morning drew closer and as the sun rose Symond woke and weakly got to his feet. He saw Henri sleeping on the chair and went over to wake him. Henri who was awake heard the footsteps and jumped up drawing his dagger.

"It's me, Symond." He said fearing Henri was about to lash out at him with his dagger.

"Oh Symond, it's you. Are you alright?" Henri asked as he sheaved his dagger.

"I'm fine, but you look exhausted."

"I am; while you lot were lying unconscious I have been busy slaying monsters and gathering supplies." He said pointing at the provisions stockpiled in the corner of the hall.

The memory of Lord Stratton morphing into a humanoid wolf sent cold shivers down Symond's spine. He could remember what happened, even though it was a bit of a haze. Then Ulric woke, moaning with pain, and drawing their attention towards him.

Henri and Symond went over to help Ulric to his feet. He was weak and unable to stand without help, so they placed him on the chair by the fire that Henri was just sat in. No sooner had they placed him in the chair Garret woke moaning. "I feel awful." He said as he slowly climbed to his feet. His legs wobbled and he fell back onto the floor. "Damn it!" Henri went over to him and helped him onto another chair that Symond had placed near the fire beside Ulric.

Symond then slumped on the floor, "Water……we need water." He said weakly.

Henri went across to the corner where he had stockpiled all of the provisions and collected the water skins. He went back over to the others and handed each of them a water skin. They took a few sips and then drifted back to sleep. He thought about waking them, but decided it was better to let them regain their strength. Exhausted himself he lay near the fire fighting to stay awake, someone needed to keep a lookout he kept telling himself, but soon he too fell asleep.

An hour later Ulric shook Henri awake, "Henri, Henri, wake up."

Henri reluctantly woke and the first thing he saw was Ulric's tanned weatherworn face staring down at him.

"You were asleep." Ulric said in a voice that implied he had done something wrong.

"I tried to stay awake, but…………"

Ulric laughed. "It's alright; if it wasn't for you we wouldn't be waking at all."

Henri sat up, "How do you know?" He asked, thinking that none of the others were conscious when he had battled with the beast.

"It was I that told him," Symond said stepping forward, "I saw the whole thing remember."

Henri thought back and remembered Symond being half conscious. "Yes I remember now." He said. It had only happened last night, but it already felt much longer ago.

"And we can assume it was you that collected these supplies." Garret said as he stepped into view.

"Yes, while you all were unconscious I went to the kitchen to gather some food and water." He said as he stood. "You said you wanted to leave at first light, so I made sure we were ready."

"You did good lad, real good." Ulric praised. "Now let us get something to eat."

Garret went and fetched a sack filled with bread, apples and a cold joint of roasted pork wrapped in brown paper. They sat and ate in silence. Henri watched as Garret ripped off a chunk of bread and stuck it on the end of his sword, holding it up to the fire. "I like it as black as your boots." He said to no one in particular. They finished their breakfast and sat back drinking their water.

Henri couldn't stop thinking about what had happened last night; he took a swig of water and asked Ulric. "What happened to Lord Stratton………., why did he attack us I mean?"

"We didn't see it coming, yet the signs were there; but even with my good eyesight, I still did not see it." Garret said. "And Bard, poor Bard." He lowered his head and cuffed away tears.

"The wine was spiced with a drug that quickly dulled our senses." Ulric said. "We all drank too much and lost our wits. Then, when we were no longer able to defend ourselves, he changed right before our eyes. He doubled in size as thick hairs covered his body; his face elongated and from his jaws grew sharp fangs. Bard was the closest; it grabbed him and with a single bite took his head clean off; paralyzed by the wine he never even screamed as the sharp fangs pierced his skull." Ulric paused to take a swig from his water skin. "It chewed his head into mush before it swallowed it. We tried to get to our feet to defend ourselves, but it was pointless. It leapt around the hall like a cricket in a field; it swatted our feeble attempts to kill it

224

aside, as if we were mere flies. I lost consciousness after that."

"That's when I came in." Henri said.

"Yes," Ulric grinned, "A young boy saving the lives of three of the king's Arcani; never thought I would live to see such a day. Now let me see that dagger of yours."

Henri was unsure at first if he should admit to having it, and then thought that it was pointless to lie about it now. He drew it from its sheath and handed it to Ulric.

"A blade forged by the Gigantes." He said as he handled the blade with care, turning it to look at both sides.

"Please let me keep it." Henri said fearing that Ulric would keep it for himself.

Ulric looked up and saw the concern on Henri's face. "This blade is worth a king's ransom." He said, "Keep it safe." He handed the blade back to Henri.

"You're letting me keep it?" Henri said surprised by Ulric handing back the dagger.

"You have earned my trust and proven your worth." Ulric walked over to a chair where Bard's sword was leaning up against and grabbed it. "Here, take this." He said walking back and offering Henri the sword.

Henri stood and accepted the offered blade. He walked into space and drew it from its scabbard, taking a few swings that awkwardly sliced through the air.

Ulric laughed as he saw the clumsy strokes. "You need to learn how to use it."

"It's easy," Henri answered, "You hold it at this end, and you stab them with the pointy end."

Symond stood, drew his own sword and with one swift movement disarmed Henri. "You have much to learn my young friend." He said as he handed back the sword.

"And you shall teach him." Ulric told Symond. "Whenever we stop and have time, teach him."

Henri sheaved his sword and sat back down beside Garret.

"You'll get the hang of it soon enough laddie." Garret said as Ulric and Symond came and sat by the fire. There was another silence as they sat listening to the sound of the fire cracking and spitting.

Henri wondered how Lord Stratton ever became a shapeshifter; was he born like it, was his mother raped by a pack of wild wolves? All sorts of thoughts circled in his mind until he could bear it no longer. "How did Lord Stratton become a shapeshifter?" He said out loud.

Ulric shook his head. "I don't know, but what I can say is that they are an age-old menace that mask their true form and prey on the weak."

"I have heard of a story," Symond spoke as he sat next to Henri, "of a man named Thetis, he was a righteous man who once served as a priest in the Chalice Temple long-ago. They said he had such a great affection for righteousness, that he would feed the poor and tend to the sick as well as his daily duties in the temple. Over time, Thetis became a name that people would cheer on hearing it, a name people would measure the other priests up to. That made a fellow priest jealous, so jealous that he fell in league with a mage who cursed Thetis. He was forced from the temple and banished into the wild, where he would by night change into a beast. They said that whoever was bitten by the beast would themselves share his curse. From that day on, the curse was passed down through the ages, and until all of them are slain, they shall roam freely in the wild."

"I heard it was a mage's experiment that went wrong." Garret said.

"It doesn't matter how it started," Ulric said stopping the conversation, "All that matters now is that we get out of here and on towards Elmham Castle."

"It's a good two days journey from here." Garret said stroking at his bushy red beard.

"Yes and we've lost enough time already." Ulric took out his map and unfolded it on the floor. "We are here," he said prodding a finger on a mark he had made, "Elmham Castle is here," he pointed it out on the map, "If we go across the plains we risk those Star Knights catching up with us."

"They've not managed it yet." Garret said.

"No," admitted Ulric, "but I could gamble a king's ransom that they will be on horseback heading our way."

"But they don't know where we are." Henri said, adding in his thoughts. "They probably won't know which way we've gone."

Ulric shook his head. "They know, the trouble we caused back in the village of Raven Wood, we may as well have sent them a letter telling them where we were. Besides that the locals there saw us enter the woods, and those damn Star Knights will have obtained that information by now. They won't have taken the path we did, they won't risk it; they will have gone around. It would be the same with the burial mound, so at best they are probably a few hours behind, maybe half a day. Hopefully that fog will have slowed them."

"With a bit of luck those wolves will have ripped them to pieces." Garret said with a bark of a laugh. "If they are close by we cannot stay on the open plains, it would be madness." He added, agreeing with Ulric.

"So what are we to do?" Symond asked.

Ulric looked back at the map and pointed at a town called Hollington. "The road between here and Elmham," he said tracing the road with his finger. "Regular carriages ferry passengers to and from the two towns. If we head south from here, then by tomorrow we will find the road and we shall pay for passage to Elmham on the first carriage we come across."

"Pay," Garret said, "why don't we just commandeer it?"

"The same people work the carriages every day, they would notice we were not one of them, and the only place we would end up then is the town's dungeons."

Ulric folded up his map. "They see countless passengers every day and will suspect nothing of us." Symond and Garret nodded their approval.

"Then let us make ready and leave this place of ill omen." Symond said as he stood.

Ulric stood. "One hour," he said, "I want to be out of here in an hour. Garret, fill our packs with the supplies Henri found, and everybody fill your water skins before we go." He ordered. "Now Henri where is the body of Bard?"

"I dragged it to an empty room across the way."

"Show me."

Henri took Ulric to Bard's headless body. Ulric searched his body for anything of use, but found nothing. He told Henri to find some tools and bury him.

Henri wandered down to the storeroom where he had seen a spade earlier. Symond accompanied him, offering his help. Together they dragged Bard's body outside where they dug a shallow grave and buried him. The body of Lord Stratton they ignored and left rolled up in a rug by the front door.

No sooner had they finished, Ulric and Garret came walking out of the front door holding their packs and hooded cloaks that they had found hanging in a closet in the hall. They handed Henri and Symond their new hooded cloaks, and packs that Garret had filled with food.

"I need to refill my water skin." Henri said fearing that he was going to hold everyone up.

"Already filled it laddie." Garret said handing Henri a full water skin.

With everybody ready they walked out of the gates and headed south towards the Elmham Road. The day was going to be cool and sunny with the remnants of the previous night's dense fog gradually lifting. The tall grass was wet with the morning dew that reflected the morning light.

Henri looked at the others as they walked ahead of him, they were scruffy, tired and didn't look like a single unit. When we had first been taken to them back at the castle of Heath Hollow, they had looked like a single unit; dressed all in black like Star Knights. They still wore the surcoats of Star Knights, but the plane black cloaks they had burned to fight off the wolves the day before. Now their cloaks they had found were a mix of Brown and green, they looked more like a band of wandering peasants then members of the Arcani.

He looked down at himself and saw the same. It made him feel comforted, he felt part of something, something big, and for the first time he was glad that he had been caught that night of the festival. He smiled to himself and found himself looking forward to the rest of the journey and walked willingly on south towards the Elmham Road.

*   *   *

Tom yawned and slumped in the saddle. It had been a long hard night; wild wolves had been prowling the plains with a vicious intent on killing anything they came across.

Commander Frey ordered a circle of fire be made and all to take refuge in it. They had found plenty of fuel and had piled it near the centre of the circle that they had made. Commander Frey had then set alight to the ring of leaves, dry brush and branches they had collected, creating a barrier that kept the wolves at bay.

A handful of times a wolf would risk the flames and jump over into the circle, only to be swiftly killed by one of the Star Knights broadswords. The night passed on slowly in much the same pattern and as the dawn neared the fuel runout and the fire burned low. They were forced to mount their steeds and flee. The wolves gave chase for a few miles, snapping at the legs of the horses as they fled.

Eventually the sun rose and the wolves gave up their pursuit, so they slowed their horses to a walk. Behind them in the distance, rising above the mist, was the burial mounds. It had taken them a full day to travel around it. They had hoped that they would have caught up with the thieves on the open plains, but thus far there was no sign of them.

They knew that the thieves had come out of the woods, they had left tracks that William was able to read and follow, but as they got to the main burial mound they had disappeared. There they stopped in front of the huge stone door to rest the horses.

William went scouting around the mound looking for further tracks on the ground. He found none and was about to give up when he had another thought, could they have gone through the mound? He climbed the mound and for an hour or more he had searched for any tracks. Finding an entrance dug above the stone doorway and a tied off rope that he pulled up from the dark shaft, he came to a frayed end where it had snapped. He had got the answers he was looking for and quickly climbed back down the mound to inform the others.

On hearing Williams's news they mounted their horses and spent the whole day riding around to the other side of the mound. Once there they picked up the trail again, but they didn't need to follow it. Commander Frey knew where they were heading; it was the only place that offered any safety on the plains.

It was that night that the wolves had attacked them and now with the morning sun shining in their faces they rode towards Stratton Manor House.

"You should keep your back straight." Edward told Tom.

Tom snapped out of his daze and straitened his back. "Sorry, I'm just tired." He said.

"We are all tired." Edward replied.

If they were tired they never looked it. No matter what, every morning they would wash their bodies and comb their hair; their surcoats and equipment was kept immaculate. Then every morning and night they would kneel together and say their Star Prayer.

Tom had heard the prayer so often now that he could recite it word for word himself. After the night's events and being forced to flee from the wolves; they hadn't been able to say their prayer or groom themselves as they normally would, but to Tom they still looked tidy and ready for anything that might happen.

Commander Frey, feeling that it was now safe, called a halt. All of the Star Knights dismounted and knelt down on the wet ground, and in unison said their prayer.

> *O heavenly stars let your divine light*
> *guide and protect us slaves that*
> *submit before you. Banish all darkness*
> *within us and let the light fill our*
> *hearts. Give us the strength to stand*
> *against the darkness, that we may*
> *bring the kingdom to light.*

Tom stopped on his horse, and in a more mockingly way, mimed the words with them. Over the last day he had managed to get the basics of riding the horse lent to him. He still felt uncomfortable on it and would much prefer to walk. His inner thighs were red raw from the hours spent in the saddle, and found walking difficult whenever he dismounted.

He thought to himself that he shouldn't mock them; after all they had saved his life back at Raven Wood. It was funny but it seemed like it had never happened, but yet he knew it had. It had taken hours for the poison to leave his body, but once it did the Commander had questioned him on what he had learned. He told him all he had found out, only to be asked again, as if they didn't believe what he had told him. Eventually they had made their plans and went in pursuit of the thieves.

The Star Knights finished their prayer and mounted their horses. Commander Frey took out his telescope and cast an eye over the grasslands ahead. He saw nothing but the breeze swishing the tall grass. Snapping shut his telescope and placing it back into his saddlebag, Commander Frey ordered them on.

By midday they had reached Stratton Manor House. They rode in through the gate and dismounted by the front door. Tom tethered his horse to an iron ring that was fastened on to the stonework and knelt beside a rolled up rug that had been left by the front door.

"What is it Thomas?" Commander Frey asked.

"A rug covered in blood Commander." He answered, holding it up for him to see.

Commander Frey thought it odd, and as he glanced around the garden he noticed a recently dug grave. "I want you to find out who is in that grave." He said to Tom. "I want to know if it is one of our thieves." He turned to Geoffrey, "Help Thomas; William see to the horses; Edward you will come with me."

William took the horses to the stables where he found a carcass of a horse crawling with maggots. He put the horses at the opposite end and placed a couple of old saddle blankets he had found lying around over the carcass.

Tom and Geoffrey picked up the two spades that had been left beside the grave and dug. They made short work of it as the grave was shallow and soon unearthed the body. To Tom's horror they found it was headless. He stepped out the grave and gagged.

"How are we going to tell if he's one of the thieves?" Tom said spitting onto the ground.

"He is," Geoffrey said tearing the surcoat off the body, "One of our stolen surcoats." He said tossing it to Tom.

Tom looked at the surcoat and filled with dread, what if it was Henri? He forced himself to look at the body and was able to rule his fear out; it was too big even without the head. Doubt crept into his mind, what if he was wrong.

"Whoever he was, he was not your friend." Geoffrey said seeing Tom's pain.

"How can you tell?" Tom asked.

"Your friend is the same age as you?" Geoffrey paused, waiting for Tom to answer.

"Yes." Tom nodded. "That's right."

"And no doubt, just as skinny." Geoffrey added.

Tom said nothing and just nodded his agreement.

"This body is of a man who had the build of years' worth of warfare, and not that of a skinny boy." He said reassuring what Tom had thought.

They shovelled the soil back over the body and went inside to report their findings to Commander Frey, finding him in the hall. As Tom walked into the hall the first thing he noticed was the dried up clotted pool of blood on the floor. The hall was a mess with goblets and empty platters scattered across the floor. The table was lying upside down with a leg missing in the middle of the room. A small pile of food had been placed in a corner at the back of the hall.

Commander Frey and Edward were standing in front a varnished wooden fireplace that still had the remnants of a smouldering fire.

Geoffrey handed the surcoat to Commander Frey. "It is as you suspected, the thieves were here."

"And not that long ago," Commander Frey answered pointing to the fire. "We must only be a few hours behind."

"Then what are we waiting for," Tom said, "If we leave now we'll be able to catch up with them." He turned to walk out to the horses when he was stopped by Commander Frey.

"No Thomas," Commander Frey said. "We do not know which direction they will have gone."

"Can't William just track them like before?" Tom asked.

"Yes he probably could; but if we're tracking them, we're also following them; and what we need is to get ahead of them."

"But we could take them on the open plains." Tom argued.

"What if William loses their tracks? We would then lose time in a pointless pursuit." He turned back to the fire and tossed the surcoat onto the charcoaled logs. "From here they will be heading for Elmham Castle and I want us to get there first."

Tom thought about it and decided it was a better idea than just wandering in the plains on the chance that they might catch up with them.

"We shall rest here until first light tomorrow morning then it shall be a full day's riding; and by tomorrow night I want us to be at Elmham Castle.

Chapter 8

Henri and the Arcani reached the Elmham Road. They sat beside the road resting in the midday sunshine, waiting for a carriage to pass by. Garret was stood on a boulder beside the road peering east and then west in the hope of seeing a carriage on the horizon.

They had walked twenty four miles from Stratton Manor across the open plains; endlessly watching over their shoulders for the pursuing Star Knights, but saw no sign of them. A hope that they might have lost them began to creep into their minds, and they began to relax, walking and joking as though they were strolling through the castle gardens back home.

A couple of hours passed before Garret saw a black smudge on the western horizon. "There's one coming now." He jumped down off the boulder. "It should be here within an hour." He said.

They waited. The sound of the wheels rumbling on the stone road and the click clacking of the horses' hooves filled the air as the carriage drew near. Ulric stepped out into the road and held his hand up.

The driver pulled on the reins, "Woe." He said brining the four horses to a stop. Two other men armed with crossbows jumped down off the back of the carriage and aimed their weapons at Ulric. They wore a dark blue tunic with a horse broach pinned on to it, brown trousers and tall black boots. Their hair had been pulled back and powdered white. The driver wrapped the reins around a bar and climbed down from his cab. "What are three Star Knights and a Sergeant doing on foot out here in the open plains?" He asked.

"Our horses were killed by wolves in the night." Ulric lied. "We are in need of passage to Elmham Castle."

The driver who had been driving this road for near on twenty years was cautious. He could see that they were wearing the old fashioned surcoats of the Star Knights, but there hooded cloaks were not the attire of the Star Knights. There was something was odd about them, but what he didn't yet know. "I have the space for you, but do you have the coin? My gaffer doesn't like me giving free passage, even to Star Knights."

Ulric pulled a purse from out of small pouch on his belt. He pulled open the strings and fished out a thick golden coin. "There's enough here to pay for passage to the stars and back." He tossed the coin to the driver who inspected it by placing it in his mouth and biting it.

Assured that the coin was good he waved for the other two men to lower their crossbows. He pushed the coin into his pouch and opened the carriage door. "Leave your packs; my men here will put them on the roof."

The carriage was one of the newly designed stagecoaches that Ulric had seen back in the capital. It was wooden framed, covered in plane black leather that protected the passengers from the weather. Two doors, one either side, led to a comfortable interior of burgundy coloured seats and matching quilted walls to keep in the heat.

They climbed inside and sat side by side on the seat nearest to the front. Opposite them were two women, one old the other young. They were mother and daughter who had spent a couple of days with family in Hollington and were now heading home.

"I plan to travel through the night, stopping once only to take a meal and water for the horses. By morning we'll reach Elmham Castle where you will all have to sign in." The driver said to Ulric. He closed the door and once the four packs were safely stowed, climbed back onto his cab and whipped the horses into motion.

The journey was one of wonder for Henri as he had never been in a carriage before. It was far more comfortable then he imagined it would be. He thought it would be rough and bumpy, but instead it was smooth with only a little swaying. Relaxed by the motion of the carriage he closed his eyes and dozed off. When he woke it was dark. A lantern had been hung from a hook on the celling and was burning dimly.

Symond was the only other person awake. He sat with the shutter down staring out into the night. A cold breeze blew in waking the old woman opposite.

"Close that shutter." She said sternly.

"Of course my lady, forgive me." Symond said as he pulled up the shutter.

The old woman pulled her woollen blanket tightly around herself and dozed back off.

"I really need to stretch my legs." Henri said in a hushed tone.

"We will probably be stopping soon enough." Symond answered.

"What time of day is it?" Henri asked thinking that it was early hours of the morning.

"It is about two hours after sunset. You should take some rest my young friend, we have a long way yet."

Henri leaned his head back and closed his eyes, dozing back off.

Soon after, the carriage came to a stop. The driver climbed down from his cab and opened the carriage door, letting in a blast of cold air that woke everybody. "It's safe to get out and stretch your legs, but don't wonder too far; we eat within the hour."

Henri climbed out of the carriage and paced around to revive his cramped legs. They had pulled up in a spot that carriages regally used. Another carriage that was heading in the other direction was already there. They were preparing to leave when they saw the other carriage pull in, so they left their fire for them.

The driver set a pot filled with a premade stew over the fire. The other two men gave the horses a little water before they came and sat beside the fire with the passengers. Each was given a wooden bowl that the driver filled with hot stew along with a small bread roll.

Henri blew at his steaming stew, dabbed his bread in the thick gravy and bit into it. "Not bad." He said as a blob of gravy ran down his chin.

When they had all finished the driver collected their bowls and placed them in the pot that held the stew. They stowed the pot back in the box at the back of the carriage and ushered the passengers back inside. The driver once more climbed up to his cab and whipped the horses on. They travelled on through the night at a steady pace without stopping. The passengers drifted in and out of an uneasy sleep, regularly being woken by the carriage wheels hitting bumps.

The morning dawned grey and cold with a strong wind that told the tale of a coming storm. It whistled around the carriage waking all inside.

"What was that?" Henri asked, startled by the sudden noise.

"It was only the wind my young friend." Symond answered. "It's getting worse."

Garret who was sat beside a shutter opened it and sniffed at the air. "There's a storm coming." He said. "I can smell it in the air."

"How can you smell a storm?" Henri asked.

Garret just tapped the side of his nose with his finger and said no more.

The driver banged on the carriage roof and called out, "Elmham Castle!"

Ulric nudged Garret aside and leaned out of the window. He saw the huge stonewalls that looked black against the grey clouds that filled the sky. "We'll be there in about an hour." He said leaning back into the carriage.

As the carriage approached the west gate it was stopped by one of the guards. He asked the driver a couple of questions and when he was satisfied by the answers given, allowed the carriage to enter the town with the strict instructions for everybody to sign in. The driver nodded his agreement and slowly pulled off, rumbling in through the gate. He pulled up in a wagon park that was already crammed and opened the carriage door for his passengers.

The first thing Henri noticed was the smell, quickly followed by the noise of many people. It reminded him of home and for the first time in a while he felt homesick. He thought of Elizabeth and wondered what she was doing right now, probably working her father's stall he thought.

"My I take your names please." A thin man with a long nose said disturbing Henri's thoughts. He wore a scarlet tunic with a chain of coins strapped around his waist; and on the tip of his nose was small round spectacles. Atop of his head he wore a large black floppy beret with a brooch of a quill pinned to it; in his hands he carried a thick ledger and quill, at the ready to write down their names.

Ulric saw the Town Steward and greeted him, "Good morning steward." He said inclining his head. "We are Knights in the Order of the Star and are exempt from the town's customs."

"May I see your warrant of exception?" The Steward asked with a raised eyebrow. Wind snatched at the pages of his book. He placed his hand on the pages to stop the wind from losing his place and asked again. "May I see your warrant please?"

Ulric took a step closer and spoke in a hushed tone. "We're looking for a quiet place to sit out the storm." He pulled out his purse and took out a gold coin, placing it on the Steward's book. "My mother never did name me." He said.

The Steward picked up the coin. "Very well, you should head for the eastern wall; there you shall find an inn called The Hammer and the Anvil."

Ulric nodded his thanks and turned back to the others. "We make for an Inn on the eastern wall." He announced.

The driver of the carriage came over to them with their packs. He dumped them on the ground by their feet and thanked them before returning to his carriage.

They shouldered their packs and walked east through the stinking streets. It took longer than they thought, and the weather was starting to get worse. The wind was blowing more constantly and stronger than before, carrying with it the distant sound of thunder. As they reached the eastern wall grey clouds gave way to black ones that threatened rain. They followed the street east until they found the Inn.

It was a two storey building painted white with thick black beams and lead framed windows. A wooden sign with a hammer and anvil painted on it hung above the door, swinging and squeaking with the wind. The lantern light glowing inside looked warm and welcoming, but before they went in Ulric led them up a flight of stairs that was next to the inn, leading them to the top of the town's wall. They looked out over the parapet towards a dark forest that dominated the horizon.

"That is where we are heading." Ulric announced to Henri.

Henri shuddered at the thought of entering that forest. The last wood he had seen was the one at Raven Wood, and those woods had looked pleasant, but the forest he looked upon now, looked terrifying, even though it was miles away. He pulled his cloak tightly around himself and shivered. "Is that where the chalice is?"

"Hidden within that forest is the ruins of the ancient city of Dimon Dor; there within the temple we shall find the chalice." Ulric took out his telescope and offered it to Henri.

He took the offered glass and scanned an eye across the distant forest, searching for the ruins of the ancient city. "I can't see it." Henri said, but what he did see scared him.

The trees were taller than any other he had seen before and had grown into cruel, twisted shapes. The trunks and branches were grey; and the leaves were as black as the night sky. A true place of horror, which would make even the mightiest of men tremble in its wake.

"Trust me, it's there." Ulric said taking back his telescope.

There was a flash of lightning that forked across the sky followed by a clatter of thunder. A heavy pouring rain fell and in seconds it turned the streets into rivers of filth.

Henri and the others ran down the stairs to the Inn; and in the short time it took them, they got soaked. They opened the door, dripping wet, and entered the warm, dry inn.

The inn had been built up against the east wall, its roof slanted down from the wall, making the ceiling higher than in any other inn. Inside was warm as there were two fireplaces, one at either end, the walls were plastered and painted white with wooden beams that had been left unpainted and had tiny holes where woodworm had eaten through it. A few of the locals sat at a table near to the fireplace on the right, talking quietly, they took no notice of the four sodden men that entered.

The Innkeeper was stood behind the bar wiping mugs with a wet rag. He was a tall burly man with a hard squared face with a close clipped beard. Above his brow he wore a strip of brown leather that kept his hair out of his face and copper bracelets on his wrists that had turned the skin under them blue.

Ulric followed by the others walked over to the bar, leaving wet boot prints across the floor.

"We need a room with a fire to dry ourselves." Ulric said to the innkeeper.

The innkeeper said nothing and looked straight past them at the wet trail they had left behind them.

There was another loud clatter of thunder.

"We wish to stay here and wait out this storm." Ulric said to regain the Innkeeper's attention.

The Innkeeper looked at them, and saw that they wore the surcoat of Star Knights, arousing his suspicion. "Why don't you go to the Star Perceptory where your kind belongs?" He said, spitting into a mug and wiping it.

Ulric took out his purse and placed another of his gold coins on the bar. "A room with a fire, and no questions asked."

The Innkeeper placed down the mug and picked up the golden Denar. "I don't want any trouble." He said looking sternly at Ulric.

"We wish to shelter from the storm, nothing more." Ulric replied.

The Innkeeper grunted, turned and took a key from a hook behind him. "Go up the stairs, third door on the left." He handed the key to Ulric, "I'll be up shortly to make a fire."

Ulric nodded his thanks and walked over to the staircase that was next to the bar. They found their room with ease and the Innkeeper shortly followed bringing a tray of mugs filled with warm dark ale. He soon got a roaring fire going and left them to themselves. They stripped off and placed their wet garments near the fire, sitting in dry blankets they had found ready in their room.

Henri shivered at the sound of the pouring rain beating against the window. He thought about the forest he had seen from the parapet, and wondered why it looked the way it did; maybe it was because of the wicked monsters that dwelt there? "Why does the forest look the way it does?" He asked aloud to no one in particular.

Nobody rushed to answer and left the question hanging in the air. There was a flash followed by another loud clatter of thunder.

"Long ago," Symond told the story, "in the age before the chalice, the city of Dimon Dor was a place of learned men. They spent years plotting the stars and searching for answers to the great questions of life. The land was at peace with many seeking enlightenment in the city. Then as the years passed and the darkness grew, they began to hide all they had discovered. Fearing that the rival city of Balharoth was stealing their knowledge, they closed their gates to all and sent the city's mages to plant a forest to hide their great city. Yet more years passed and the city was swallowed by the forest and hidden away. Most had forgotten its location, but one wondering wise man named Adullam was able to find the city. So impressed by Adullam's knowledge, they granted him leave to study their old texts. After years of study he found an answer to expel the darkness. The chalice was then created and the last king of Dimon Dor wanted it for his own."

"What happened then?" Henri asked eagerly wanting to hear more.

"War. The king sent his armies north into the kingdom of Balharoth; there they proceeded to burn and kill, but it was not an easy fight. It took years and much spilt blood before the kingdom of Balharoth fell. With the war won the chalice fell into the city's hands; but all was not yet won.

To the west the boy sent from the heavens had gained support of the men that dwelt there and had raised an army. He forged a kingdom of his own and vowed to reclaim the chalice that was his by the rights of his divinity, so the second war for the chalice began. The two great armies met on the Plains of Pendor, where the army of Dimon Dor was defeated. Elnar the Great then took back the chalice and founded the Order of the Star to guard it. Those that survived the battle, fled back to Dimon Dor where they were impaled for their cowardice by their king.

The Grand Imp Georus, who had remained neutral throughout the war, was appalled by how the darkness had corrupted a once great city. He went into the forest and cursed the city to eternally dwell within the forest. From that day, the forest turned dark and the kingdom of Dimon Dor fell from the pages of history."

"So what happened to the people there?" Henri asked.

Symond shook his head. "No one knows for sure, but the history books say that they were cursed to be one with the forest that they had planted, and that even today they dwell there still."

"That is why we need you." Ulric said. "If the ruins are still inhabited, then we will need you to sneak into the temple and take the chalice."

Henri thought for a moment. "What if I get caught?"

"We will be close by, should anything go wrong." Ulric reassured him. "Anyway it might be deserted."

"How do you know the chalice is even in the temple?"

Ulric opened his pack and pulled out an old map, handing it to Henri. It was not like ordinary maps that were drew onto parchments, this one was stitched like a tapestry. In the upper right was a star with eight elongated points, the same as on their surcoats. The pictures showed a procession of Star Knights carrying the chalice east to Dimon Dor where they placed it in the temple, under which was written: Here lies the truth of men's curse, until the mountains doth crumble away and the darkness devours all, let it remain hidden.

Henri handed the map back to Ulric and feeling satisfied that his question had been answered he checked his garments. They were still a little damp but he still put them back on.

"Since you're dressed, you can go down stairs and tell the Innkeeper to bring up some hot food." Ulric said.

Henri strapped on his weapons and said nothing, walking out the room and down the stairs, something felt odd, wrong, but what he didn't know.

The Innkeeper was busy talking with the locals and didn't notice Henri come down the stairs. He didn't dare disturb him, so instead he went outside in to the pouring rain.

Striding purposely towards the inn was a group of Men-at-Arms who wore black and white quartered surcoats that clung to their chainmail. They never saw Henri so he ignored them and went up the stone stairs to the parapet. He looked out over the parapet and noticed the wide river that ran at the foot of the castle; the water looked icy cold and murky. He wondered why he never noticed it before. There was another flash of lightning and a cracking of thunder. I must be mad for being out here, Henri thought to himself. He glanced at the distant forest and said aloud to himself. "I must be bloody stupid." He turned and went back down the stairs. There he was met by a scene that took him by surprise.

On their knees being shackled one by one was Ulric, Garret and Symond. There packs and garments were piled on the wet ground beside them. They were asked something that Henri couldn't hear because of the rain, and then roughly pulled to their feet and led away in chains.

*   *   *

Tom and the Star Knights had arrived at Elmham Castle the day before the thieves. It was late when they had arrived and the town's gates were closed. The guards who saw them ride towards the gate called out to them, asking them who they were and what they wanted. Commandeer Frey had called back that they were knights of the Order of the Star and that they had urgent business with their lord. The captain at the gate saw the white star on their surcoats and ordered for the gate to be opened.

Commander Frey beckoned for Tom and the others to follow him as he walked his horse in through the gate, reining in beside the Captain who had come down to greet them.

The Captain of the gate introduced himself as Captain Marment and explained that he needed to take the names of all in Commander Frey's company. They gave their names and were then allowed to enter the town.

The sound of the hooves clip-clapping echoed in the night as they rode their horses in single file through the narrow cobbled streets towards the Star Perceptory.

Tom was amazed by the size of the town and of the stonewall that ringed it. He too had come from a town with a castle, but it was not like this one. The castle at Heath Hollow was small and had no wall to protect the town. In places the stonework there was in a bad state of repair and crumbling. Here the walls were strong and high, as if they had been built to keep out giants. The castle too looked just as impressive. He counted six round towers on one side alone and guessed that there must be just as many on the other side.

They reached the Star Perceptory that was in the northern part of town where two Sergeants opened the gates for them. They dismounted and asked to see the Commander in charge of the watch. They were led into a small room with a small fireplace and benches, and made to wait. An hour passed before the Commander of the watch came and greeted them. He apologised for the wait and led them straight to the Marshal.

The Marshal was dressed only in his long nightshirt and bedcap, and despite being woken he greeted Commander Frey warmly. "My brothers I bid thee welcome."

"I am Commander………."

"Frey, yes I know who you are." The Marshal interrupted. He was in his seventies and his body was hunched with age. His once strong mind was now fading like a fire that had burnt up all its fuel. He sat in a chair by the small fireplace and gestured for Commander Frey to take the seat facing him.

"News of our quest has reached you then?" Commander Frey said taking the offered seat.

The Marshal's shaky hand pointed to his desk that was littered with parchments. "Commander Bartholomew, be so kind as to hand me the letter from the Grandmaster."

The Commander that had escorted Frey and his company to the Marshal went over to the desk, picked up a parchment with the wax seal of an eight pointed star on it, and then handed it to the Marshal.

"Thank you Brother Bartholomew, now be a righteous man, and fetch an old man a blanket."

Commander Bartholomew a young man eager to please bowed and left the room to fetch the Marshal a blanket.

"We have been informed of the impending crisis and have been instructed to aid you with whatever your needs be." The Marshal shakily handed the parchment to Commander Frey for him to read. "Six Knights are listed," he said, "Yet only four do I see; and the letter does not mention a Sergeant in your company." He looked at Tom with suspicious eyes.

"His name is Thomas, a fieldworker from Heath Hollow." Commander Frey said, seeing the Marshal's look.

"You have the relevant lord's permission?" The Marshal asked with a raised eyebrow.

"Yes; the thieves have taken an innocent young boy and Thomas's job is to identify him."

"Very well, if you feel the need for him, though I must counsel you to be cautious. Great darkness dwells in those who are not one of us."

Commander Bartholomew came back with a thick woollen blanket and placed it around the Marshal's frail shoulders. He bowed and stepped behind the Marshal, standing rigid waiting for any further instruction.

"Tell me Commander Frey," the Marshal said, pulling his blanket tightly around him, "Tell me of your journey."

Commander Frey told the tale of their pursuit of the thieves. He spoke of the ambush on the hill road and of the loss of two brother knights.

The Marshal leaned forward in his chair and keenly listened to the tale. He regularly stopped Commander Frey and inquisitively asked a few questions. Satisfied by the tale he leaned back in his chair, thinking. He exhaled heavily. "Very well, what is it we may aid you in brother?"

"Have you heard of any reports of Star Knights entering the town in the past day or so?" Commander Frey asked.

The Marshal shook his head. "No such report has reached my ear." He turned to Commander Bartholomew, "What about you, have any of the town's stewards reported any Star Knights?"

"No Marshal." He said stepping forward. "I would have been informed should any of entered." He took a step back and stood rigid once more.

"Then I have every reason to believe that they will try and enter the town within the next day or two." Commander Frey said.

"So what would you have me do?" The Marshal asked. "Post knights on the town's gates?"

Commander Frey rubbed at the growing beard on his jaw and shook his head. "No, if they saw Star Knights they would not risk entering the town; and we need to trap them."

"We will need the lord's help in this matter." The Marshal said. "Good relations we have with the lord and help us he will; but that is for the morrow. Now let us retire to our beds, and on the morrow we shall speak with the lord."

With the meeting at an end Commander Bartholomew escorted them to a large chamber with five beds and a roaring fire, where he bid them a goodnight and left them. They spoke little before they climbed into bed and fell fast asleep.

The morning dawned to the sound of a ringing bell that called the Star Knights and Sergeants to Morning Prayer. Tom was left alone in the chamber while Commander Frey and the others went to the Temple. He was not permitted to freely walk the Perceptory alone, so instead he sat topless on the window ledge with his knees hugged up into his chest, staring out through the open shutters.

The town below was starting to wake up; he could hear distant shouting and barking dogs. The morning was sunny but chilly with a cold breeze that prickled at Tom's skin. He thought the view from the window beautiful, light reflected from the rooftops as birds flew in a near cloudless sky; but one thing did spoil his view, the dark forest that was like a vast shadow on the horizon. He shuddered every time he gazed upon it and decided to look no more at it. He climbed down from the ledge and got dressed.

Commander Frey and the other Knights came back an hour later. He informed Tom that he was to accompany him with the Marshal to an audience with the lord. They left soon after, walking to the courtyard where the Marshal was already waiting with the horses.

Tom was surprised by how different the Marshal looked, last night he had looked frail and weak, but now he was properly dressed and mounted on a great black warhorse, Tom thought he looked immortal, like a hero of the golden age.

They both mounted their horses and were escorted by four other Star Knights up to the castle. They were stopped at the gates by guards wearing black and white quartered tunics; the Marshal flashed a pass with the lord's seal on it and they were allowed to enter.

The castle was bigger than Tom thought it to be; the walls were higher than the town's wall and much thicker. The huge round towers stood even higher and had their own portcullises and ballista machines, so that if the castle walls were breached they could be turned into a mini fortress of their own. Every angle of the walls was covered by arrow slits and murder-holes, from which there was no cover. It would be a place of death in a time of siege Tom thought.

They dismounted outside of the tall, squared keep where stable boys took their horses by the reins and led them to the stables. The Marshal ordered the four escorting knights to wait by the keep's entrance until he returned.

A grossly fat man with a long beard wobbled out from the keep and down the few stairs to greet them. He wore an orange robe so big that it could have been used as a bed sheet; around his shoulders we wore the chain of his office, a chain of coins with a key hanging from the middle.

"My dear Lord Aide, you grow bigger by each passing day." The Marshal said in a friendly tone.

"I fear you may be right." He slapped his belly and smiled. "Now what may I do for you."

"I come seeking an audience with your master."

"My master will be most happy to receive you." The fat Lord Aide said bowing and gesturing for them to follow him. He led them in through the keep's entrance and up to the top of a spiral staircase. By the time they had got to the top he was sweating and breathing heavy. He waddled on leading them to a long hall filled with old armour where the lord received his guests.

The lord sat in a throne-like chair at the far end of the hall listening to petitions. He looked up, saw the Marshal and dismissed the old farmer who had been petitioning for more patrols across the river to protect the southern fields. He signalled for the Marshal to approach him. "Marshal Nicolas my old friend." He said holding out his arms.

The lord was a middle-aged man with long black hair that was beginning to grey at the roots. He wore an ankle length purple robe made of cotton and matching sandals on his feet.

"Lord Hubert." He embraced the lord as a brother.

"Come let us talk in more privacy." He led them into an adjacent room where they could sit and talk in privacy where they all took a seat around a circular table.

"What is this talk of bandits attacking the southern farms I hear?" The Marshal asked.

The lord shifted in his chair. "A week ago, a village fifty miles or so from here was attacked and burned. Rumours of strange creatures roaming the wild have unnerved the farmers. They report missing cattle and beasts that terrorise the outer villages. I sent a company of outriders to investigate the claims, but they have yet to report back."

"That is indeed troubling news." The Marshal said. "Perhaps it would be wise to evacuate the southern villages."

"No," the lord said shaking his head, "That would only cause panic; and besides that we need the farmers to gather their crops; winter is fast approaching my old friend."

"I shall order prayers for a solution." The Marshal said.

"So what is it that brings you to my hall this morning; I assume that it wasn't to offer prayers."

The Marshal put his shaky hands together and placed them on the table. "We are in need of your help." He said leaning forward in his chair. "Commander Frey here is on a quest to retrieve a stolen relic from our Perceptory at Baleford."

"You have travelled far Commander." The lord said with admiration.

"Yes my lord, and with your help, here will be the end of my journey." Commander Frey said.

"So how is it I may help you?" The lord asked.

The Marshal answered. "The thieves will at some point over the next day or so try and enter the city, we would be most grateful if you could apprehend them."

The lord thought for a moment. "Would it not be best for your knights to watch the gates?"

"No, they know we are after them. If they saw us, they would not enter and take another route. It's best to corner them in the town." Commander Frey explained.

"Very well," the lord said as he stood, "I will send in the Head Steward to take a description of the thieves; I will then issue a warrant for the arrest of any matching their description. I will then inform you and give you leave to identify them. Should they be the men you seek, then I shall release them to your custody."

"My thanks Lord Hubert, once more you have answered the Order's call for help." The Marshal thanked.

"Forgive me good knights, but I have many petitioners filling my hall and they won't resolve themselves." He bowed and left the room.

The Head Steward soon came and took a description of the thieves from Commander Frey. He could tell the Steward very little other than they were disguised as Star Knights and that one of the thieves was an innocent person called Henri who had been swept along with them. He ordered that none of them were to be harmed, but imprisoned only. The Steward scribbled down all the details and left to make it official.

With their business concluded the Lord Aide came and escorted them back to their horses that were waiting for them outside the keep. They rode back to the Perceptory assured that all was in place and that they were ready for the ending of their quest. All that they could do now was to wait.

They waited all that day to hear nothing. Commander Frey had regularly checked for any messages that might have been left at the gate, but none had been left. Tom had been left alone in the bedchamber while the others were at prayer or honing their skills on the training field.

The night came and passed to a new day. Like the morning before, a bell rang and the knights and sergeants went to the temple for Morning Prayer. Tom once more was forbidden to attend the Temple; instead he lay on his bed cot with the shutters of the window wide open, listening to the morning. The day passed slowly on and by midmorning the wind had blew storm clouds over the town. Heavy rain beat against the tiled rooftops of the rich quarter and the streets were quickly flooded.

Tom shot up off his bed and rushed over to the window. It was raining so heavy that it was hard to see very far. He watched the lightning forking across the sky, causing blue flashes that illuminated the dark clouds. His attention was drawn back into the room as the door opened and Edward came rushing into the room.

He saw Tom and said, "Come quickly, Commander Frey has had word from the lord."

"Have they found Henri?" Tom eagerly asked.

"They have arrested three people matching our description; Commander Frey has already gone to the dungeon. He sent me to fetch you; we are to meet him there."

Tom snatched up his cloak and followed Edward out of the door.

262

Ulric, Symond and Garret had been talking quietly when they heard the sound of many heavy footsteps rushing up the stairs. Their door was kicked open, and rushing in came six Men-at-Arms who wore the lord's surcoats. They were roughly restrained and dragged out into the pouring rain, wearing their under garments only. The Men-at-Arms gathered up their packs and garments from their room and tossed them onto the soaking wet ground before them.

"Tell me where the other member of your company is." A man dressed as a Steward asked Ulric.

Ulric looked up and saw the Steward that he had spoken with earlier.

"Where is he?!" The steward shouted at him.

Ulric looked back down at the ground and said nothing.

A flash of lightning briefly lit up the streets and Symond noticed Henri peering from the bottom of the stairs that led up to the parapet. He quickly looked at the ground not wanting to give Henri's location away.

The Men-at-Arms pulled them to their feet and led them through the deserted streets to an underground prison that had been built by the southern wall of the town. It had only one entrance that was constantly guarded day and night by two guards.

Henri had followed them, sticking closely to the shadows of dark alleyways and hiding behind anything he could. His heart was pounding and he felt certain that he would be seen, but he never was. He watched from the shadows of an alleyway opposite as the others were taken in through an open entrance that looked more like an entrance to a cave then a prison. A road ran in through the entrance and led down to the cells.

Panic swept through his mind. He felt defeated with grief and even considered turning himself in just so he could be back with the others. Falling to his knees, thinking back of what he had been through since leaving Heath Hollow, a little voice spoke. Remember the woods; you made it through them. Remember the burial mound and the giant spider that you set alight too; but most of all do you remember the shapeshifter at Stratton Manor House that was slain by your hand. He found some strength in the words and pushed aside any fears.

Standing back to his feet he peered back at the prison's entrance. The thin Steward followed by the Men-at-Arms came out of the entrance and left, heading back towards the castle. Two other guards flanked the entrance and it was these guards that Henri needed to get past, but how? He tried to think of a way to get past, fire, he thought, it had worked that night he had snuck into the castle of Heath Hollow. No, no it was raining too heavy; he would never get one started.

Looking around he saw a horse tethered to a small cart at the end of the street. He quickly made his way over to it using the back streets; it took him longer but he got there unseen. He untied the reins and slapped the horse's rump as hard as he could. The horse reared up and bolted off down the street.

The two guards heard the commotion and tried to stop the bolting horse, not noticing as Henri slipped in through the entrance to the prison.

Inside was lit by torches fitted on the walls between storerooms and cells; Henri went in and looked around in a room that was close to the entrance. It had a small desk that was dented and scratched; on a hook above the desk was a set of long keys. He took them and quickly left, following the road that led further into the prison. It slopped down into the holding area and Henri scuttled from cell to cell looking for any of the others.

Most of the cells were empty and he was beginning to have doubts that they were even down here. He came to a T-junction where the road split to the left and right. Stopping for a moment to make sure no one had seen him; he heard no call of alarm and decided to go left first.

He crept along softly calling out, "Ulric......., Symond..., Garret." Hearing no response he crept further along until Garrets voice startled him.

"We're over here laddie."

He went over to the cell at the end, in the far corner, and there was Garret and Ulric.

"Good lad, now get us out of here." Ulric said.

"Where is Symond?" Henri asked.

"I'm here my young friend." Symonds said from a cell opposite.

Voices echoed down the long passageway. "Quickly Henri get us out!" Ulric snapped.

Henri fumbled with the keys as he tried to find the right one. It was the sixth or seventh key that he tried before he found the right one and heard the lock click open. The voices down the passage were growing louder. He snatched the keys from the door and went to free Symond.

"No, we have no time." Ulric said.

"We can't just leave him here." Henri snapped.

"Henri, Ulric is right, you must go now or share my fate." Symond said sharply. "We will meet again my young friend, we will meet again."

Ulric grabbed Henri by the arm and pulled him along the passage, making him drop the keys. He could hear footsteps and voices ahead, and wanting to avoid whoever it was coming their way; he shoved Henri in an open cell. Garret followed along with Ulric, who closed the door behind him.

"Silent." Ulric said in a hushed tone.

The footsteps were heavy and their voices clear as they neared the cell where Ulric, Garret and Henri were hiding.

"We have not yet found him." A voice said. "But rest assured the lord has men looking for him now."

"Were they wearing the attire of my order?" Another voice asked.

"Yes Commander, we found their surcoats; they are now being kept along with their packs and weapons in the storeroom next to the guardroom."

"I wish to have the prisoners and their belongings transferred to the Perceptory's prison for questioning." The Commander said.

The sound of their voices faded as they passed. Ulric opened the cell door and peered out and saw the two figures walking down the passageway. He waved for Garret and Henri to follow him.

They made their way to the entrance as quickly and quietly as they could. Ulric and Garret went into the storeroom beside the guardhouse to retrieve their weapons and packs. They dressed and calmly walked out from the prison; where the guard at the entrance asked who they were and what they were doing.

"Orders." Ulric said calmly, holding up his pack. "We are to take this lot to our Perceptory."

The unsuspecting guard allowed them to pass, so they hurriedly passed the other guard who was leading a horse tethered to a small cart into the prison. They walked towards the eastern gate with ease and passed no other guards along the way. The rain that they had cursed earlier, they now thanked; it was because of the rain that the streets were empty and they were able to reach the eastern gate so quickly.

The eastern gate was guarded by a handful of men that Ulric and Garret quickly dispatched. Leaving their bodies where they fell, they opened the gate and slipped out of it, crossed the bridge; and ran for the forest of Dimon Dor.

Chapter 9

"Raise the alarm!" Commander Frey yelled at the steward.

The steward raced back down the passage yelling, "Guards, guards, guards!"

Commander Frey's foot scuffed against a set of keys that were lying on the floor. He stooped down to pick them up and began thinking of what could have happened. Had they bribed the guards to let them out?

The steward came back with one of the guards that had been guarding the entrance. He saw the Commander standing by the open cell door and looked at the floor sheepishly.

"Tell me what happened here." Commander Frey said in a stern voice.

"I….. I……," The guard stuttered.

"Where are the prisoners?" The steward asked in a harsh tone.

"Two of them were placed in that cell and….."

"Well they're not there now!" The steward snapped, red-faced with anger. The shout echoed down the passageway and was followed by an awkward silence.

"You said two of them were held in this cell." Commander Frey said questioningly. "Three were arrested were they not?"

The steward nodded his head. "That's right." He rounded on the guard, "So where is the other one?"

The guard looked up from the floor and pointed to the cell opposite. "We put him over there; he's an easterner, so we kept him separate from the others."

Commander Frey walked over to the cell and peered through the cell's bars. It was dark, but he could see the outline of a man. "Tell me how your companions escaped." There was no response from the man. He sat motionless in the far corner of the cell with his head down facing the floor. "Who has visited the cell since they were brought here?" Commander Frey asked, turning away from the cell and facing the guard.

"No one sir, only two knights and a sergeant from your order, who came to collect the prisoners' belongings."

"You let them pass?" Commander Frey asked.

"No, we only saw them leave; we assumed that they had passed on an earlier watch." The guard said sounding truthful.

"None other than me have orders to pass; did you leave the entrance at any point?" Commander Frey asked suspiciously.

"No sir." The guard looked at the floor and scratched his head, "Well for a brief moment when a horse and cart came clattering down the street. It nearly hit us. We only just managed to get out of its way."

"So you left your post." The steward said with implication.

"It was only for a short moment." The guard said, fearing that he would be punished.

"That's all it took you fool!" The steward shouted. He turned to Commander Frey and said, "I will have more guards patrolling the streets and posted on the all gates."

"We must move quickly to the eastern gate; if they plan to leave the town then that's the way they would go." Commander Frey said striding off.

They went back to the entrance were Edward, Geoffrey, William and Tom met up with their Commander.

"What has happened?" Edward asked seeing the troubled look on Commander Frey's face.

"Three of our thieves have escaped; they maybe still in the town, so we need to move quickly." Commander Frey explained. He turned to the steward and said, "Have the prisoner dressed and transferred to our Perceptory, and try not to lose him this time." He added sternly.

A column of Men-at-Arms came marching towards the prison. They were soaking wet as the heavy rain hadn't eased and they came to a halt by the steward. Their Captain spoke with him for a moment and then waved his men on.

"They are heading for the eastern gate. I have told the Captain that you will accompany him should you wish it."

The Commander nodded his thanks and ran out into the pouring rain. Tom and the others ran after him and they soon reached the eastern gate. The scene that greeted them was grim. Six bodies lay motionless on the saturated ground. Their blood mixed with the rain, puddled around the bodies.

The Captain of the Men-at-Arms issued orders to close the gate and clear the bodies. He went from body to body to check that they were dead; but one was still alive. "Commander you had better come and see this!" He yelled to be heard over the rain.

Commander Frey went and knelt beside the wounded guard. "Who did this?" He asked.

The wounded guard wheezed and spat blood. "Star………, Knights." He looked young, too young to have been needlessly killed by thieves.

The Captain pulled out a long needle like knife and slipped it up through his ribs and into his heart, ending his misery and pain.

Commander Frey stood up and walked back over to the others. "It was the work of our thieves." He said. "They have escaped the town and left us with no choice, but to enter the Black Forest."

The thought of having to enter such a place weighed heavily on their minds. Tom could see the horror on their faces and it scared him. He had never seen them look so nervous before and suddenly he felt vulnerable.

Commander Frey led them to the top of the gatehouse, where he took out his telescope and looked east towards the forest. There on the horizon were three shadows running towards the forest. "Is one of them your friend?" He asked offering Tom his glass.

Tom looked through the telescope; he saw the three figures running, but struggled to make anything out because of the heavy rain. Then just as he was about to give-up looking, one of the thieves turned and looked back; and he instantly recognised the face. It was Henri. "Henri, Henri!" He yelled, hoping that he might hear him. He never did.

Commander Frey took back the telescope and told Tom to be quiet. "He won't hear you in this storm." He added.

"If we're quick, we will catch up with them." Tom said excited by seeing Henri, and knowing that he was still alive.

"No." Commander Frey said. "By the time we would get anywhere near them; they would have reached the forest; and we will need more men if we're to enter that dark place.

Tom looked out over the parapet. "What are we going to do then?"

Commander Frey looked through his telescope. The forest looked dark and horrifying; a place of pure misery and evil. He removed the glass from his eye and snapped it shut. "We need to report back to the Marshal." He said turning to leave.

Tom stood alone for a moment, staring towards the forest. "I'm coming Henri." He said aloud to himself before turning and following the others.

They went back to the Perceptory where Commander Frey informed the Marshal of the recent events. He listened intently as the Commander spoke of the thieves escaping the town and seeing them heading towards the forest. Having heard the report he stood and walked over to the window, staring out to towards the forest. "So there is no other choice, other than to enter that cursed place."

"No Marshal," Commander Frey said, "I ask you to spare me as many knights as you can."

The Marshal turned away from the window and sat back down at his desk. He pulled a blank parchment towards him and began to write orders with his quill. "I'm issuing orders for five hundred knights to be placed under your command." He said holding up sealing wax over a candle and stamping the drippings with his seal. "Until the completion of your quest; understood?"

"Understood Marshal; I shall return and report back when all is concluded."

"Very good Commander; now go and rest, your knights will be ready in a couple of hours." The Marshal handed over the parchment. "May the light of the stars be with you always Commander."

Commander Frey took the written order and went to the temple to pray for the protection of the stars.

*　　　*　　　*

The last few days had been a pleasant change for Elizabeth. She had been allowed to leave her bedchamber after she had promised not to attempt to run off again, which she did with sincerity. Those thoughts had long since left her head; now the only thoughts were of John, her rescuer. Since that terrible night at the marketplace, she had heard nothing from him; he hadn't even been to visit her to see if she was alright. She often wondered why, as she knew he cared for her, he had made that obvious. Perhaps he had changed his mind and decided not to marry a woman as foolish as her. No, John is not like that she thought, he would never change his mind so readily.

Her father however, had completely changed since that night. Now, instead of being hard and demanding of her, he was now more understanding and caring towards her. Every day he would come and sit with her, speaking of her childhood memories. One morning he had bought her the last of the flowers from the garden; but it was not just her father that had changed, the old handmaiden had also. After John had brought her back that night; the old handmaiden had taken her back to her bedchamber and wept as she hugged her tightly.

For days now nobody had mentioned the marriage, and deep down Elizabeth missed the attention it had given her. She was unsure if it was even still going ahead and at times had wanted to ask, but never dared to hear the answer she didn't want. But what was that? She had been over and over it in her mind, always coming to the same conclusion. Henri was a good man and would make a good husband, but that's all he had to give. He was not rich, nor would he have enough money to buy his independence from the lord anytime soon; and where would they live, in a dung heap on the edge of town? No, that's not what she wanted for herself. The more she thought about it, the more she realised that she wanted the position that marrying John would bring, along with the wealth and the finer things in life.

Elizabeth now walked the bare and dead garden with her sister. They were both dressed in long fur overcoats with matching hats as the weather had turned wet and windy in the past days. They had walked at first in silence before Elizabeth had confided in Catharine. "I'm in love with John." She blurted out in an enthusiastic manner.

Catharine was taken aback by the sudden confession. "You are?" She said surprised by Elizabeth's sudden change of mind on the matter.

Elizabeth stopped and smiled at her sister. "I have been foolish lately, can you forgive me."

Catharine returned the smile and said, "It's yourself you want to say sorry to." She gave Elizabeth a hug and linked her arm, leading her along the garden path. "So tell me what changed your mind, was it because he's handsome?" She said with a small giggle.

Elizabeth thought for a moment then answered. "I must confess that he is handsome; but that is not why I changed my mind."

"Then why?" Catharine asked.

Elizabeth thought for a moment. "Because in what has been a difficult time for me, he was the only one who listened. He understood me and never once told me what I should do." She said looking at her sister.

"I'm sorry if I was a bit forceful," Catharine said, "But you needed to hear it. Father only wanted to find a man who could provide for his daughter."

"I know." Elizabeth said. "But now I fear that he won't marry me."

"What nonsense is this?" Catharine said stopping and turning her sister towards her.

"It's just that, since that night things have changed."

"What things?" Catharine asked.

"Well since that night father has been kind to me, and even mother's handmaiden has been kind with me."

"They care about you Elizabeth, we all do." Catharine said compassionately.

"I know, but what if the Lord Aide has called the whole marriage off because of my foolishness."

"He won't have done that."

"How do you know? Since that night I've heard nothing more about the marriage; nor has John been to visit me." Elizabeth began to let her emotions get the better of her. "I've had no letter, no word, nothing since that night, and I'm worried why."

"I'm sure it's nothing." Catharine reassured Elizabeth. "Have you spoken to father; he will be able to help you with this."

"No," Elizabeth shook her head, "Not yet."

"Well I think you should," Catharine said, "Let us go together."

Elizabeth smiled and let Catharine escort her to their father's private chamber. They knocked and were greeted by a servant who opened the door for them. Their father was sat at his desk signing some documents that another servant placed in front of him.

He looked up, saw his two daughters and said, "Wait a moment." He finished signing all of the documents and placed his quill back in its pot. "I'm glad you have come, I was about to summon you both."

"Father, Elizabeth wishes to speak with you about the marriage." Catharine said.

"That is the very reason I wanted to speak with you Elizabeth." Their father dismissed his servants and said to Catharine, "You go and help out at the stall." He ordered. "I wish to speak with Elizabeth alone."

Catharine was reluctant to go at first; she wanted to hear what her father had to say, but then decided that it was pointless to stop as Elizabeth would tell her later anyway. "Father," She said as she curtsied and left the room.

"Come sit you down." Elizabeth's father said gesturing to the vacant chair before him.

Elizabeth went and sat on the chair. Her heart was pounding and she had convinced herself that her father was about to give her the news that she would have cheered a week ago. Instead he looked at her with a saddened face. "What is it father, has the marriage been called off?" She said fearing the worst.

Her father shook his head, "No Elizabeth, it's worse than that."

"Worse, how do you mean worse?" Elizabeth asked feeling suddenly alarmed by her father's words.

"It's John he's gravely ill."

"No, he can't be; how?" Tears welled in Elizabeth's eyes.

"The cut above his eye got infected and he has been burning with fever for the past two days."

Elizabeth shook her head as tears rolled down her cheeks. "What is being done for him?"

"The physicians have bled him to draw out the bad blood, but the fever still remains strong. They say the only word he has spoken is your name."

Elizabeth felt cold with guilt. All this time she had been wondering why John hadn't been to visit, even convincing herself that it was because he no longer cared for her or their arranged marriage. Now she knew, she felt the urgency to do something. "I must go and see him." She said.

"Yes you must." Her father opened the desk's draw and pulled out some bark from a willow tree wrapped in brown paper. "Crush this up and mix it with hot water; it will help with the pain." He handed the paper over to Elizabeth and added, "I will have my hand servant escort you."

Elizabeth stood and walked out of the room, followed by her father who called out for his hand servant. A man dressed in a green tunic with yellow leaves; with a blank expression on his round face came running to meet his master's call.

"You are to escort my daughter to the Kinge household and are to await there until she is ready to depart, is that understood?"

"Yes master." He dutifully replied and bowed.

The Kinge household was on the highest street near the castle. It had tall iron railing that fenced off its boundaries. The hand servant led Elizabeth in through the gates and towards the double doors that was the entrance to the house. The hand servant knocked and waited.

The door was opened by one of the Kinge's household servants; he was a young boy no more than fifteen with a mop of dark hair. He wore a black tailed coat with white turn backs. On seeing the hand servant's tunic he recognised who the women standing behind him was. He ushered them inside to a large hallway with a polished oak staircase. The servant spoke directly with Elizabeth. "I'm glad to receive you Lady Elizabeth." He said bowing, "My master has been talking of you in his delirious state."

"Tell me," Elizabeth asked, "Is he as bad as my father says?"

The servant closed his brown eyes, lowered his head and nodded. "Yes, Lady Elizabeth."

"I must see him." Elizabeth said fighting to hold back her tears.

"Of course Lady Elizabeth, but you will have to wait as the physicians are with him now."

"Very well," Elizabeth said. "But as soon as they have finished I want to see him."

"As you wish Lady Elizabeth." The servant gestured to a padded chair at the bottom of the stairs. "You may wait here; I'm sure that they won't be much longer."

Elizabeth took the offered chair and waited. It wasn't long before she heard the opening and closing of a door, followed by footsteps coming down the stairs.

Two physicians both wearing long black robes and masks with an elongated bird-like beak, walked down the stairs. They were discussing whether they should bleed the patient again or not. When they reached the bottom of the stairs they saw Elizabeth and the two servants standing beside her. They went over and made their report.

"The patient is still burning high with fever." One of the physicians said as he removed his mask. He was old with a round red face and grey curly hair. "We have put more incense on the braziers and may have to bleed him more in order to draw out the toxic."

"Will he live?" Elizabeth asked fearing the worst.

"Only time will tell." The old physician replied. "Rest assured he is in the best possible hands."

Elizabeth suddenly remembered the willow bark that her father had given her. "What about this." She said. "This should help." She handed the old physician the folded brown paper containing the willow bark.

He unfolded the paper and sniffed at its contents. "You know how to give this?" He said handing it back.

"Me? I think it would be better if you gave it to him." Elizabeth said not feeling very confident with herself.

"The heavenly stars are more likely to show pity on a beautiful young lady, then of an old goat like me." He said with a smile. "Crush it well so that he doesn't choke, give it him three times a day and no more; I will be back on the morrow to see how the patient has progressed for the better." They both bowed to Elizabeth and walked out of the front door.

Elizabeth took a deep breath to calm her nerves, and then asked John's servant to take her to see him. She was led up the stairs to the master bedchamber where he opened the door for her. Inside the room was dark with a heavy smell of incense lingering in the air. Before she entered she took off her fur coat and hat, handing it to the servant as she stepped in. The servant closed the door behind her and went to tend to his duties.

The first thing Elizabeth noticed was the roaring fire that cracked and spat in the fireplace to her right. Against the opposite wall was a large four-poster bed where John lay burning with fever. A small table littered with pots and beakers was beside his bed. The air was stuffy with the burning incense and Elizabeth began to cough. She rushed over to the thick heavy crimson curtains that were drawn across the windows, blocking out any light. She pulled open the curtains, flooding the room with grey light, and discovered a door that led out onto a balcony that overlooked the garden. Twisting the key that was in the lock, she opened the door. Cold air blew in and out again, taking the smoke of the burning incense with it. She breathed in the fresh air before going to John's bedside.

He was covered in thick blankets sweating and breathing heavily, to Elizabeth surprise he looked better then she had imagined. His face was half covered by a blooded bandage that dressed his wound; the other half was red as if he was hot instead of being pale and ill looking. She put it down to her inexperience with the sick and tried to speak with him. "John, it's me, Elizabeth." She said placing a hand on his forehead. It felt cooler than she thought it would be.

John stirred at her voice, but said nothing.

Elizabeth tried once more. "John it's me, Elizabeth; can you hear me?"

John turned his head to face her. He never opened his eyes and spoke in a whimper of a voice. "I'm dreaming." He said.

"No," Elizabeth said, "It is truly me."

"Then I have died and gone to the heavens."

Elizabeth blushed and took hold of John's hand. "What may I do to help you?"

"The touch of your hand is enough to drag me away from the mouth of death." He coughed and Elizabeth handed him a beaker of water from the table beside the bed. She held it to his lips as he took a sip. "I feel much better already." He wheezed.

Elizabeth went back to the door, opened it and shouted for a servant. Her father's hand servant, who had been waiting for her at the bottom of the stairs, came running up the stairs. "Lady Elizabeth, are you alright?" He asked fearing something bad had happened.

"Yes, I'm fine; now go find John's servant, ask him to bring freshwater, clean linen and a kettle." She ordered.

Her father's hand servant nodded, "Yes my lady." He said scuttling off to find John's servant.

Elizabeth went back to John's bedside, sitting on the edge and holding his hand. Soon after, her father's hand servant and john's came bringing a bucket of freshwater, clean linen and the kettle. They placed the items by the end of the bed.

"Forgive me Lady Elizabeth, but I must protest." John's servant said as he rushed over to the balcony door to close it.

"It's too hot and stuffy in here," She said, "He needs some fresh air."

"But the physicians have ordered that……."

"I will deal with them," John snapped from his bed, "Do as the lady asks."

John's servant reluctantly conceded to his master's will and then left Elizabeth alone with John.

Elizabeth picked up the bucket and took it to the bedside table, where she refilled John's beaker and an empty washbowl. She then took a cloth from the pile of linen and dipped it in the water in the bowl, then rolling it up and placing it on John's forehead.

"That feels good." John said as the wet cloth cooled his clammy forehead.

Elizabeth smiled and told him to rest. She filled the kettle with water and hung it over the fire. While it slowly came to a boil she crushed up the willow bark in a dish, making sure that there were no big pieces left. She then emptied John's beaker in to the bucket and poured some of the crushed up bark in to the beaker. The water in the kettle was now boiling, so with a wet cloth Elizabeth took it off the fire and poured some of the hot water in to the beaker, stirring it for a short while.

"Here drink this." She said helping John to sit up.

"What is it?" He asked.

"Something that will help you, now drink it up." She said as though he had no choice in the matter.

John sipped and grimaced at its horrid after taste. "It doesn't taste as though it will make me better." He said handing back the beaker.

Elizabeth looked at the blooded bandage that covered his right eye. "I had better change that." She said.

"No!" John snapped, "Sorry," He said realising that he had spoken too sharply, "I think it best if we left that to the physicians; after all I am paying them for that sort of thing." He added with a smile.

"Very well," Elizabeth conceded, "But I do insist on you drinking this." She handed John back the half full beaker and helped it to his lips.

"Thank you." He said as he finished the water. "I feel much better already."

Rain spots began to pelt the windows; Elizabeth rushed over and closed the balcony door. She stood quiet and closed her eyes, listening to the sound of the rain beating against the window. Her stomach was fluttering with a mixture of nerves and guilt. She was about to tell John that she would marry him; when the guilt of what had happened to him flooded her mind. It was all her fault; if she hadn't have ran off that night then John would be well and not bedridden with fever. "John, I'm so sorry; it's my entire fault." She said bursting into tears and going back to his bedside.

John looked up at her with his one eye and said, "No."

"Yes it is; if I were………"

"All things happen for a purpose. My lady I would have paid a thousand times more than this, if it meant saving your honour."

Elizabeth blushed. "You truly are my knight in shining armour; but now I must go and let you rest."

"Promise me that you will visit every day."

Elizabeth smiled and untied a green ribbon from her hair, "For my brave knight." She placed the ribbon in his hand and said, "I will return in the morning."

"And I shall hold you in my thoughts until you return."

Elizabeth walked to the door and opened it. "I will marry you." She said before she left, closing the door behind her.

John smiled and put his hands behind his head. It was the answer that he had wanted, but thought that it would have taken longer, much longer. He waited until Elizabeth had left before he went and reported the good news back to his father.

In the following days Elizabeth visited John every day as she had promised him. Each day as she grew to know him better, the more she fell in love with him. She had stayed longer each day, caring for John, until all she went home for was to sleep. Her earlier thoughts of Henri grew less and less each day, until he became a faded memory, and she no longer thought of him at all. Now her only thoughts were of John, and their forthcoming marriage.

*   *   *

Henri, Ulric and Garret slumped onto the ground exhausted and wet through to their bones. They had run across the open field, making straight for the forest of Dimon Dor, taking cover under the trees there. They panted to catch their breath and drank a little of their water.

"What will happen to Symond?" Henri asked fearing for him. From all of the small company of Arcani, Symond was the only one who seemed to care for Henri.

"I don't know, but he knows how to handle himself in such situations." Ulric said as he took another swig of water. "Is anyone following us?" He then asked.

"I saw men on the battlements," Henri replied, "I think they were looking straight at us."

Garret stood up and peered out from the treeline towards the castle. "I see no one," He said leaning against a tree; "There's no one following us, the field is empty."

"Well it won't be long before they discover where we left the town; we need to move on." Ulric stood. "Quickly and as quietly as we can, we do not want to wake the forest."

"How does one wake a forest?" Henri asked confused.

"Remember the story of Dimon Dor we told you back at the inn." Ulric said looking at Henri as if he were stupid.

"Yes," Henri nodded, "But that can't be true; surely."

"I have no wish to find out, so we move quickly, and as silently as we can." Ulric said looking hard at Henri.

Ulric led the way with Garret a step behind him. Henri followed closely behind them, eyeing up the forest. The trees were tall, by far the tallest trees Henri had ever seen. Their long grey trunks were no bigger than a man's waist at their thickest, and the leaves that grew on them were black and as tough as leather. A smell of age-old dampness hung heavy in the air. If the woods by Raven Wood felt sinister and oppressive, then these were worse, much worse. A gentle breeze blew inside and Henri was sure he could hear voices calling out to him. Other than that it was eerily quiet, a place that seemed void of life and where time itself mattered little, and came to a stop.

They walked on for hours, not daring to stop, until they couldn't bear the pace any longer. Needing to rest they all sat up with their backs against a tree and tried to sleep. They had little, as each one would drift off, bad dreams would haunt them and wake them again soon after.

After a couple of hours Ulric pulled out a loaf of bread from his pack. He tore it into three pieces and handed it out to Garret and Henri.

"What time of day is it?" Henri asked as he bit into his piece of bread.

Ulric shook his head. "I don't know." He truly didn't, as no matter what time of day it was the forest seemed the same, day or night. It was still raining outside as they could hear the sound rain beating on the leaves above, as well as the occasional droplet that would drip down to the forest floor.

Henri was certain he could still hear his name being called and wondered what it was. He remembered the dream he had back at Raven Wood and realised that he was now in the same forest hearing the same voice. He said nothing to the others; not wanting to think about it he stood and said, "Hadn't we better be moving."

Ulric stood and brushed the stuck leaves and mud from his surcoat. "Yes, we had better keep moving. This is no place to be lingering."

They walked on heading eastwards, going deeper and deeper into the forest. Hours passed by with no change in the atmosphere, until, like before they stopped to rest. Sitting close to each other in a small clearing, they began to hear a distant humming and singing of a soft melody.

Ulric signalled to the others to lie-down and stay hidden. The soft melody got louder and louder as whatever it was got closer.

Garret knelt up and peered towards where the sound was coming from. "Women," He said with excitement, "Three beautiful women coming this way."

Ulric stood and looked at the three women; one of them was carrying a wicker basket filled with mushrooms and other goods. The women were beautiful with curves in all the right places. They wore long dresses that brushed against the ground as they walked and when they saw Ulric they immediately rushed over to him.

"O thank the stars," One of the women said as she wrapped her arms around Ulric. She wore a low cut green dress that matched her eyes, and had red fiery hair that hung loose down past her shoulders.

The other two went to Garret and Henri, throwing their arms around them. Garret happily embraced the blond haired woman with deep blue eyes and full lips that smiled up at him. "I am in need of a strong man." She said as she rubbed a fingertip down his chest. She wore a navy-blue dress that clung to her eye-catching figure.

The other woman with long straight dark hair and oval brown eyes embraced Henri. She wore a low cut red dress that emphasized her ample breasts. "I welcome the gaze of a brave man." She said seeing Henri glance at her chest.

"Sorry." He flushed with embarrassment and quickly looked away.

"What are three women doing wandering alone in this forest?" Ulric asked the red haired woman stood before him.

"We were part of a convoy that was attacked days ago; we fled into this forest where we have been lost ever since." She smiled and ran a fingertip along his bottom lip. "We are ever so grateful to have crossed paths with you."

Ulric returned the smile and said, "The pleasure is all ours."

The three women flattered and flirted with Ulric and the other two, until Ulric and Garret blindly believed everything they said. They made a small fire and cooked a mushroom stew with the few things they had in their wicker basket.

Henri thought it strange that three women should be so calm and domestic at such a time; especially in a place such as this. He could see the lust in the eyes of Ulric and Garret as they watched the women, who played to their lusting gaze.

They ate the stew, which was by far the best meal they had eaten in a long time, and lay on the ground, feeling content. Ulric asked them their names, and they avoided the question by changing the subject.

"Tell me, what are you brave men doing in this dark forest?" The woman in the green dress asked Ulric.

"We are on a sacred quest for the King." Ulric unwittingly said.

"Then you must be truly brave men to have been chosen for such a quest." She said stroking Ulric's chest.

Ulric smiled and was consumed by the flattery. "So we are, but tell me your names."

"No need to worry about names." She stood and began to dance erotically. "A brave man like you deserves a reward." The other two women joined in, dancing exotically around the fire. The whole time they kept their eyes on their chosen man, as they twisted and twirled around the fire, and each other.

Henri watched fully indulged by the erotic dancing, but at the same time he thought it odd. They seemed to move smoothly like they were gliding over ice rather than stepping on solid ground. His eyes began to feel heavy as the dark haired woman in the red dress came and took his hand.

The other two also took Ulric and Garret by the hand, pulling them to their feet and dancing seductively around them. They wrapped their arms around their chosen man, embracing them tightly.

"How old are you?" The dark haired woman asked Henri.

"Old enough." Henri replied red-faced.

"It matters not, as tonight I desire young flesh." She began to stroke Henri's hair at the back of his head.

Henri pushed her hand away, "Sorry, but I can't."

The dark haired woman took a step back and undid her dress, revealing her ample breasts. "A brave boy like you may take what he wishes."

It took all Henri's will to resist her charm, but resist it he did. "You are a beautiful woman, but I wish to save myself for another." He saw a flash of anger sweep across her face.

"No man can resist me!" She said pushing him to the ground and leaping on top of him. The nails on her finger tips began to elongate and she ran a sharp nail down Henri's right cheek, cutting him deeply. "I will take what I want." She said with a sinister smile.

This would have been Henri's end had it not been for the contents of his pouch spilling out onto the ground. A small mirror he had found whilst he had been looking for supplies back at Stratton Manor House fell out beside him. The dark haired woman glanced down at the mirror and saw her true reflexion; an ancient hag with rotten flesh hanging from bone.

She screamed at the sight of her true form and began to disintegrate into thin air before Henri's eyes. After a brief moment, all that remained of her was the red dress that she had been wearing. The other two seeing what had happened morphed into ravens and flew off, screeching.

The spell that had clouded their minds now lifted. Ulric shook his head, "What was I thinking." He said as he regained his senses. He saw Garret lying on the ground motionless. "Garret, get up!" He shouted over to him. There was no response, so Ulric went over to him and found that he was dead.

A small pool of blood had gathered at the back of his head, where the blond haired woman had driven her nails in deep to suck out his blood. Ulric knelt down beside his body, closed his eyes and bid him goodbye.

Henri stood to his feet, shaking with the thought of how close to death he had come. He saw Ulric kneeling beside Garret's lifeless body and numbly asked, "Is he alright?"

Ulric shook his head, "It's just me and you now." He stood and walked over to Henri. "What about you; are you alright?" He asked, seeing blood oozing out from a cut on his cheek.

"I think so." Henri flinched as he cuffed away the blood with the sleeve of his tunic. "What were they, demons of some sort?"

"You need stitches in that." Ulric said pointing to his cheek. He went to his pack and took out a needle and thread. "Sit down, this is going to hurt." Ulric threaded the needle and knelt down beside Henri. He pinched the cut together with his finger and thumb, and then carefully stitched the severed skin back together.

It hurt more than Henri thought. The sharp pain of the needle piercing through his skin was more than he could bear. He kept flinching which made Ulric lose his grip and the pain even worse. "So what were they?" He asked to try and take his mind off the pain.

"They are the Baobhan Sith." Ulric answered. He snapped off the needle and tied off the last stitch. The cut was deep and had taken eight stitches to close it.

"The boo-boo what?" Henri said confused.

"Once many years ago," Ulric began the tale. "The temple in the city of Dimon Dor, housed the most beautiful women from all over the island. They dedicatedly served the temple there for many years, until the city fell to the darkness, and was cursed. The temple maids were cursed to linger for all eternity, their beauty faded with time, and their desire to keep it grew stronger with the passing years.

Somehow they acquired the knowledge to stay young and keep their beauty. They would roam the forest or venture out to the southern fields where they would prey on lonely travellers and shepherds. They drink the blood of their victims, which in turn gives them vitality." He looked over at the red dress on the ground. "We have to build a cairn over the place where she departed this world."

"Why?" Henri asked.

"An old man once told me that the weight of stones keeps the door to the spirit world closed, so we need to find stones so that she may not manifest again, the last thing we need now, is an angry blood sucking woman seeking revenge."

"What of the other two; will they come back?" Henri asked, fearing that they would want revenge for their fallen sister.

Ulric went and picked up the small mirror that had saved their lives, "The Boabhan Sith fear their true image only, So long as we carry this we will be safe."

They then scouted around the forest floor finding enough boulders to make a small cairn. They piled them up over the red dress to stop the creature from manifesting back into the world. By the time it was finished it was as high as Henri's waist.

Next they placed Garrets body along with his sword and pack inside the hollow of a tree trunk. They blocked the opening with a mixture of boulders and fallen branches as best they could. Without another word being spoken, Ulric and Henri shouldered their packs, and silently walked on towards the ancient ruins of Dimon Dor.

Chapter 10

The ancient people of Dimon Dor had laid the foundations of the city to the plan of an eight pointed star. Eight roads perfectly aligned with the needles of a compass led in and out of the city. The many buildings were flat roofed and perfectly built. On every street corner there was a water fountain with a strange face with large, dark oval eyes and a narrow mouth where water had once flowed from.

At the centre of the city was a huge step pyramid that served as the temple. It had been painted white and had once had many statues of the old kings of Dimon Dor lined around the lower ring. Years ago people from all over the island would travel to the temple to pay homage to the stars and the Gods that dwelt there.

Written in the old scrolls that are now kept in the great library in Elon Dor, it says that the city had been built to honour the Star People. At the start of every new cycle the Star People would descend from the stars to bring enlightenment to the city and its people. They were honoured as Gods and the ancient people gifted them with many Precious stones they had mined from the mountains. Throughout the cycle one hundred people would be chosen to ascend to the stars with them as slaves to the Gods. In return the Gods would gift men with the knowledge of how to build and of the crafting of metals. In time the city grew to be a place of wonder and majesty, a place where the wise men of old would gather to debate on the great questions of life. The people that dwelt there were joyful and peaceful; they would welcome all who sought enlightenment in the city. Until one cycle the Gods never returned.

The city fell to panic and fear. The wise men began arguing amongst themselves as to why they had never returned. They blamed the other kingdoms and closed their city to them. What became to be known as the darkness grew and spread across the land until all were infected by it. The city fell to its own greed for knowledge; cursed and forgotten it became, consumed by the forest their distrust had planted. Now the city was desolate; thick vines had grown over the stone building, slowly pulling them apart. The pavements where people once walked, now gave way to trees pushing up through the stone slabs.

Ulric and Henri approached the city on the northwest road. Small monuments to long lost citizens of the city were dotted alongside the road. Henri went from one to the other, staring at the strange symbols carved into the stonework. "What do these symbols mean?" He asked Ulric.

"Keep your voice down." Ulric said in a hushed tone. He came and stood by Henri, looking at the carvings on the monument. "I don't know," He said after a while, "It is the ancient symbols of Dimon Dor, I cannot read them."

Henri thought it odd that they should write with symbols rather than words. "So what were they built for?" He asked unsure of what they were.

"They were built in memory of the dead." Ulric answered.

"Like a grave you mean."

"Yes and no. Their bodies are not kept here; them they burnt on priers. These they built so that they would be remembered forever." Ulric answered.

Henri looked at the monument and wondered who it was for and what life they would have had. "So what did they do with the ashes then?" He asked.

"They say that they mixed the ashes with oats to make porridge. All family members would consume this porridge. That way the deceased would forever remain a part of them."

Henri shuddered at the thought. "It sounds crazy to me." He said.

"Yes," Ulric agreed, "We are in a strange place, so stay alert." He added.

Henri followed closely behind Ulric. They had both been keeping a constant lookout for the Baobhan Sith, fearing their return for revenge Ulric kept the mirror in his hand. They walked as quietly as they could along the broken road. As they neared the city, the monuments alongside the road became more regular until they were packed side by side.

Ulric stopped and climbed up a tall monument. He took out his telescope and looked ahead at the dormant city. He was looking for any movement that would let him know if the city was still inhabited by anything. Seeing nothing to alert him he snapped shut his telescope and climbed back down to continue on.

The road took them into the city where it was eerily still and quiet. A heavy atmosphere of sorrow clung around the abandoned buildings. Henri's eyes were everywhere; he thought he had seen shadows moving in the corner of his eye, but each time he looked, nothing was there. It was strange, after all the years the city had been abandoned all the inhabitants possessions were still in the place where they had left them. All that was needed, Henri thought, was a good tidy up to make the city habitable again.

The city was almost clear of trees and for the first time in what Henri thought ages he could see the sky. It was a clear night and bright stars were dotted across the dark sky. "I thought that people lived here; that's why you needed me." He said thinking that finding the chalice was going to be easy.

Ulric stopped and turned to look at Henri. "It might be," He said, "Remember what I told you; the people here were cursed to be one with the forest. They could blend in to the surroundings without us ever seeing them. Besides, rumour has it the Wild Folk as they have become to be known, have lain dormant for years."

"So why don't you go into the temple then?" Henri said not fully understanding the situation.

"Inside the temple dwells a spirit that endlessly watches over the chalice. I do not have the skill to pass undetected; you on the other hand have a talent for such a thing." Ulric glanced around the buildings. "We need to keep on moving; the longer we stay here the more likely it is we are to wake the Wild Folk from their slumber." He spun around and continued on towards the temple.

Henri followed. "I'm not sure I can do this." He said feeling suddenly scared and less confident then he had before.

Ulric never stopped or turned to face him. "Yes you can," He said still walking, "All this way, at the back of your head a little voice has said you can't; yet you have. That night when you stole from the Lord of Heath Hollow, the same voice told you the same, yet you did." The temple now came within sight and Ulric stopped and pointed at it. "Here you stand, on the threshold of regaining your honour, and the same voice speaks again. You can do this, you know you can." Ulric said to urge Henri on.

"I'm scared." Henri admitted.

"We all get scared sometimes; it's whether we let that fear conquer us or not, that's the difference." Ulric placed a hand on Henri's shoulder, "Remember why you are doing this." He said.

Henri thought of the pardon and independence he had been promised by the Lord Aide. If he earned that then he could make an honest trade and save enough money to marry Elizabeth; but how long would that take, would she even wait until he had saved up enough money? Niggling doubts clouded his mind and the doubts only grew stronger the more he thought about it.

"Without the chalice the king's grip on power shall weaken, and the kingdom will rip itself apart with war."

Ulric looked hard into Henri's eyes. "We need you to do this; the kingdom needs you to do this."

The thought of the kingdom's survival resting on him, a Richards who the people in the town of Heath Hollow looked down upon, made him laugh. "Let's go save a kingdom them." He said with a forced smile.

Ulric patted his shoulder. "Good, then let's get this over with."

They walked on towards the temple, which seemed to grow bigger and bigger as they approached it. They came to the foot of the step pyramid and walked around its base until they found the entrance on the southern side. Huge stone stairs covered in thick ivy led up to the entrance of the temple.

Ulric led Henri to a small building opposite that looked out onto the temple's courtyard. The roof had collapsed in and Ulric made a small fire with the broken timber that had fallen to the floor. They dropped their packs and placed them in the corner of the room. Before Henri entered the temple he rested and took a small meal of stale bread and mouldy cheese that Ulric had quickly prepared.

The whole time Henri was resting, Ulric stood at the doorway keeping a watch for any other movement. He saw none and was satisfied that they had not woken the Wild Folk. "It is time." He said to Henri.

Henri stood and exhaled deeply to calm his nerves. He said nothing and followed Ulric out of the doorway and towards the temple. They stopped at the foot of the stairs where Ulric handed him a torch.

"Go quickly and as quietly as a mouse." Ulric said. "When you have the chalice, come back to this building," He pointed back to the building where they had just come from, "I will wait for your return there."

Henri looked up at the massive step pyramid. "Come with me." He said feeling suddenly very scared by the realisation of what he was about to do.

Ulric shook his head. "No, I must wait out here in case something should go wrong."

"What could go wrong?" Henri nervously asked.

"I said in case something should go wrong. Now go, before you convince yourself not to do it."

Henri began to climb the stairs. To take his mind off the thought of the spirit that dwelt inside, he began to count the steps. One, two, three, four, five; they went on and on, going higher and higher until Henri paused to ease the burning in the back of his legs. He looked back down and saw the outline of Ulric quickly walking back to building with the fire. Looking back up to the pyramid he swore; he was still only about halfway up. He continued to climb the stone stairs, losing his count, until he finally came to the entrance.

He stopped before a huge opening that was flanked by two strange statues. They were tall, thin with elongated heads and large eyes. He wondered if these were the Star People that the ancient people used to worship. Above

303

the entrance were the same strange symbols that he had seen on the monuments on the road into the city. Holding out the torch, he peered in through the entrance.

There were more steps on the inside, these led down into darkness. Painted on the walls were depictions of stars moving across the sky, and a huge pyramid with one of the Star People standing on top. At the foot of the pyramid was thousands of kneeling people; they looked as though they were in some kind of ancient ritual.

Henri went in through the entrance and cautiously climbed down the stairs. They brought him out to a chamber with three doorways that led to a labyrinth of passageways. He hadn't expected to have to find his way through a maze to get to the chalice. Instead he thought that it would just be placed on an over decorated table or something where he would simply just pick it up and take it back to Ulric.

"Henri." The loud whisper came from out of nowhere.

Henri spun around, looking all around the chamber to see if anyone else was with him. Nobody was.

"Come this way." An illuminated green mist came from out of the right hand doorway.

Henri was unsure at first of the green mist, but something told him to trust it, that it would take him in the right direction. He took a step through the right hand doorway and the green mist retracted along the passageway. Slowly he walked along the dark, narrow passageway, step by step, until it led out into another chamber, only this one had six identical doors.

Henri looked around, he couldn't see the green mist that had led him here, and he couldn't remember which door he had come from. Panic swept through him, he was going to die here he thought to himself. He fell to him knees in despair. "I should have stayed at home." He said out loud to himself.

The green mist suddenly returned, filling the chamber. Henri waved his hand in front of his face and was unable to see it. He shot back to his feet holding out his torch in front of him. At the far end of the chamber, an illuminated, misted figure appeared. Henri couldn't make out any features. All that he could make out was that it was tall and thin. In a clear voice that echoed around the chamber it spoke. "Within thee thy heart doth hide; but thy heart I doth see." The mist suddenly disappeared to reveal mass amounts of gold piled up around the chamber.

Henri was awestruck by the amount of gold. He began to think about what he could do with that vast amount. Buy his own castle with horses and servant to tend on his every need; he could go home rich, and make those people who had looked down on him his servants. The thought made him smile. Then thinking back to what Ulric had said about the kingdom falling to war and ruin if the king doesn't gain the chalice. What good was gold then? He knew what he must do, and it wasn't what he wanted.

"I bid thee to take thy fill." The voice echoed.

It took all Henri's willpower to resist the urge to fill his pockets. "I have come for the chalice." He said aloud in a nervous voice that betrayed his fear.

The misted figure faded. "Why doth thy heart desire men's curse?" The voice echoed all around the chamber.

Henri in a loud voice answered. "The kingdom stands on the doorstep of war; the king needs the chalice to keep the peace. No amount of gold could change that."

The green mist filled back into the chamber and then quickly disappeared again. The gold had vanished leaving Henri in an empty chamber. Where the six doors had been now there was only one that remained.

Henri cautiously walked over to the doorway and peered through it. It led to another long passageway, only this one was had been painted blue and had stones that sparkled as the light of his touch reflected off them. He slowly walked the passageway, the sound of his footsteps echoing down the passage. As he walked further he came across a painting on the wall. It was a scene of what he thought the underworld must look like. Mountains of fire were spewing their fury over a black scorched land. There were no trees or life in the picture, just a hostile barren land with a red sky filled with black clouds. He wondered what the picture was; maybe it was hell, or the ancient's vision of the future?

He continued on until he came across another picture painted on the wall. This one was at night and the sky was filled with bright stars. In the centre of the stars were faces, like the faces on the statues outside of the temple. The land in this picture looked lush and green with young trees growing up through the fertile ground. A little further along the picture was a fallen star lying on a hilltop. Walking out of the star was a naked man and woman. Henri suddenly realised that the pictures were retelling the story of how life came to be and the faces in the stars must be the Gods of old, the Star People worshiped by the ancient peoples of the city.

There were two more pictures along the passage; the first was of Dimon Dor at the height of its glory; the second was an apocalyptic scene. Fireballs rained down from the heavens; people were running for their lives from skeletons on horseback that chased them. Town and cities were burning; crops were rotting in the fields and a black smoke with a demonic face was spreading across the land. The picture made Henri shudder with fear. Was this the vision of the future if the king never gained the chalice?

Henri, disturbed by the painting, quickened his pace and soon came out into another chamber. Unlike the last one it had no other doors. He turned to go back the way he had come, only to find the passageway had closed behind him. This time he was sure he was doomed, he was trapped with no hope of escape.

There was a sudden wind that blew around the chamber, blowing out Henri's torch. It was pitch-black until in the corner of the chamber a pale-blue glow pulsated as it spoke. "If thee doth not flee the path Thou has set upon, then thou heart shall know pain."

"What do you mean?" Henri called out confused.

The blue pulsating light disappeared as the green mist filled the chamber. It quickly vanished again, leaving Henri in an unfamiliar garden.

It was strange, one moment he was trapped in a dark chamber, the next he was standing in somebody's garden. The sun was shining and he could feel a cold breeze blowing in his face. The garden's borders were empty and he noticed two people walking ahead of him on the path. He rushed over to them and asked. "Can you tell me where I am?" The two figures ignored him and continued on. One was a woman wearing a fur overcoat with a matching hat; the other was an elegantly dressed man. Pompous snobs, Henri thought. He watched as they walked a little along the path and stopped, facing each other. The face of the woman he recognised immediately. "Elizabeth!" He called out to her. There was no response as Henri ran over to her. He tried to grab her, but his hands just went straight through as if she wasn't there. "Elizabeth it's me, Henri!" He yelled at her. Still she never responded.

Then he saw a sight that hurt him more than any sword thrust ever could. The man embraced Elizabeth and then passionately kissed her. He expected her to pull away and chastise the man, but instead she seemed to welcome it, even smiling afterwards. They once more linked arms and walked on, as Henri looked on in anger and despair at what he saw.

It can't be, Henri kept thinking to himself. Elizabeth must have known his feeling for her; she had never told Henri that she had loved him, but her actions had given him hope. Elizabeth wasn't like that; she would never do such a thing, he tried to reason with himself. Confusion clouded his mind and he was unable to do anything other than keep going over it in his mind.

The chamber darkened and the blue pulsating light returned. "Doth thy still wish to tread this path of pain and sorrow?"

Henri didn't want to; all he truly wanted was to go home marry Elizabeth and live a quiet life. Yet something deep down within himself said he needed to go on, that the kingdom's future rested on his next move. Why did he have to suffer when the chalice was not even for him? He told himself that the apparition was not true and that he needed to continue on; and even if the apparition were true, then at the very least he would have his independence.

He took a deep breath and answered. "I cannot avoid my fate, only embrace it."

"So be it." The voice echoed all around the chamber. "Thy path is set."

Green mist filled the chamber and Henri's torch reignited. Out of the mist a whisper said, "There shall come one, and never again shall there be another."

Henri shuddered; he had heard that before back at the village of Raven Wood; when the old seer had spoken with him outside of the inn, before he had vanished into thin air. "What does that mean?" He called out. There was no answer.

Orbs of light shone through the mist. They danced around him, twinkling and twirling before coming together at the far end of the chamber. They shone so brightly that it forced Henri to close his eyes. A door opened and all of the green mist was sucked out of the chamber.

Henri struggled against the suction. He tried to keep his balance by dropping his touch, but the force was too strong and he was sucked in through the doorway. He fell down a slope that twisted its way down to another chamber. He hit the bottom and rolled out into the centre of the chamber. He got to his feet and rubbed himself down. His torch was at the foot of where he had just slid down, still lit. Hurt from the fall he limped over and picked it up, holding it out in front of him.

This chamber was a long rectangular shape with eight columns that held the stone ceiling in place. The walls were cased in smooth, dark granite that gave it the effect of the night sky. At the far end of the chamber was a closed doorway. Henri went over and tried to open it, but it wouldn't budge. He slumped down onto the floor and rested, letting his hurting body regain some strength. His mouth was dry and he wished he hadn't left his water skin with his pack.

Then a sound of scraping stone drew Henri's attention towards one of the near columns. He stood back up and peered into the gloom; nothing but empty darkness. He tried the door again, but it still wouldn't open.

The sound of bare footsteps flapping on the stone floor alerted Henri. He spun around and drew his sword that had been Bard's. Holding out the torch in front of him, he called out into the gloom. "Who's there?" He took a few carful steps forward. "Ulric is it you?" It wasn't Ulric, but one of the Wild Folk that he had spoken of.

It stepped into the light and its appearance made Henri shudder. Its skin was grey and looked more like tree bark then skin. Vines grew over its body, covering its modesty. Where its eyes should have been were empty black sockets and in its hand it carried a club with a wickedly sharpened stone sticking out of it. It stood sniffing at the air.

Henri noticed that it was at least twice the size of him, and heavily muscled. A creature he decided that would rip off his limbs should it get hold of him. It never sensed him, so he carefully began to step away from it.

The creature heard the soft footsteps and angrily charged straight towards Henri. He was able at the last moment to roll out of its way. It ran straight into the wall, knocking out a chunk of stone from it. It spun around sniffing the air once more and then charged again at Henri.

This time Henri was able to take a clumsy swing of his sword as he dived out of the way. He caught the creature on its upper thigh. It gave a cry of pain as it came to a stop and sniffed at the air. Henri noticed the blood that seeped out from the cut was black. It sensed Henri and charged him again and again, each time taking cuts as Henri took swing after swing to try and bring it down.

Henri began to tire and found that he was slowing down. He needed to kill the creature quickly, but how? He couldn't just fight it, it was too strong. With all the cuts it had taken, it hadn't slowed down any, so carrying on just diving out the way was not a good idea. What he needed was to escape the chamber. Then he had an idea.

Moving quickly, he made his way back to the door, ducking and diving out of the way of the creature's charges as he went. He stood in front of the door and called out. The creature instantly rushed angrily at Henri. Holding his nerve until the last moment he dived out of the way.

The creature slammed straight through the door, sending splinters of wood scattering across the adjacent chamber. It tripped and fell into a pool of water that was in the centre of the chamber. It gave a deafening screech as its body slowly disintegrated in the water.

The green mist rose from the water and covered the floor. Henri got back to his feet and entered the chamber. He walked around the pool carefully, fearing that he might fall in he kept a hand on the wall. At the far end of the chamber, he came to a double doorway that was flanked by two statues like the ones at the entrance to the temple. The first was draped in a purple robe that went from its neck down to the floor. In its hands it held a crown of stars. The second was identical to the other; only in its hands it held a pyramid.

The door swung open to reveal a set of stairs that went up. There were torches fixed on to the wall that burst into life as Henri put his foot on the first step. He cautiously climbed the many stairs, taking at step at a time until it bought him out into another chamber. This one had a hole cut into the roof and Henri could see stars in the night sky. Moon light shone in to light the chamber and Henri could see no other door then the one he had come from.

"The doors of destiny are open." The voice echoed all around Henri.

Two doors hidden in the wall opened. One was dark with the green mist concealing whatever lied within. The other led out of the temple. Henri could see the distant trees and the flat rooftops of the crumbling buildings. A cold wind blew in, as if it were trying to tempt Henri out.

He was close to giving up and walking out, even taking a couple of steps towards the doorway that led out of the temple. Blowing out a tired sigh and rubbing at his face. No, he told himself, he was so close that he couldn't just give up now. He needed the chalice, the kingdom needed the chalice; all that he had been through had to be for something, he told himself. He turned to the doorway with the green mist and called out, "Where is the chalice, I need it."

"The doors of destiny are open." The voice said again.

Henri felt beyond tired. He decided that he must go on and taking a deep breath he entered in through the misted doorway. There were more stairs leading up. As he climbed them feelings of death and sorrow plagued his already troubled mind. Soft, haunting chanting echoed down the stairs; it made him cry and he didn't know why. By the time he reached the top he felt awful. His arms and legs felt like they were made of stone; his head was spinning and he began to have hot flushes.

He came to a small chamber at the top of the temple that was filled with old rusted armour and weapons. There was an elegant fountain in the centre and Henri went and slumped by it. He rolled over to scoop up some water in his hands when he noticed a twinkle. He quickly pulled his hands out, fearing what it might be. As the water settled,

Henri could see the outline of a chalice. He picked it out of the water and gazed at it.

The chalice looked old and crude. It was made of a dark metal that Henri had never seen before. Around the top was decorated with small stars and four faces that looked as though they were chanting. Its thick stem was decorated with trees, each representing one of the ancient kingdoms, and on its base were elegant square patterns that crossed over each other in a pragmatic manner.

Henri was so amazed by the simplicity of the chalice, that he begun to doubt that it was the chalice he was looking for; it was not how he had imagined it to look. He turned it over and over in his hands, looking for any indication that it was the chalice of the old legends. Remembering what the old stories said he scooped some of the water from the fountain with it. He held it up in front of him, waiting to see if it would glow blue as the stories of old said. It did nothing, so Henri, dry mouthed, closed his eyes and drank the water.

He kept his eyes closed as the cool liquid revitalised his tired body. A sudden sense of failure swept through him. What was he going to tell Ulric? That he couldn't find the chalice, or that it wasn't here. No, to do that meant defeat, and he could never go home having failed his quest. Deciding to go back the way he'd came and find the right chalice, he opened his eyes and saw that the chalice in his hands was glowing blue.

Out of shock, he dropped the chalice, hitting the floor with a *clang*, Henri stepped back; what had he done? The great kings of old had drank from the chalice and were said to have been cursed. If kings were sent mad by it what chance did he, a fieldworker have. Despair at the helpless thoughts swept through him. I've got to get out of here and back to Ulric, he thought. Accepting the realisation that it was too late for him, but the kingdom could still be saved from war; he quickly picked up the chalice and turned to go back out the way he had come, but it was closed.

The chamber suddenly filled with green mist. "There shall come one, and never again shall there be another." The voice repeated it over and over again. "There shall come one, and never again shall there be another."

The floor rumbled and opened up below Henri's feet. He clung on to the chalice as he fell down on to sloped stone and began to slide down into darkness. After what seemed to be an endless slide of darkness, it brought him out at the bottom of the temple, where he thudded to a stop on the cold stone road below the pyramid. Painfully getting back to his feet, he glanced around. The slide had brought him back out of the temple on the opposite end of where he had entered. He limped as quickly as he could around the base until he came to the side with the stairs to the entrance.

Ulric, who had been keeping a vigilant watch for Henri's return, saw his shadowy figure coming from around the base of the pyramid and ran over to help him. He put Henri's arm over his shoulder and led him back to the building where he had been waiting.

"What happened in there?" Ulric asked as he sat Henri on the floor by the fire. He saw the chalice in Henri's hands, and before Henri could answer his question, snatched it from him. "Could it be?" He said, holding it with trembling hands.

Henri nodded. "It is the chalice you seek."

"How do you know? It could just be an ordinary chalice the temple maids used for daily ceremonies." He looked hard at Henri. "Was there anything inside to indicate that this is the chalice of knowledge?"

Henri thought back to the temple where it had glowed blue when he had filled it with water; but he couldn't tell Ulric that he had drank from it. That he would never tell anybody, through fear of what could happen to him. "It was the only chalice I saw in there, and it was guarded by a strange creature like one of those Wild Folk you spoke of." He said, hiding his true thoughts.

Ulric looked at Henri curiously. "What did it look like?"

Henri told Ulric of his encounter of the strange creature inside the temple and gave a detailed description of the creature.

"It was a Wild Folk," Ulric answered, "One that has been tormented by the spirits that dwell there. Tell me did you encounter any spirits."

"No," Henri lied; wanting Ulric to think he had passed undetected by the spirits and had done a good job. "The only thing I saw was that creature."

Ulric nodded his head and took a water skin from his belt, tossing it over to him. "Here, take a drink of this." He walked to the door and peered out across to the temple. "There's a small lake in the eastern part of the ruins; we'll refill our skins and fill the chalice; if it glows blue then we know we have the right one. If it's not then you'll have to go back in."

"Why don't we use this water?" Henri asked offering back the skin, thinking it to be the easier option.

"No!" Ulric said a little too sharply. "You look as though you need it. Besides we'll need to refill our skins before we go back anyway."

Henri was so dry that he could have drank a whole river, so he put the skin to his lips and tilted it, gulping down the warm liquid. It tasted warm, bitter and left a horrible aftertaste in his mouth. "Well we did it." He said wiping his mouth with the back of his hand. "Do you think the king will reward us for our efforts?" Henri asked, pleased by the thought of a king being indebted to him.

Ulric smiled at his deception and turned to face Henri, "The rewards shall be all mine."

"And mine…," Henri coughed and gagged as his throat began to burn. "Something's…….. Wrong." He wheezed. "I……. can't……. breathe."

"What's the matter?" Ulric asked, knowing that it was the poison he had slipped into the water skin. He watched on as Henri grabbed at his swelling throat and jerked in panic on the floor.

317

Henri was in a blind panic as he was unable to breathe. His body jerked and shuddered as his face turned blue.

"Sorry lad, know that if it were my choice I'd have let you live; but the Lord Aide never wanted you to return." He said grinning.

Henri gasped as he tried to get to his feet. He had wanted to kill Ulric for his betrayal, but not having the strength he fell back on to the ground. The last thing he saw was Ulric standing over him smiling. His vision blurred and then faded; the last thing he heard before he slipped into darkness was the blast of a distant horn.

Now that the chalice had been removed from the temple, the Wild Folk awoke from their slumber. Their horn blasts broke the silence of the forest as they gathered in strength to reclaim the stolen chalice.

Ulric picked up his pack and took the Gigantes dagger from Henri's twitching body. He slipped out of the doorway and headed towards the small lake in the eastern part of the ruins where he planned on drinking from the chalice and claiming it for his own.

Chapter 11

It was a sight that had not been seen in an eon of time. Five hundred Star Knights led by Commander Frey, marched, on foot, in a neat column towards the forest of Dimon Dor. They were well equipped with each knight having armour, a tall tower shield, spear, and a war bow with a quiver of arrows.

The people of Elmham Castle had gathered and followed the Star Knights from their Perceptory to the eastern gate. There the town guards stopped them and told them go back to their daily business, but they refused. Instead they climbed up to the battlements and watched the Star Knights march out of the gates. The people looked on in both fear and wonder at the sight. They began to gossip of what was happening; some said that the Star Knight were abandoning them to the beasts that had been reported in the southern fields. Others said that they had been sent by the lord to drive back the beasts and reclaim the fields. Some were not sure and thought it an ill omen for the coming winter. They watched on in horror as they realised the Star Knights were heading towards the forest.

"The Wild Folk have awoken to reclaim what was once theirs." An old beggar with no hands proclaimed.

Panic swept through the people and they began to flap about in terror of the wrath of the Wild Folk.

"We need to leave the town quickly!" A nervous young man shouted out.

"No, no, no, we'll be better off staying here behind these strong walls!" Another man shouted.

With the town in a panic, the lord dispatched his guards to clear the battlements and restore order to the town. It took the remainder of the day, and by the time a nervous order was restored, distant horn blows carried by the wind were heard throughout the town.

Commander Frey led his knights from the front. He tried not to show any fear, even though he felt it, preferring to stare straight ahead at the dark forest before them. While he had been waiting for his command to assemble, he had questioned the captured thief that was now being held in the Perceptory's prison. After a few attempts of interrogation, he had spoken not a word, not even giving his name. What Commander Frey needed to know was who he was working for, and how they were able to break into the vaults at the Baleford Perceptory and steal the map.

The Captain of the prison had recommended that a spell in the rack would have him talking, but Commander Frey had refused saying that any man would confess to anything just to end the pain. It was not a good way to gain truthful information in his opinion. He tried one final time before his command was ready and waiting for him, but got nothing but silence; so he left to safeguard the chalice.

Commander Frey led his command into the forest where they took the north-eastern road that would lead them straight the ancient ruins of Dimon Dor. They marched on with the sound of their heavy boots and clanking of weapons on armour echoing through the forest. After hours of a quick pace they came to a stop on the outskirts of the ruins.

As Tom looked up the wind blew a gap in the treetops to reveal a starlit sky. He felt uneasy in the forest, like someone was constantly watching him. It was a horrible place he thought, a place of pure evil and torment.

Distant horn blasts sounded through the forest and the Star Knight instinctively made a circular perimeter beside the road. Commander Frey ordered a small fire built in the centre and ten knights to scout on ahead into the ruins and to report back any findings. They raced on ahead, taking only their swords with them.

Tom went and sat by the fire. He was given the task of keeping it burning in until he was told otherwise by Commander Frey. Hearing more distant horn blows, he began to shake with fear of what might be blowing them.

Commander Frey carrying an armful of more wood came and sat beside Tom, dropping the wood to the ground. "There is no shame in being afraid in such a place." He said seeing Tom's pale worried face.

Tom picked up a twig from the ground and twiddled with it. "What's blowing them horns?" He asked nervously.

Commander Frey rubbed at his jaw and shook his head. "I do not know for certain, but if the old scrolls are right, then it will be the cursed people of Dimon Dor, now better known as the Wild Folk."

Tom snapped the twig and tossed it onto the fire. "So what does that mean?"

"It means, Thomas, that we are too late. The thieves must have the chalice."

"How do you know that?" Tom asked wondering how he could possibly know that.

"Years ago, when the chalice was placed in the temple, a bargain was struck between Grandmaster Everard of Beolog and the spirit that dwells there. The chalice was to remain forever hidden in the temple; and in return the spirit would cast the cursed people into an eternal slumber; but the spirit warned of a time, when one shall come and remove the chalice and awake the curse's wrath. None but the Order of the Star knew of this; and the scrolls with the map of the chalice's location remained secret, kept deep in our vaults for hundreds of years; but somehow, someone discovered our knowledge."

"So do we need to put the chalice back in the temple to send the cursed people back into their slumber?" Tom asked, thinking more out loud then asking.

Commander Frey shook his head. "No, we have only to make it safe again."

"And how are we going to do that?"

"First we will need to regain it, and then we will have to hide it someplace else. For the old scrolls say that for as long as the chalice is in danger of man, then the cursed shall seek it." Commander Frey stood.

"Where are you going?" Tom said, not wanting to be alone.

There was another horn blast that lingered on the breeze.

"That is the sound of the cursed people waking." Commander Frey said. "I need to make sure my men are in position."

"They won't attack us will they?"

Commander Frey nodded. "We need to be ready." He walked off ordering the knights to close up any gaps in their perimeter until all the Knights were stood shoulder to shoulder in a circle, facing out into the forest.

For what seemed to be an eon of time the knights stood rigid with expectation of a sudden attack; but as of yet there was no sign of the Wild Folk. The long drawn-out horn blasts sent shivers down their spines; yet they never spoke of retreat or showed any signs of faltering.

A small gap opened up to allow the ten scouts back in. Two were carrying a body by its arms and legs. They went over to the fire and laid it on the ground.

At first Tom had thought it to have been one of the scouts, thinking that they had been attacked by the Wild Folk. But as they carried the body into the fire's light he saw the face and was grief-stricken.

"Henri!" He rushed over to his friend. There was no response; he just lay there seemingly lifeless. "Is he dead?" Tom asked the two knights that had set him down.

"Yes and no." One of the knights answered as he placed a sword on the ground next to Henri. "He looks it and breathes not, but his heart still beats."

"Where did you find him?"

"He was lying beside a fire in a building near to the temple pyramid."

Commander Frey came back to the fire. "You two join the defensive circle with your fellow brothers." He ordered. "Leave that sword here, Tom shall watch that the prisoner doesn't try to escape." The two scouts went off and took up their positions in the defensive circle. Commander Frey knelt down beside Henri and rolled him on to his side.

"Is this your friend?" Commander Frey asked.

"It's Henri." Tom said. "Will he live?"

"Maybe," Commander Frey said, "keep him on his side."

"Why?" Tom asked.

"Looking at him, I would say he has been poisoned." Commander Frey stood. "For some reason it has not killed him and it seems to be lodged in him, so keep him on his side and his body shall reject it."

Another long drawn-out horn blast filled the forest; only this time it sounded closer.

"I must go, my men will need me. I shall be back soon to see if he has awoken; I will need to speak with him then." Commander Frey left them alone by the fire.

Tom looked at Henri and thought he looked different. For some reason when he looked at him he never saw the scruffy, daydreaming boy, with the stupid idea of stealing the lord's gold, instead he saw a manlier figure with a deep cut on his right cheek that seemed to suit the frame of his face.

A horn blast quickly followed by two more startled Tom. He wanted Henri to wake so that they could get out of this wicked place and go home; but something deep down within him, told him that he would never leave this place. "Come on Henri wake up." He said believing that if he did things would seem better.

Henri awoke, vomiting black bile out onto the ground. His vision was a little blurry but he recognised the face staring down at him. "Tom?" He weakly said.

Tom helped Henri to sit up. "I thought that I would never see you again." He took his small tin canteen and unstopped it, offering it to Henri.

Henri took the offered canteen and drank deeply. He felt weak and his body trembled as the cool liquid trickled down to his unsettled stomach. "Where am I Tom, how did I get here?" He asked.

"Commander Frey sent out scouts, they found you and brought you back here." Tom looked at Henri with concern. "What happened to you?"

Henri took another swig of water from the canteen. "That bastard Ulric, where is he?" The memory of Ulric telling him of the small lake in the eastern part of the ruins suddenly came back to him. "I need to get to the lake in the east part of the ruins." He said trying to stand.

Tom pushed him back down onto the ground. "You need to regain some strength before you do anything."

Henri reluctantly sat rigid, staring aimlessly into the fire, his memories of all that had happened flooded back to him.

"Who is Ulric?" Tom asked breaking Henri's thoughts.

"A bastard who tried to kill me," Henri looked hard at Tom, "I'm going to kill him; that bastard." He spat.

Another loud horn blast shattered the still forest.

"You might not get the chance." Tom said shuddering from the sound of the horn.

"Wild folk." Henri said.

Tom nodded. "They seem to be getting closer."

The thought of a horde of Wild Folk bearing down on their position never seemed to bother Henri. In truth he had been through so much of late, that even the most evil of monsters coming to devour them, would not have unsettled him.

"I've seen too much to be scared of a few simple creatures." Henri said. "Besides I've already killed one of them."

"You have, where?"

"I was in the temple, when it charged at me again and again; but I outsmarted it."

"So how did you kill it?" Tom asked impatiently.

"It fell into a pool of water and disintegrated."

Tom laughed. "So you didn't really kill it then."

There was an awkward silence before Henri spoke again. "I've seen something else Tom."

Tom looked at Henri and could see that he was troubled. "What is it Henri?"

"I was in a chamber at the temple; it was dark one moment, the next I was standing in a garden." Henri took his gaze from the fire and looked straight at Tom. "I saw Elizabeth."

"What, she was in the temple?" Tom said confused.

"No, she was not really there."

"Then what was it?"

"Some sort of magic that made shadows look real."

"Magic, that made shadows look real." Tom repeated in disbelief.

Henri nodded. "They showed me Elizabeth in the arms of another man."

Tom thought back to when he had seen her last. He remembered the green ribbon she had given him and pulled it out of his pouch. "She told me to give you this."

He handed the ribbon to Henri. "She told me to tell you that she's sorry."

"Sorry?" Henri repeated the word and thought about what she meant by sorry. Then it suddenly dawned on him what sorry meant. "How did she know I was going to ask her hand in marriage?"

Tom looked sheepishly. "It slipped out when I was talking to her sister, the morning after the festival."

Henri looked angrily back to the fire. "Does she love another Tom?"

Tom picked up a stick and poked at the fire, sending glowing embers up into the air. "I don't know." He admitted. "She never spoke of another to me."

"Heh," Henri spat, "don't suppose my independence was real either."

"Your independence?" Tom said.

"The Lord Aide had promised me my independence when I returned home; but when Ulric poisoned me, he told me that the Lord Aide never wanted me to return." Henri could feel his anger rising and tossed the ribbon onto the fire. "I was stupid for ever believing it."

Tom was unsure whether Henri meant the promise of his independence or marrying Elizabeth. He was about to ask when their conversation was interrupted by Commander Frey who came and sat beside them by the fire.

"I am Commander Frey of the Order of the Star." He introduced himself to Henri. "Are you Henri Richards?"

328

"Yes for all the bloody good it's done me." Henri answered.

"First of all are you alright?" Commander Frey asked.

Henri nodded, realising that his body was no longer weak and shaky.

"Good." Commander Frey said. "I need to ask you a few questions about the men you were traveling with."

"Are you real Star Knights or just more bastards dressed up to bugger my life up?" Henri asked harshly.

"Henri," Tom stepped in to reassure his friend. "Believe me, these are real Star Knights."

"I am sorry for all the troubles you have been through, and know that I intend on keeping you safe and to escort you home." Commander Frey said, trying to soften Henri's anger.

"What do you need to know?" Henri asked angrily.

"Everything," Commander Frey said, "their names, whether they are part of any order, who they are working for?"

"They are the Arcani." Henri said.

As Commander Frey heard the name he rubbed at his jaw as though it all suddenly made sense to him. "And they are working for the king?"

Henri nodded. "Yes, they were being led by a man called Ulric."

Commander Frey was intrigued by the word *were*. "What do you mean by, were?" He asked.

"We started out as a small company of eight men; two were killed in Raven Wood, Laurence in the woods by the village. Bard was killed by a shapeshifter at Stratton Manor House; Symond was captured back at Elmham Castle, and Garret had his blood drained by some sort of blood sucking demon. I and Ulric were the only ones who made it to the ruins."

"So where is Ulric now?" Commander Frey asked.

Henri fell silent, unsure if he should say anything or not. "He has the chalice and has gone to a lake to see if it is the real chalice."

"By the stars I pray it is not." Commander Frey said knowing it was.

"It is the right chalice." Henri admitted.

"How do you know?" Commander Frey asked.

"Because," Henri said, "when I filled it with water it glowed blue."

The news alarmed Commander Frey. He was silent for a moment as he thought about what he should do. A loud horn blast that sounded very close gained his attention. He shot to his feet and saw Edward rushing over to him.

"The cursed people are massing to the north of our position." Edward said.

Commander Frey nodded and asked, "How many?"

"Thousands." Edward replied.

Henri and Tom followed the Commander as he rushed over to the northern section of the defensive circle. There standing a few hundred feet away was thousands of Wild Folk. They were grim looking things, smaller then what Henri had seen back at the temple. They wore tree bark as armour and carried weapons made from stone. Some carried banners made from leaves that grew up out of their backs as a branch grows from a tree trunk.

Commander Frey pulled out a long whistle from his pouch and blew two quick blasts. Every other knight took a step back and closed up, making a smaller circle. The others then closed up on them to make the defensive circle two men deep.

"My brothers," Commander Frey called out, "we hold our ground, let no brother take a step back in fear. If we are to die in this dark place, then let us die obedient to our laws!"

The Star Knights called out in unison, "For the order!"

"Do not lose heart for a fallen brother, for they have gone to take their place amongst the stars!"

"For hope!" The Star Knights called out.

"We have waited for this day, trained from infancy for it, now let us now embrace it, and delay it no longer!"

"For the stars!" Their war cry echoed through the forest, and what became known as the Battle of the Black Forest began.

*   *   *

The day of the wedding had quickly arrived. Now that Elizabeth was willing to marry John Kinge the date of their marriage had been brought forward. The Lord Aide had made hasty preparations, claiming that it was in everyone's best interests to marry before the winter set in. The date was set so soon that Elizabeth feared that John would never recover from his illness in time. Then suddenly, to Elizabeth's surprise, he was his fit normal self again. He had thanked Elizabeth saying that it was her hot willow water that had restored his health. Elizabeth blinded by what she thought was love, accepted his thanks willingly and never suspected anything unusual.

On the morning of the wedding Elizabeth sat on the edge of her bed, waiting for her father to escort her to a small temple just outside of the town. She was nervous and begun to have doubts about the marriage. Was it too soon? She thought she knew John well enough, but what if she was wrong. Her thoughts were interrupted by a knock on her door.

"Enter." Elizabeth called out.

Her mother entered. She was dressed in a long pale-green dress that looked heavy, and was low-cut enough to show off her ample cleavage. Her straw coloured hair was pulled up and tied in two buns either side of her head, where a long netted hairpiece that ran down the length of her back had been fitted.

"You look beautiful daughter." She said coming to stand before Elizabeth. She was dressed in a plain white wedding dress that had been the custom for hundreds of years. Her hair had been tied up and fitted into an elegant headpiece that had pearls dangling from it.

"Thank you mother," Elizabeth replied, "you look beautiful too."

Her mother smiled and said, "Has my handmaiden told you what to expect tonight?"

Elizabeth blushed. "Will it hurt?" She asked.

Her mother sat beside her on the bed. "For the first time, yes," she said, putting her arm around Elizabeth. "There will also be a little blood."

Elizabeth looked into her mother's blue eyes. "Do I have to do that?" She asked. "I don't know if I am ready."

"It is your duty as a wife to have sons." Her mother answered. She could see the anxious look on her daughter's face and tried to reassure her. "It gets better with time, and you will in time come to enjoy it."

"It's not just that mother; it's….. It's…"

"What is it Elizabeth?"

"How do I know if John will always love and care for me?" Elizabeth looked away from her mother and stared at the floor, hearing how weak and needy she sounded. "What if he grows to hate me because I can only produce girls?"

"Nobody could hate you Elizabeth, it's impossible. You are a beautiful young woman full of life. John ardours you, I have seen it in his eyes. All this is nerves, nothing more."

"But what if I only have girls like you mother; will he still love me then?"

Elizabeth's mother stood up and walked over to the window, staring out of the misted glass. "Your father still loves me."

"Yes but that's father."

"On my wedding day, I told your grandfather that your father looked like a toad, and that I could never love a toad. And he told me what I will tell you now." She looked from the window back at Elizabeth. "He said that love should never be freely given, but earned over time. Years later your father earned my love." She went and sat beside Elizabeth once more, looking straight into her eyes. "After you and your sister were born, I was with child once more. All seemed fine until there were complications giving birth. It was stillborn, a boy, a boy your father had wanted to continue his line. He could have divorced me, I even expected him too, yet he stuck with me, even after the physician had told him that I would never have any more children."

Elizabeth could see tears welling up in her mother's eyes. "Sorry mother, I didn't know."

"You were only young Elizabeth, and your sister still at the wet-nurse's breast." She forced the unhappy memory away and smiled. "But today is a happy occasion and I know you will honour the family name."

Elizabeth hugged her mother. "Sorry I have been silly; I know John will take care of me."

"You have nothing to be sorry for; all women feel the same on their wedding day." She smiled once more at Elizabeth. "Now I must go and see if all is well downstairs. Will you be alright now?"

Elizabeth nodded. "Yes I'll be fine."

Her mother strolled out of the room, leaving her sweet scent lingering in the air after her.

Elizabeth stood and went to look out of her window. She could see a mass of peasants crowding at the gates. The household servants were trying to usher them back to keep a path clear for when the carriages would arrive to take her and her family to the temple. She wondered why they gathered outside of peoples home at weddings. Was it just so that they could glimpse the bride in her dress as some said? Maybe it was because they would never have such a lavish wedding and would look on wishing it was them; after all most of the peasants couldn't marry while they were still the lord's property, so they just lived together in pretence of marriage. The thoughts shocked her; she mustn't think like that, she told herself, after all one didn't need marriage to find love. It was a matter of honour, she decided, a great honour to dedicate yourself to another for all your life.

Her bedchamber door opened and in burst Catharine. "Have you seen the throng at our gates?" She said excitedly. She was wearing a long flowing pale-yellow dress. Her hair had been tied back in a bun at the back of her head and had two locks of tightly curled hair flanking her face.

"It seems in all this excitement that you have forgotten how to knock." Elizabeth said as her sister came springing over to the window.

"Look at them," Catharine said ignoring Elizabeth's remark. "I bet they have never seen such a thing before."

"They will have seen a marriage before." Elizabeth corrected her sister.

"Not one as lavish or important as this." Catharine said turning and looking at her sister. "You look beautiful."

"Thank you," she said twirling. "You look beautiful yourself."

Catharine smiled, "I know. Maybe I'll attract a marriage offer myself."

There was a cheer from the crowds outside as two elegant carriages decorated with fake silk flowers came to a stop by the iron gates. Coachmen jumped down from the back, opened the doors and lowered a set of small steps. A troop of town guards that had escorted the two carriages, now held back the crowds as they tried to push closer to the carriages to steal one of the many silk flowers as a keepsake of the day.

"Look at the carriages;" Catharine said excitedly, "don't they look wonderful."

Elizabeth looked out of the window. The carriages did look wonderful, perfect even; but it all seemed too perfect, and a nagging thought that something would go wrong whirled around in her head.

"Elizabeth what's wrong?" Catharine asked, seeing the look on her sister's face. "You've not change your mind about this marriage again have you?"

"No, it's not that."

"Then what is it?"

"It's just me and my silly thoughts," Elizabeth said turning away from the window and looking straight at Catharine. "I keep thinking that something is going to go wrong."

Catharine hugged her sister tightly. "You're nervous, that's all; father won't let anything spoil this day."

"I know, I know; now let me go before you crumple my dress."

"Sorry," Catharine said as she rubbed out a light crease she had made on her sister's dress.

There was another knock on the door as their father came in. He stood for a moment looking at his two daughters. "The both of you are more beautiful than the greatest of poets could ever describe." He said. "Catharine your mother awaits you downstairs."

Catharine kissed Elizabeth on her cheek and said, "I will see you at the temple." She formally curtsied to her father and left them alone.

Elizabeth's father walked over to Elizabeth, took her hand and kissed it. "You do me proud Elizabeth." He said. "Now is the moment that every father both fears and dreams about."

Tears welled in Elizabeth's eyes. "I will still be your daughter." She said. "And you may visit as often as you please."

"And I shall visit as often as duty allows me." This time her father leaned in and kissed her forehead. "It is time." He said.

"May I have just one more moment alone?" She asked.

Her father nodded. "I shall await you downstairs."

"Thank you father," She said.

He kissed her on the hand once more and walked out of the room, leaving Elizabeth alone with her thoughts.

She went and sat on the edge of her bed, looking around her room. She had grown up in this room feeling safe and certain of life; never imagining that this day where she would leave to have a household of her own would really come. Now it was here, she felt both scared and excited about the future. Blowing out a deep breath to calm her nerves, she stood and slowly walked to the door. Old memories of her childhood swept through her mind, causing tears to roll down her cheeks. She pulled the door shut behind her and said softly, "It is no longer my room."

Elizabeth carefully walked down the stairs where her father, mother and sister were waiting for her at the foot of the stairs. A few household servants were waiting also; and when they saw Elizabeth descending the stairs, they begun clapping. Once she had reached the bottom she linked her arm with her father's. Two servants went and pulled open the doors and a wave of cold air rushed in. The crowd gave a cheer as they stepped out and walked towards the two carriages. Catharine and her mother climbed into the first carriage. Elizabeth was led by her father to the second carriage where he helped her into the carriage.

Elizabeth watched her father climb in behind her and sit on the seat opposite. He looked at her and smiled. "Are you alright?" He asked her.

She nodded, "yes father, it's both a happy and sad day." She said looking back at family home.

"I know," he said, "I feel it also."

The two carriages jerked to a start and rumbled on down the cobbled street. The troop of town guards walked on the flanks, using their long spears to keep back the crowds that lined the streets. It took a while to reach the small temple, and when they did, they were greeted by temple maids that sang a soft, haunting melody as they arrived.

The carriages came to a stop at the foot of the steps that led up to the temple. The coachmen opened the doors and lowered the steps for them. Elizabeth took her father's hand as she climbed out of the carriage. She looked up at the small temple and felt a cold shudder. The crowds cheered at the sight of her and her family. Her mother and father waved to them before they turned and led their two daughters up the stairs.

Once at the top another party of temple maids greeted them. They wore white hooded robes that clung to their athletic bodies and had white powdered faces with a red stripe that ran from the middle of their forehead, down their nose and lips, to their chin. Each carried a small silver bowl filled with white rose petals. They split into two groups, the first led Catharine and her mother into the temple to take their seat inside where the invited guests waited.

"Are you ready?" Elizabeth's father asked. "Because if you don't want to do this, now is the time to tell me."

Elizabeth wondered why her father would say that now; not so long ago when she had been against this marriage; he had punished her and told her that she had no choice in the matter. All that seemed a lifetime ago now, now she was certain that she wanted this marriage. She had found love with John Kinge and his love had found her. "I'm ready father." She answered him.

The temple was a circular shape with a domed roof that was held up by thick marble pillars. Inside was made to look like the sky at night; the walls and ceiling were black with varied sized white stones dotted around in irregular patterns. Sparkles of light reflected off the stones as hundreds of candles lit up the interior. The guests were seated in wooden pews that circled around the chamber, leaving the aisle and a raised centre where the High Priest with John Kinge now waited.

As Elizabeth was led in through the doorway, temple maids lined around the circular wall began to sing a song so soft and true that is made Elizabeth shiver. Four temple maids walked ahead of Elizabeth and her father, tossing out white rose petals to line their way. The guests all stood as she passed by and wives whispered, commenting on her dress. Elizabeth knew they would be looking for any faults with the day, just so they could say it was an ill omen for the marriage; but Elizabeth didn't care, they were just jealous. She was trying her best not to cry and smiled as she passed them by.

The singing stopped as her father led her up the four steps to the raised centre where John smiled warmly at her. "You look beautiful." He said to her.

The High Priest of the temple was old; his hair was pure white and his face looked like an old wrinkled up piece of fruit. "Who brings this woman for holy matrimony?" He asked in a hoarse voice.

"I do, Edgar De'lacy." Her father said stepping forward. "I bring my daughter, Elizabeth De'lacy, to wed John Kinge."

"And do you Lady Elizabeth De'lacy, consent to marrying John Kinge?" The high priest raised his bushy white eyebrows as he spoke.

"I do." Elizabeth answered.

The old priest turned to John. "Is this the woman you wish to wed?"

"Yes," he confidently replied, "I wish to marry Elizabeth De'lacy."

The old priest took Elizabeth's hand and led her next to John. He placed John's hand over hers and said. "You came to this temple as two willing to become one. Today before these witnesses and the stars, you shall swear the sacred oath of matrimony."

A man dressed in a dirty red and yellow quartered tunic came bursting through the temple's door, interrupting the ceremony. He scanned around the chamber looking for the Lord Aide, seeing him sat stone-faced and rigid at the front, he rushed over to speak with him.

The High Priest raised a bushy eyebrow and coughed to regain their attention. "Do you John Kinge swear before the stars that from this day on, till death shall part you; that you shall love and honour Elizabeth De'lacy and no other, as befitting the title of wife."

John looked into Elizabeth's eyes and answered, "With all my heart, I so swear."

The High Priest then looked to Elizabeth. "And do you Elizabeth De'lacy also swear before the stars that from this day on, till death shall part you; that you shall love and honour John Kinge and no other, as befitting the title of husband."

"Yes, I swear it also." She nervously replied.

The crowd began to mutter and the distant sound of ringing bells could be heard.

The High Priest raised his hands to hush the guests. "From this day forward," he had to raise his voice to be heard over the muttering. "From this day forward, let the light of the havens bless the oath you have both sworn this day. Go now in union as one body."

John leaned in and kissed his new wife. He led her back down the few steps where the Lord Aide was waiting. "Father what did that man want?"

"The lord has died." The Lord Aide coldly answered.

*   *   *

The Wild Folk gave a mighty scream that seemed to make the trees shudder with fear. From the mass horde hundreds of Wild Folk armed with slings stepped forward. They placed pebbles in their slings and spun them around their heads to build up momentum before letting them loose.

Commander Frey ordered the inner circle to use their bows to return fire. "Nock, draw, loose!" He shouted to his knights. The arrows tipped with black feathers sailed through the air and rained down upon the slingers. Few missed their target, but still the slingers had the better of the skirmish. The constant barrage of pebbles raining down began to take effect on the Star Knights. One was hit straight between the eyes, killing him instantly. Others had ribs, arms and fingers broken by the bombardment. Seeing that they were losing the fight Commander Frey ordered his knights to crouch down and take shelter under their large tower shields.

The sound of the pebbles hitting their shields was like a hard rain hitting a rooftop. It seemed to go on for hours before it suddenly stopped. Commander Frey looked over his shield and saw that the slingers were falling back. He kept his men tucked under their shield until he was sure it wasn't a fake retreat to fool his men out from their cover. There was another spine shivering scream, and Commander Frey could see that the Wild Folk were massing for an attack.

He shouted the order, "Stand!" The Star Knights stood as one and locked their shields together, ready to receive the charge.

The Wild Folk began to walk menacingly forward, chanting as they went.

"Now is the hour, now is the time!" Commander Frey called out.

The Star Knights yelled out, "For the stars!" Then they began to bang on their shields with the flat of their swords. Clank, clank, clank, they steadily beat.

The Wild Folk broke into a run and clashed with the Star Knights as a wave clashes around a rock. The clashing of steel on stone could be heard for miles around.

The Star Knights held their ground and desperately stabbed out at the Wild Folk before them. The inner circle thrust their spears over the shoulders of the knights in front to keep the Wild Folk back, but they seemed to ignore the casualties they had taken and pressed on.

The Wild Folk had thick hard grey skin that was hard to penetrate; if a sword thrust was angled wrong, it would bounce harmlessly off their bodies. The few of them that had been killed piled up at the Star Knights feet, where their black blood spilled out onto the ground.

The battle slowly turned in to a pushing contest, where both side pushed against the other in hope of gaining ground. Commander Frey could see that despite the Wild Folk's advantage of numbers, his knights were winning the contest. Normally that would be good, but here where he was surrounded it was a problem. Gaps appeared in their circle where they had advanced too far. "Hold your ground!" He yelled at them. The knights who were the best disciplined force in the kingdom stopped advancing. "Close up, close up!" Commander Frey shouted the order. The Star Knights fell back to their position and locked shields in a tight formation, resealing their defensive circle.

The Wild Folk watched them fall back and let a gap open up between the two armies. They reformed and charged again at the knights. This time the impact of the charge forced the Star Knights back a few steps. One knight was knocked to the ground and was dragged off back towards their skirmishers where they hacked him to pieces. Two other knights were killed by savage blows to their head that split their helmets in two. Others were taking wounds, some small, others worse, causing knights to fall away from the fighting to dress them.

"Hold your ground; close up!" Commander Frey yelled.

The Star Knights defensive circle gradually shrank as knights were either killed or wounded. They fought on valiantly, killing twice as many as they lost. The front-rank had melted in to the inner circle as the casualties took their toll.

Another gap appeared. "Close up, close up!" Commander Frey bellowed the order; but it was too late. A hand full of Wild Folk broke through the gap.

Henri who had been helping to dress wounds saw the threat, and without needing to think he drew his sword and rushed at them. He barged straight into one, knocking it to the ground, and stabbed down in fury. The others that had broken through noticed Henri and rush towards him. Ducking out of the way of a stone hammer that was swinging for his head, he quickly slashed out at its exposed flank. It screamed as black blood poured out from the wound; but he had no time to finish it off as he quickly parried a thrust that would have slashed open his stomach. He was forced back as he made quick clumsy parries that saved his life. Three knights that were wounded, but still able to fight, rushed over to help Henri. With quick fluent movements they killed the few Wild Folk with ease.

Commander Frey rushed over. "Close up!" He roared as he helped Henri back onto his feet. "We owe you thanks Henri; now go back and help the wounded."

"Why I can fight; you need all the help you can get." Henri said trying to force the issue.

"You are but a child, and have no place on a battlefield." He said placing his hand on Henri's shoulder. "Your time may yet come, before the end; but until then keep clear of the fighting, both of you." He turned away from them and went to encourage his men. "Hold your ground, close up!"

There was a long horn blast, and the Wild Folk fell back. Their slingers advanced and began a barrage of stones that rained down on the Star Knights. Commander Frey used the time to reassemble his knights. They reformed their defensive circle and crouched down, taking shelter under their shields. There were no longer enough knights to form an inner circle; instead Commander Frey held back a small reserve unit to fill any gaps that would appear in the circle.

The bombardment ceased and the Wild Folk took up their chanting. They brought forward from their ranks a tall, heavily muscled creature. Henri saw the creature and instantly recognised it. "Commander, Commander!" He yelled.

Commander Frey ran over to Henri. "What is it?"

"That creature I've seen it before; well one like it anyway." Henri said. "Their strong and can take much punishment before being killed."

"They mean to force a hole in our defence." Commander Frey looked at Henri. "We will have to stop it."

"You won't," Henri bluntly said. "I've seen one of them run through a solid door with ease; you won't stop it."

"So what do you suggest?"

"We let it in."

Commander Frey shook his head. "It would be the end of us all."

"And if you fight it head on, many of your knights shall die." Henri could see the concern on the Commander's face. "If we open up and let it through I will trip it up; then you make sure you have knights ready to finish it off."

Commander Frey rubbed his jaw. "How are you going to trip it?"

Henri looked around on the ground and saw thick vines. He quickly tore one up and said, "With this; me and Tom will hide behind the knights and raise it when they open up."

Commander Frey was unsure, but acknowledged that it was the only thing they could do. "Alright," he nodded his agreement, "you make certain it falls."

They both went to prepare for their plan. Henri rushed over to Tom who was dressing a deep cut on a knight's arm. He told him of the plan and they found three thick vines that they quickly twisted together.

They finished just in time as another war cry sounded from the Wild Folk and they charged forward. Henri and Tom picked out the spot where the creature would hit, and laydown behind the knights.

Commander Frey watched on anxiously. "Hold!" He called out. "Hold!" A few feet before the creature hit, he gave the order, "open up!" The knights momentarily opened up as the creature came crashing through.

Henri and Tom pulled the vines tight and were jerked along with the creature as it tripped on the twisted vines and crashed onto the ground. The group of Star Knights that Commander Frey had gathered pounced on the fallen creature, slashing and stabbing at it until it was dead.

The knights had quickly closed the gap and were fighting off the second assault. It went on in the same pattern as the first. The Wild Folk charged and charged again trying to break the Star Knights; but they held steady.

"Close up!" Commander Frey yelled the order. The dead Wild Folk piled up at their feet, which the Star Knights used as a barrier that the Wild Folk were forced to climb over.

Henri looked at the wounded and thought that it was only a matter of time before the knights were overrun; that they couldn't hold forever. What they needed was to keep the Wild Folk away, make them fear the Star Knights. He looked at the fire and the stockpiled bows with arrows beside them, and had an idea. "Tom!" He yelled. "Grab a bow and a quiver of arrows."

Tom grabbed a bow and quiver of arrows from the stockpile. "Why, what are you planning now?"

Henri began tearing off the dead knights surcoats and tucking them into his belt. "We're going to climb that tree." He said pointing to a tall tree within the defensive circle.

"What for; you do know there's a battle going on?"

Henri ignored Tom and ran to the tree and began climbing it, knowing that Tom would follow him. "Pass me up that bow." He called down to Tom.

Tom passed up the bow and quiver. "What now?" He called up to Henri.

"Go back to the fire, bring back a torch, and get yourself another bow and quiver. I'll wait here for you."

Tom nodded and raced off, soon returning with the torch and another bow and quiver. He passed the things up to Henri and climbed up into the tree. They climbed up to where there were many branches close together. Using it as a platform, they placed down their quivers and wedged the torch between two branches so that it couldn't fall down. They tore the surcoats into strips and wrapped them around the arrow tips.

Henri nocked an arrow and set it alight. "Let's make it rain fire." He said to Tom as he drew back the bow string and let loose the flaming arrow. It flew down through the air and struck a Wild Folk in the neck.

There was a sudden panic as the Wild Folk feared fire. The hit Wild Folk suddenly burst into flame, and as it bumped into others, they too were set alight and sent into a blind panic. Henri and Tom continued loosing fire arrows into the dense mass of Wild Folk. Many were set alight and as fear swept through them, they retreated back out of arrow range.

Commander Frey came and stood at the bottom of the tree, sternly calling them down. They both climbed down to be greeted by his angry face. "Did I not command you both to keep clear from any of the fighting?"

"We did," Henri said defensively. "We climbed that tree, to keep out of the way, where we found bows and arrows, so we were simply trying to help."

"I have already been told what you did!" Commander Frey snapped at him. "However your disobedience has saved us; but now my knights shall take over from you."

"So how does this end?" Henri asked.

Commander Frey turned away from them and said. "Without the chalice, they will never stop, not until we have all fallen." There was another horn blast followed by a bombardment of stones that fell down upon the Star Knights. They once again took cover under their shields, waiting out the bombardment.

Henri gripped with anger, thinking that it was his fault these knights were going to die here. No it wasn't his fault; Ulric had used him, tricked him and then tried to kill him. It was his fault and he now held the power; he knew where he was and he wanted revenge.

So not thinking of honour nor valour, but for the need of revenge, he ran, jumping over a crouching Knight and off into the gloom of the forest before anybody could stop him.

"Henri, wait!" Tom yelled after him. Out of instinct he ran after him, jumping over the same crouching knight that Henri had, and slipped off into the forest.

"Come back!" Commander Frey yelled.

But it was too late.

Chapter 12

The lord's hand servant had found him dead in his bed. He had entered the bedchamber in his usual manner, bidding the lord a good morning and pulling open the heavy curtains. When the lord never responded with his normal grumpy response of, *is it indeed*, he knew instantly something was wrong. He rushed over to the bed, looked down at the lord's wrinkled pale face.

"My lord," the hand servant screamed, "my lord!"

The two guards that were posted outside of the bedchamber's door heard the commotion and rushed in. "Fetch the physician!" The hand servant yelled at them. One of the guards turned and ran out of the door to fetch the physician.

After half an hour the guard returned with the same physician that had treated John's fake illness. "Let me through, let me through." The physician said pushing aside the small crowd that had gathered around the bed. The crowd was already muttering with suspicion. The lord had been popular, and was liked by both rich and poor alike. He was considered to have been fair, and served justice equally to all. Though he was old he had shown no signs of being ill or weak. The physician quickly checked for a pulse, and shook his head. "He has come to pass." He announced to the uneasy crowd of servants and guards.

"How did he come to pass, he has neither been ill nor complained of any ailment?" The hand servant said feeding to the crowds suspicions. He turned to a servant in a dirty red and yellow quartered tunic and said, "Go and fetch the Lord Aide; we will need his presence to calm the siltation." The servant nodded and sped off out of the bedchamber.

"You need to clear the room;" The physician said. "I cannot answer your question until I have examined the body, and I cannot do that with all these people around the bed."

"Right everybody out!" The hand servant called out, waving his arms in the air to usher them all out. Once the bedchamber was clear the physician begun his work. He pulled down the sheets and begun checking the lord's body for any signs for what could have caused his death.

The Lord Aide arrived, his face cold and rigid, betraying no emotion. He spoke to no one as he made his way to the lord's bedchamber, where the crowd anxiously waited outside of the chamber door, muttering of murder. When they saw him approach, they fell silent and parted to allow him through.

"Sorry my Lord Aide, but none are to enter while the physician examines the body." The lord's hand servant said standing in front of the door. The Lord Aide shot him a look with his piercing grey eyes that made him immediately stand aside.

"Forgive me my Lord Aide." He said allowing the Lord Aide past.

The Lord Aide entered the bedchamber and saw the physician covering the body back up with the bedsheets.

He closed the door behind him to stop the crowd from peering in and went over to the bedside. "Have you come to a conclusion of death?" He asked the physician.

The Physician looked up into the Lord Aide's emotionless face. "There are no suspicious signs on his body and I can say with certainty that he died peacefully in his sleep."

"Good, then I shall make public your findings and quash any talk of murder that always comes with the death of a lord." The Lord Aide went back and opened the door. "The physician has concluded that the lord has died of natural causes in his sleep." He announced to the waiting crowd. They were unsure of the Lord Aide's announcement and were still suspicious about his sudden death. The crowd reluctantly dispersed off, spreading rumours of treachery and murder throughout the castle.

Downstairs in the great hall, where the lord was supposed to have given his blessing on the marriage, the wedding guests were arriving to feast and make merry. They spoke of an uncertain future with a new lord. What if they had one like their grandparents had? He had gone mad and had executed any who he didn't like. Many supported the new idea that they should be able to choose who was lord over them; but that was rebellious talk that could have you imprisoned and your assets seized; so they stayed quiet, hoping for another just lord.

Elizabeth and John had arrived in one of the carriages decorated in silk flowers. Bells rang out and crowds gathered at the castle gates, but it was not to celebrate the marriage. The news of the sudden death of the lord had swept through the streets like a flash flood. Outside of the castle gates was densely packed with peasants waiting for an official announcement. The two carriages were forced to stop a good way from the gate because of the crowd. The coachmen shouted for them to make a path, but they ignored them and continued on shouting for answers.

"What's happening; why don't they move?" Elizabeth asked John.

John looked out of the carriage window. "The people want answers," he said, "the masses are always nervous when a lord dies."

The castle gates opened and a troop of guards came storming out. They pushed and shoved people aside to clear a path for the two carriages to pass. The coachmen cracked their whips above the horses' heads to move them on, but had to keep on stopping to wait for the guards to clear the path again.

Elizabeth could see the crowd pushing back against the guards, trying to force their way into the castle. One guard was pushed to the ground and trampled on by the rushing crowd. He managed to push himself onto his knees before he was shoved back down onto the ground. A face she recognised dashed from out of the crowd and shouted in through the open carriage window.

"You whore, you told me you would never marry him; you said you loved Henri!" Henri's mother, Mary, shouted at her.

Elizabeth was shocked by the sudden appearance of Mary; she could remember their conversation that night when she had found out she was to marry John Kinge. She had said she would never agree to the marriage and even told Mary that she had loved Henri; but she had been saying all sorts of things in anger. Since then she had grown up; the world was not like one of those stories she had grown up reading about. Marriage was not just about love; after all, love would not buy her the things she needed.

Mary spat at Elizabeth; it missed her, hitting the floor by Elizabeth's feet.

"Arrest that woman!" John yelled to the guards; but they never heard as they were hard-pressed by the crowd, and Mary, her point made, slipped off into the crowd and vanished from sight. "Are you alright?" He asked as he put his arm around her.

"Yes," she replied, red-faced with embarrassment. "I never said I loved him," she added, fearing that John would be angry with her.

"It matters not," John said, "all that matters now is that you are my wife." He pulled his arm from around her shoulders and poked his head out of the carriage window. "Hurry up; these peasants are upsetting my wife!"

Elizabeth heard the words, *my wife*, and felt a shiver run down her spine. It didn't seem real; somehow it felt like a dream from which she would wake up from and still be the same person she was before. The carriage jerking to a start snapped her out of her daze as it rumbled in through the castle gates. The gates were quickly closed behind the two carriages to stop the crowd from rushing in. Servants dressed in red and yellow quartered tunics came and opened the carriage doors and escorted them into the great hall.

The great hall was a large rectangular shape with a large fireplace built into the back wall. It was painted white with small red and yellow shields painted around the top of the walls. Above the fire place hung the lord's war banner, it was quartered red and yellow with two stags locking horns. The long tables that had been place in a U shape were decorated with fake silk flowers. Silver platters and jugs of rich foods and wine filled the tables. The candles were already lit and made the room glow with their light.

As John and Elizabeth entered the guests clapped and raised a goblet of fine wine to the newlyweds. They went and took their seats at the head of the top table and John made a quick speech to the guest. "My noble friends," he begun, "today we feast and make merry, for the day is a happy one. Today our two great houses become one and united together in union by this marriage. You have all been invited here today to bear witness to our union, and our love for each other. Today is also a day of sorrow for we must mourn the loss of the lord." This caused the guests to mutter. "A day of change is upon us all; but a day for which we can look to a brighter future." John raised his goblet, "for a brighter future for us all."

The guests raised their goblets and drank to a brighter future, but was it going to be a brighter future? The guests, like the peasants at the gates were worried and felt anxious about the future. They knew something was afoot with the lordship, and they feared the coming change.

Elizabeth felt awkward about feasting in the lord's great hall. He was supposed to have been present to show his support for the marriage. It seemed wrong to her that they should feast and make merry in his hall so soon after his death.

The guests took their seats around the tables and begun the feasting. They spoke of the lord's sudden death with horror and anxiety. Some even quietly pointed their fingers at the Lord Aide, saying him to be an ambitious man who would not let anybody stand in his way for power.

Elizabeth could see the suspicious glances aimed at her husband and wondered why they looked so suspiciously at him. "Why do they look at you as though you have committed a crime?" She asked with annoyance.

John glanced around the hall, and those who were staring at him quickly looked away. "I think that they envy me because I have married the most beautiful woman in all the kingdom." He said as he took Elizabeth's hand and kissed it.

The servant in the dirty red and yellow tunic came into the hall and made his way over to John. He whispered in his ear and stood aside waiting to escort him to his father who had summoned him.

"Forgive me my wife, but duty calls." John pushed his chair back and stood up. "I will be back soon; enjoy the feast and appease our guests."

"How long are you going to be?" Elizabeth asked feeling worried by being left alone to appease the guests.

"Don't worry, I shall be back soon to celebrate with you." He saw how concerned she was and added, "I will tell your father to escort you in my absence, let him make the small talk with our guests." He smiled and formally bowed before walking away. John went and quickly spoke with Elizabeth's father, then was led out of the hall and up a set of stairs that led to a hallway with many rooms used for administration purposes. The last room at the end of the hallway was the lord's office. John walked straight in; and sitting at the lord's desk was his father signing multiple pieces of paper. The servant left them alone and closed the door behind him as he left.

"How are our guests?" The Lord Aide asked without taking his eyes off the pieces of paper.

"They are nervous, like many within the town." John replied. "What news of the sudden death of our dear lord?"

The Lord Aide set down his quill and looked up at his son. "All went as I planned. The physician has examined the body and has concluded that he died peacefully in his sleep."

"So we are to go ahead with our plan?"

The Lord Aide nodded. "There have been reports of trouble in the streets; I have sent guards to arrest any inciting violence and to restore order in the town." He rang a small bell that was on the desk. The servant entered back into the room and the Lord Aide passed him a piece of paper. "Take this to the town's crier and have him announce it immediately." The servant bowed and went back out of the room to carry out the Lord Aide's commands.

"What is the crier to announce father?" John asked.

"Martial Law. I want the streets calm and clear. Any found in the streets by nightfall shall be presumed to be inciting unrest and shall be arrested." The Lord Aide picked up his quill and continued scratching his signature on the many pieces of paper. "I want you to have your men ready to execute the second part of our plan."

"Yes father, they have been told what to do and won't let us down."

"Good," the Lord Aide said, "I will soon announce the lord's last will to our guests. Many of them will not like it, so I want armed guards at the ready in case any of them should lose mind and turn to violence."

"I shall assemble them at once father."

"Do it quickly and then return to your wedding feast, tell nobody anything other than I shall make an announcement shortly, is that understood?"

John nodded. "Yes father." He turned and left his father still signing pieces of paper and went to muster some guards.

Back inside the great hall Elizabeth was making polite conversation with some of the guests. Her father escorted her around and did most of the talking. Many times she was asked for any news about the lord's sudden death, and each time she told them she knew nothing, she was met with a look as though they disbelieved her. She was glad when she saw John return, smiling and shaking hands with some of the guests as he walked over to Elizabeth.

"Is all well?" An old merchant with a bold head and bushy grey eyebrows asked John as he came and stood beside Elizabeth.

John nodded and smiled at him. "Very well, the Lord Aide shall make an announcement shortly."

The old merchant grunted and walked away from John, fearing what that announcement would be.

"John what took you so long?" Elizabeth asked. "I thought you weren't going to be long."

"Duty." John calmly replied. "The lord has died and there is much to do." He took Elizabeth's hand and kissed it. "Forgive me; this is a day we should be celebrating, not burdened with the chains of duty."

"No, I'm sorry; a true man must always answer the call of duty." Elizabeth said, giving John a reassuring smile.

"This day I have truly been blessed by the stars to have married such a noble woman." John took her arm, "now let us continue on with the feast." He turned to Elizabeth's father and said, "Arrange for the gift giving."

Elizabeth's father formally bowed, "as you wish." He went off to gather the servants and made the announcement to begin the gift giving ceremony.

Each of the guests in turn came before the table where John and Elizabeth were sat. They offered their congratulations and wished them many strong sons. Servants took the many gifts of silver and gold goblets and platters as was the custom. The last person to offer gifts was Elizabeth's father. He approached them with his wife and Catharine by his side. Each of them offered their congratulations and wished them many strong sons. Then her father bid them to look out onto the courtyard below. Everyone went to a window and looked out onto the courtyard. There were two matching pure-white horses.

"My gift to you both on this most momentous day." Elizabeth's father said holding out his hands.

"Father they're beautiful." Elizabeth said rushing and embracing her father.

"They truly are a most noble gift." John said bowing to his new father-in-law.

Just then the Lord Aide came busting into the great hall. He was surrounded by officials and a small troop of grim looking guards that filed in around the hall. The excitement with the guests ended and gave place back to uncertainty; they fell silent waiting for the announcement. The Lord Aide was stone-faced and seemed as calm as a goblet of water as he went and sat at the head of the top table. The officials lined up behind him and the lord's hand servant stood at his side, holding a scroll with the lord's unbroken seal on it.

The lord's hand servant held up the scroll for all to see, to show that it had not been tampered with. "This is the last will of our lord and is to be honoured by all." He waited for any reaction from the guests, but there was none, so he continued on. "The physician has examined the lord's body and concluded that he died peacefully in his sleep. Funeral arrangements shall be made and held before the week's end so that he may rest in peace amongst the stars."

He now broke the wax seal on the scroll and unrolled it in his hands. Speaking in a clear voice he read out the will. "These being the last words and will, of Lord Aelfgar Middlemore, Lord of Heath Hollow. All assets and power that was bestowed to me by the king, I do hereby pass to the Lord Aide, John Kinge the senior. Let his words be law and let no man contest my last will, save the king who has divine right to contest all." The hand servant went on with more personal requests that nobody seemed to be listing to. Instead the guests muttered with suspicion and the old merchant that had spoken to John not so long ago stood and spoke his mind.

"It stinks," he said, "the whole thing stinks! The lord I knew would never have left all power to you."

The Lord Aide nodded to a guard who rushed over to the old merchant and dragged him out of the hall. "Is there anybody else who wishes to speak out against the lord's last will?" He said in a loud voice that commanded obedience. "Tomorrow I shall be officially made Lord of Heath Hollow; all are expected to swear loyalty to me. Any that do not will be outlawed and have their assets seized, as the king's law commands." He stood and walked out of the hall, followed closely by the other officials.

The silence shattered as the guests spoke with horror and disbelief at the announcement. They quickly left the hall, fearing for their future.

Elizabeth's father rushed over to John. "Daughter might I have a word with your husband." Before she could answer he had grabbed John's arm and led him out of earshot. "I thought that your father was to name me Lord Aide?"

John smiled. "He will, tomorrow when all have sworn their fidelity to my father." He placed his hand on his shoulder. "The town is on a knife's edge and my father wishes to keep the peace. He will let his appointment as lord settle with them before making too many changes."

"What of the king; will he confirm your father's lordship?" Elizabeth's father asked fearing that all their work would be undone by the king appointing another.

"Our deal with the Arcani will gain the king's blessing on the lordship." John said looking back at his bride. "Your daughter is afraid; I would ask you to escort her back to my house where she shall be safe."

Elizabeth's father feeling assured by John's words nodded. "Very well; I will return to speak with your father once I have escorted my daughter to her new home."

"My father will happily receive you." John said with a smile.

They went back to where Elizabeth waited with her mother and sister, and John instructed Elizabeth to go with her father to their home. Elizabeth's father kissed his wife and told her to wait here with Catharine for his return.

Elizabeth said her farewell to John and bid him to hurry home to her. He embraced her and said, "Fear not, I will be quiet safe; now go, let me do my duties so that I may get home to you sooner."

"Come now Elizabeth; let me escort you home." Her father said.

Elizabeth said farewell to her mother and sister, and let her father escort her to her new home. They went out of the great hall and out into the courtyard where one of the carriages waited for them. Climbing back inside Elizabeth blew out a breath of frustration. It had all gone horridly wrong; on all of the days the lord could have died, he had to die on this one. As soon as she thought it she felt a sudden pang of guilt. That was not fair, she said to herself; but she couldn't help the way she was feeling. Most of the day John had been tending to his duties and had abandoned her to appease the wedding guests by herself. Later she would discuss it with him and tell him that she thought it unacceptable.

Her father smiled from the seat opposite her. "Sorry that the day never turned out quite like you wanted it to."

Elizabeth returned a forced smile and said, "There will be plenty more days father."

"But you only have one wedding day; and today's event has spoiled it for you."

The carriage jerked to a start and Elizabeth looked out of the window as it passed out of the castle gates. The crowds that had been pushing and shoving with the guards earlier were now gone. The streets were empty and they passed only a few guards patrolling the streets. The carriage was forced to stop as a wagon was blocking the road.

"Why have we stopped father?" Asked Elizabeth, feeling scared.

"I don't know." He poked his head out of the carriage window and saw the wagon blocking the road. "There's a wagon in the way; they'll soon have it moved and then we'll be on our way again."

The coachmen jumped down and begun moving the wagon. Then there was a twang and a thud sound as crossbow bolts flew through the air and struck the coachmen in the chest.

Elizabeth's father hearing the noise poked his head back out of the carriage window, where he saw the dying coachmen spitting out blood onto the cold cobbled road. Before he had time to think the carriage door was pulled open and two men Elizabeth instantly recognized stood pointing their daggers at them. It was the same two men that John had rescued her from when she had run away that foolish night. The older looking one climbed into the carriage.

"What do you want?" Her father asked him, surprisingly calm.

"This." The one that had climbed in plunged his dagger into his chest and turned to grab Elizabeth. He pulled her out into the street by her arms, screaming, where he cut away her dress and tossed it to his companion. "Worth a few coins that." His companion smiled and ravished the carriage, taking anything of value.

Elizabeth screamed and in defiance of her attackers, kicked out at them. They laughed at her feeble attempts before the older one booted her in the face. She lay barely conscious wishing for death to come and take her, it never did. She lay there bleeding from her nose as her attackers took what few valuables they could before taking off, leaving her lying motionless on the cold ground in just her undergarments.

An hour later patrolling guards found her and took her back to the castle where they informed her that her father was found dead along with the coachmen. She had screamed and screamed until the physician was forced to use poppy seeds to calm her. She lay pacified by the poppy seeds, seeing the two faces of the attackers, and swore that one day she would see them hung for their crimes.

It was a day of deep sorrow and change for both Elizabeth and the town of Heath Hollow. The uneasy calm balanced on a knife's edge just waiting for something to nudge it over the edge.

*   *   *

From the five hundred Star Knights that had set out from Elmham Castle, only around two hundred remained. The defensive circle was now more of a cluster of men around a small group lying on the ground who were too badly injured to fight. The dead knights were left where they fell along with the many Wild Folk.

"Close up, close up!" Commander Frey called. He was now fighting alongside his men and had a deep cut on his upper right arm that was bound with a strip of cloth from a dead knight's surcoat.

The Star Knights were exhausted and dry mouthed, but doggedly fought on. They had kept the Wild Folk back for a while using the fire arrows, but they had run out and the fire had quickly diminished as they were no longer enough men to keep it burning. Now the Wild Folk went back to their tactic of sending waves of attacks and bombarding the knights with stones as they fell back to regroup. It was like an ocean wave slowly corroding away a rock over time.

"Close up, close up!" Commander Frey wearily called. He knew the end was near, that his men couldn't withstand much more.

The Wild Folk once more fell back to reform for the final push that would finally end the battle. Their slingers ran forward and began to pelt the Star Knights with their stones. A few knights were hit as they were slow to raise their shields.

"Brothers," Commander Frey called out, "my brothers of the star. Today you have fought with all the valour and honour that our order requires. I am honoured to have fought beside you in this dark place; now smile, for the next time they come we shall take our place amongst the stars."

"For the hope of the stars!" They defiantly shouted.

The Wild Folk gave their war cry and charged for the remaining Star Knights. The Star Knights braced themselves for the clash; but it never came. From the gloom of the forest came a flash of a bright blue light. A vast wave of an illuminated mist went sweeping through the forest. It swept over the Star Knights and Wild Folk, blocking out all vision.

When the mist cleared the Wild Folk were gone. Commander Frey sent out two scouts, who once they returned, reported that all was clear and the Wild Folk were gone. He ordered his knights to rest until he came back.

"Commander, where are you going?" Edward asked.

Commander Frey placed a hand on his shoulder. "You are in command until I come back." He beckoned to two knights nearby, "you two are to come with me."

"But where are you going?" Edward asked.

"To find Thomas and Henri." He turned and rushed off, followed by the two knights, to find Henri and Tom.

*   *   *

Henri could hear the battle as it raged on behind him. To his right three Wild Folk that had seen him dash off from the others leapt out in front of him. He quickly sidestepped to the left to avoid a stone axe that one of them had swung for his head, feeling it brush close to his head as he tripped on a tree root and went rolling onto the ground. They lunged at him as he clumsily parried the blows and tried to get back to his feet. From out of the gloom Tom came charging straight into the Wild Folk, screaming out in a rage.

Henri quickly got to his feet and stabbed down at a Wild Folk Tom had knocked to the ground. He then parried a thrust to his stomach and smashed the pommel of his sword in its face. While it was still dazed by the blow to its face, he back swung his sword down into its neck. It screeched as it fell to its knees pouring out black blood onto the ground and died. The last remaining one was grappling with Tom on the ground. Henri rushed over and stabbed it in its neck, splattering Tom's face with its black blood.

"What are you doing?" Henri asked angrily. "Go back to the Star Knights where it's safe."

"No, I'm coming with you." Tom replied just as angrily to Henri. "You will need my help." He added pushing off the Wild Folk's dead body from off the top of him. He wiped his face with the sleeve of his tunic and stared at Henri. "You needed my help then didn't you?"

Henri turned away from Tom's gaze knowing he was right. "Very well, but keep up and try not to do anything stupid."

"Like what?" Tom asked. "You're in as much danger as me. Why don't we both just go back to the Star Knights?"

"No Tom, I need to stop Ulric. I don't know why, but something deep down inside me is telling me that only I can stop him; besides that I owe him some revenge for poisoning me and taking my dagger."

"Then I will come with you and help you." Tom said wondering why it mattered about a dagger. "Where is he?"

"He's in the eastern part of the city, by the lake there." Henri answered.

"What if he's not there?"

"He is, I can feel it; I don't know how I know it, but I do." Henri said feeling suddenly very confident with his self. "Now let's go and gain my revenge."

They ran off into the city and headed east searching for the lake. The city of Dimon Dor seemed to be alive with strange sounds of distant chanting. The buildings were dimly glowing blue and strange orbs were floating and dancing around the buildings.

Henri stopped at a crossroad to catch his breath and tried to gain his bearings. He looked down the streets and couldn't figure out where they were or which way was the right way to go.

Tom stopped besides him puffing and panting. "Which way do we go now?" He asked.

Henri blew out a breath and shook his head. "Not sure." A few moments passed in silence as they both looked for anything that might tell them which way to go, but they found nothing. Then from out of the gloom a misted shadow formed, and with its long bony finger, it pointed down a road to Henri's left. "Who are you?" He called out to it.

"Henri?" Tom said confused. "Who are you talking to?"

"Don't you see it?" Henri said turning to face Tom. "It's right there." He turned back to point it out to Tom, but it had disappeared. "It was right there."

"What was?" Tom asked confused and unnerved by Henri's actions.

"Nothing," Henri said, "it's nothing. It's this way." Before Tom could say anything he ran down the road that the misted shadow had pointed down.

Tom followed, feeling awkward about Henri. He didn't seem the same to Tom, something had changed about him but he couldn't quite figure out what.

The road eventually ended and gave way to trees. Henri and Tom kept going until they came before a small lake. They knelt down in the treeline looking out, and there by the lake's edge was Ulric.

"You wait here Tom." Henri said.

"No, I think it would be better if we stuck together."

"No Tom, Ulric is a dangerous man; you wait here. If all goes bad make your way back to the Star Knights." He patted Tom on his back and crept off to confront Ulric.

Tom reluctantly stayed put and watched as Henri went to claim his revenge, knowing that he would be needed.

"Ulric you bastard!" Henri yelled.

Ulric was kneeling down at the lake's edge. He had scooped up some water with the chalice when he heard the familiar voice. "Henri, you're alive?" He said still looking at the chalice; it begun to glow blue, and a sinister grim spread across Ulric's face. "I wonder how you could have survived; there was enough hemlock in that water to have killed a giant."

Henri drew his sword and pointed at Ulric. "Why, why did the Lord Aide want me dead?" His hands shook with anger and he had to fight to control himself.

Ulric laughed and turned to face Henri. "You were causing problems with a marriage proposal to some rich merchant's daughter and his son. She was rejecting the marriage on the grounds of already being betrothed to you. So the Lord Aide paid me to take care of it."

Henri's head spun with both anger and hope. If he could get home and speak with the lord, tell him of the Lord Aide's plan with the Arcani of trying to kill him. He knew the lord would grant him his independence as a reward; then we would marry Elizabeth and live a better life then he had.

Ulric held up the chalice and said, "Maybe I should claim it for my own." As Ulric put the chalice to his lips Henri charged forward, holding out his sword.

Ulric had expected this and was ready for it. He quickly stepped to the side and tripped Henri up. He went crashing into the water and Ulric quickly placed his boot on his back, holding him under the water. Henri fought desperately and was able to shove Ulric boot off of his back. Ulric stepped back and let Henri get back to his feet. He drew his sword and pointed it at Henri, still holding the chalice. "Because I like you Henri, I'm going to give you the chance to walk away. Go now, the Lord Aide will never know you're still alive."

Henri didn't move. "What of the chalice? I can't trust you to take it to the king."

"And I will not part from it." Ulric quickly responded.

Henri swung a clumsy blow that Ulric parried with ease. Ulric then quickly thrust his sword at Henri's neck, which he was just able to duck under.

"Very good Henri, but I tire of this pointless exercise." Ulric said grinning. He suddenly made lightning quick strokes that Henri was just able to block. He slipped on the mud and fell on his back at the water's edge. Ulric stepped over him and went to deliver the final blow; when suddenly Tom tackled Ulric to the ground. From the corner of his eye Ulric had seen him coming and was able to move his sword to meet the threat.

Tom saw the blade at the last moment but was unable to stop. He fell helplessly on to Ulric's sword and the momentum sent them both crashing onto the ground. The sword had penetrated him at an angle so that it went in through the stomach and the tip came out of his upper back. The pain was like fire sweeping through his body; then he began to spasm and gag before he fell silent, and death claimed him.

Henri seized his chance. He quickly dived on top of Ulric and smashed down on his face with the pommel of his sword until it was a bloody mess. "You bastard!" He screamed at Ulric, "you bastard!" Standing back to his feet he began stabbing down at Ulric's body repeatedly until he was exhausted and fell to his knees. He saw his dagger strapped at Ulric's waist and angrily took it back. Tears filled Henri's eyes as the true cost of this quest dawned on him. He got up and pulled Ulric's sword from Tom's torso and flung it into the lake, before falling back to his knees beside his friend's lifeless body.

He then saw the chalice and picked up. It was no longer glowing blue as the water had spilled out of it. Henri turned it over and over in his hands thinking. The king needed this to keep his power and maintain the kingdom's unity; but for what? So the rich lords could keep people like him and Tom slaves, while they grow richer. Tom was a good person, but the rich lords would never know he even existed and wouldn't even care. He thought that if he had never drank from the chalice that this would never have happened; but what then? He would have gone home to more backbreaking labour for the lord. No, he was already cursed by being a lowborn. Maybe a new king would make a fairer life for all. A life where lowborn had the same chances as those higher up.

Henri stood to his feet, to hell with the kingdom he thought. He looked at the chalice one last time before throwing it in anger into the deep lake where it sank to the bottom, to lay hidden forevermore. Instantly there was a flash of blue light, followed by a thick blue mist that covered all. Henri fell beside Tom's lifeless body. "Sorry Tom." As the mist cleared the forest went eerily quiet again.

When Commander Frey arrived at the lake Henri was lying beside the body of his friend. He told Commander Frey what had happened before slipping into a state of shock that clouded his mind.

"The chalice, where is the chalice?" Commander Frey asked Henri.

Henri never spoke and just pointed to the lake. Commander Frey understood what he meant and said, "I am truly sorry for your friend; he always spoke of you with high regard." He turned to the two knights that had come with him and ordered them to carry Tom's body back to the others.

Back where the battle had taken place, the Star Knights had built a funeral pyre with whatever wood they could find and poured the oil they had carried from Elmham Castle over the pyre. They placed the three hundred and six bodies of the fallen Star Knights on the pyre along with Tom's. The other one hundred and ninety four circled around the pyre, wearing their hooded cloaks pulled over their heads, each holding a flaming torch. They chanted out the names of the fallen and when Henri heard Thomas, he burst into tears and felt numb inside. When the chanting ended each in turn tossed their torch onto the pyre, setting it aflame. Each of the Star Knights lowered their heads as the flames flickered high. Henri just stared as the fire consumed the bodies.

Commander Frey came and stood beside Henri, placing his hand on his shoulder. "We must leave this place."

Henri shook his head and remained rigid, staring aimlessly at the flames.

Commander Frey took his hand off Henri's shoulder. "All things happen for a singular purpose."

Henri turned to face Commander Frey and said, "So what happens now?"

"We take you home." Commander Frey smiled and signalled for the other Star Knights to move out. "Let his sacrifice not be in vain."

Henri reluctantly moved off with the Star Knights and left the pyre burning brightly, never looking back as they marched silently through the forest.

* * *

When the Star Knights and Henri had arrived back at Elmham Castle, the people had cheered and made merry, but the Star Perceptory had been a sombre place. They never cheered, nor celebrated the victory in the forest, but instead mourned for the loss of three hundred and six brothers.

Commander Frey was even more saddened by the news of his prisoner having escaped. He conducted an investigation, but found no answers. Henri had told him everything he knew of the Arcani, but the question of how they were able to steal the map of the chalice's whereabouts remained a mystery. The day after he had concluded his investigation they had left for Heath Hollow.

It was the early hours of the morning when Henri and the Star Knights had arrived back at Heath Hollow. The sun was yet to rise and the streets were deserted. The whole town was asleep apart from the teams of gong farmers that worked throughout the night.

It had been three weeks since the Battle of the Black Forest and Tom's death; Henri was still raw with anger, he no longer blamed himself for Tom's death, he blamed the Lord Aide. It was him that had tricked Henri on to the quest for the chalice, him that had paid for Ulric to kill him, and it was him that Henri had sworn revenge upon. It was all the Lord Aide's fault.

Henri's plan was to tell the lord everything, of how the Lord Aide tried to have him murdered, just so he could marry his son to Elizabeth. Commander Frey had promised that he would testify to the truth of Henri's words and recommend that the Lord Aide should be arrested, and that Henri be given his independence as a reward for his courage.

Commander Frey and Henri rode side by side along the narrow cobbled streets, with two other Star Knights following behind. At first Henri had been reluctant to ride, saying that he had never rode a horse before. So a couple of hours every day Commander Frey had tutored him in horsemanship and swordsmanship. Commander Frey was astonished on how quickly Henri learnt the skills; he was now able to defend himself with ease against more experienced knights.

They rode past the empty marketplace and Henri was surprised by how big it looked when it was empty. He thought it funny as he had been there many times before when it was empty, but he had never noticed just how big it really was. They rode on the main road that led up the hill straight to the castle. They passed through the richer quarter of the town and Henri stopped his horse, looking down the street where Elizabeth's family home was.

Commander Frey reined in beside him and said, "come Henri, we must speak with the lord first."

Henri wanted nothing more than to just speak with Elizabeth; somehow she could soothe his anger and fill the void that Tom's death had left. He nodded his agreement and nudged his horse into a walk. "I only want to speak with the lord, not with the Lord Aide." He said to Commander Frey.

"I have given you my word; we will go directly to the lord." Commander Frey replied trying to hide the annoyance in his voice as Henri had told him that many times before.

They rode in silence with the sound of the horses' hooves clapping loudly on the cobbled street, until they came before the castle gates. They were closed, so Commander

Frey dismounted and banged on the thick wooded gate with his fist. Moments later a guard slid open a small viewing window.

"Who are you and what do you want?" The guard asked.

"I am Commander Frey of the Order of the Star; I come seeking an audience with the lord."

The guard glanced down and saw the white eight pointed star on a plain black surcoat. He shut the viewing window and opened the gate. "Luckily for you the lord is an early riser." He said gesturing for them to enter.

Commander Frey nodded his thanks and mounted his horse. He led Henri and the two other Star Knights in through the gate and through to the courtyard where they dismounted and were led by a steward to a small waiting room. The steward took their names and told them to wait for his return.

Soon after the steward returned and led Commander Frey and Henri to the lord's office. He opened the door for them, and there sitting behind a desk littered with parchments was a face that took Henri by surprise. The steward closed the door behind them and went to fetch some guards as the new Lord of Heath Hollow had instructed him.

"Where is the lord? We wish only to speak with him, and not with a mere Lord Aide." Commander Frey said in a harsh tone.

The new lord looked at Henri with his grey cold eyes and said, "Lord Aelfgar Middlemore passed from this world, and left his lordship to me."

Henri shook his head in disbelief. "You're a liar!" He said in anger. "You tried to have me killed because Elizabeth wouldn't agree to marry your son; but you failed, I'm still alive and have come to report your crime."

The door opened and four guards led by a man Henri recognised from the vision he saw back in the temple at Dimon Dor. He was finely dressed and wore the Lord Aide's chain of office around his shoulders.

"Commander this is my son John, the new Lord Aide and recently married to Elizabeth De'lacy." He held up a warrant of arrest form his desk. "This boy is wanted for theft and desertion, and is now to be held until a suitable punishment for his crimes is agreed upon."

Commander Frey stepped forward and took the warrant of arrest from the new lord. He glanced at it and turned to Henri, giving him a glance that told him everything. "Sorry Henri, I will plead your case with the king."

The guards roughly grabbed Henri and stripped him of his weapons, then dragged him out of the office, across the courtyard and over to the same small cell in the ground that he had been held in before. He felt crushed and defeated, all had been for nothing. His best and only friend was dead, the woman he loved and thought he would marry, was now married to his enemy's son. The chalice that could have saved the kingdom for the king was now at the bottom of the lake in Dimon Dor. Now the kingdom would war for the throne; lowborn men would win their independence, and would come home rich from the spoils of war. Not Henri, he was cursed for drinking from the chalice, and was certain to hang at the new lord's pleasure.

As the guards tossed Henri down into the dark wet cell, the sun rose in the east and a new day dawned. He was warned by the spirit in the temple that this path would be one of pain and sorrow. Believing it to be the right thing to do, he had taken the chalice so that the kingdom would have peace, then he had threw it away in anger. But now he had paid the highest of prices because of that belief, and now he was cursed, because of men's curse, because of the Chalice of Knowledge.